MW00324250

BREWED FOR LOVE

LEIGH RAFFAELE

SOUL MATE PUBLISHING

New York

BREWED FOR LOVE

Copyright©2017

LEIGH RAFFAELE

Cover Design by Ramona Lockwood

Published in the United States of America by
Soul Mate Publishing
P.O. Box 24
Macedon, New York, 14502

ISBN: 978-1-68291-584-4

ebook ISBN: 978-1-68291-514-1

www.SoulMatePublishing.com

This book is dedicated to Dave, the love of my life, who had confidence in me even when I didn't. Your love and encouragement guides me to keep going. We both have attained our dreams, you with your farm and me with my writing. Thank you for giving me this opportunity. You're my own true hero, an example of what romance novels are all about!

This book is also a gift . . .

To Josephine — who supplied me with mountains of books over the years and couldn't wait for me to get published.

To Anthony — who brought this story and Evan to life, just by being himself!

Acknowledgements

Special thanks:

To David — whose protective nature for the women in his life is the model for the heroes in all my stories.

To Adam — whose strength, determination, and tenacity to never give up are the models my heroes embody.

To Anthony — whose kind heart, caring nature, and loyalty were the models for Evan. Without him, there would be no Evan.

And to all the critique partners I've had along the way. Your support and encouragement push me to be a better writer.

Michelle Cunnah, Susan Kass, Kate Lutter, Maria Imbalzano, Anna Sugden, Kathleen Pachecho, Miriam Allenson, Julie Schroeder, Nett Robens, and Beth-Ann Kerber.

Lena Pinto and Judy Kentrus, thanks for your support and encouragement. Hold on . . . it's going to be an interesting ride!

Acknowledgements

Chapter 1

It sounded so simple a week ago. Made perfect sense.

Go in unnoticed, collect foot-traffic data, profit levels, logistics. Leave without thinking twice. Job done.

Click. Click. Click-click.

Eleanor Langston Bainbridge clutched the mechanical counter in her right hand and peered through her car's foggy, driver's-side window. The chilly October morning had her rubbing the glass with the butt of her hand, clearing a miniature circle as she held her breath to keep the window from re-fogging. Part of her job was spying on the "little guys," the part she wasn't at all comfortable with.

A group of three entered the modest coffee shop across the street.

Click, click, click. She automatically depressed the counter's button.

A shiver ran through her, and she knew it wasn't the nip in the air that bothered her. By doing her job, she'd ultimately set someone up to lose their business—the ugly side of a being a field rep for MoonBurst Coffee. God, she hated being in this situation, but she needed the salary increase that came along with a promised promotion. Without it, she'd surely lose her apartment.

That promotion would maintain the ballooning rent increase, helping her keep her home. With rents in Manhattan as tall as skyscrapers, finding another decent-sized, affordable apartment would be near impossible.

Squinting through the re-fogged peephole of the car

window, she monitored the glass door of the coffee shop storefront across the street.

Until her boss, Bruce, told her she'd be off to Cedar Ridge, New Jersey, she never knew the place existed. The rural town in the north-western part of the state brimmed with unique shops that lined the proverbial four corners that encompassed a village center. Although, it looked like a Norman Rockwell painting, Bruce said not to let it fool her, and after researching it, she had to agree.

The village council's idea to turn their quaint village into the tourist mecca of northwestern Jersey had paid off big time. Modeled after the southern shore town of Cape May, the residents had painstakingly restored all the Victorian buildings and houses in painted-lady fashion. What appeared to be newly installed cobblestone streets transported visitors back to a simpler time. And her company, MoonBurst Coffee, wanted a piece of the financial tourist action.

Her ringtone startled her, then she relaxed, recognizing the melodic chimes she picked for Mary Claire.

"Thank God you called," Eleanor told her best friend. "My nerves are shot. I don't think I can do this."

"Of course you can do this. You're *Eleanor Bainbridge*," her best friend said in a snooty, aristocratic tone. "And *Bainbridges* never fail. You're good at everything."

That was the problem. The expectations her mother forced on her were nearly impossible to achieve. Growing up, the pressure was insurmountable with no room for failure. If she failed now, she'd have no choice but to go back home to that large, shallow mansion that echoed of Mother's disapproval.

"Nora, you still there?"

"Yes." Eleanor nodded. The use of the nickname Mary Claire and her father called her gave her comfort. "I don't know, MC, this situation's got me rattled. There's something different this time."

"How so?"

"Something's not right," she said, scanning what seemed to be rush-hour traffic.

"Is someone watching you?" Mary Claire rushed. "Call 9-1-1!"

"No. No. It's nothing like that. This place is picturesque and charming. The kind of town in books where everyone is friendly and kind. What happens if that's how the people really are?"

"Not going to happen. Those places are exactly where they belong: in books. They don't really exist. Now, take a deep breath and do what you always do and hurry back so you can come help me babysit the horses."

MC was wrong. Those types of towns did exist. Although, Nora doubted her best friend even realized she actually lived in one. And nothing would make Nora happier than to spend a weekend at Mary Claire's parents' farm. Everything from the cozy, comfy house, to the acres of paddocks and green pastures called to Nora's heart. Maybe it was Mary Claire's loving parents who made her to want to run away from everything she knew; or maybe it was the quiet of the land that spoke to her soul. Whatever it was, Nora jumped at every chance to help Mary Claire's family for all they'd done for her.

"Listen to me, girl. We've been friends since high school," Mary Claire scolded. "I know you better than anyone. You've done this a million times. Now gather yourself and those designer duds you're wearing and get out of your car."

Of course MC knew she was still in the car. Nora wished she had as much confidence in herself as her friend had in her. She hesitated then finally said quietly, "This time is *really* different."

"Of course it's different." Mary Claire laughed into the

phone. "It's your last time. After this, you're home free, so to speak."

"Nice pun." She sure did need this last field study to go well. Without it, she'd be homeless thanks to the soon-to-be astronomical rent. "What am I going to do if this doesn't work? I *can't* move back to Bainbridge Manor."

"Don't worry. You've got this. You won't have to move back in with Mommy Dearest and Daddy Warbucks. You'll still be on your own, where you belong. Besides, if you move, where will we have our Friday night game nights?"

The last thing on her mind was game night right now. But her friend did have a point. She needed to pull herself together and get it done. Period.

"Thanks, MC. I needed that pep talk."

"I'm here for you, girl. Now go get 'em!"

Nora ended the call and noticed the chill nip at her again. Maybe it was nerves, or maybe it was just the cold. She needed coffee. *Hot* coffee. If she had been back in her neat but tiny office right now, she'd be working on cup number three. Free coffee, one of the perks of her job. Although, by afternoon, she switched to decaf. Even though she was only thirty-one, all that free caffeine hyper-wired her system.

She picked up the trademarked blue and orange MoonBurst Coffee travel mug from her car's console, then shook the bottom back and forth knowing it was bone dry, but hoping one more gulp would miraculously appear.

When she noticed movement out of the corner of her eye, her attention quickly honed in on the coffee shop.

Click.

One more person entered.

Click. Click.

Two more.

She reached for the tablet positioned on the front passenger seat. The demographic chart of the proposed new franchise gleamed brightly in the dawn of the early morning.

She tapped open the statistical chart entitled Bean & Brew, keying in the numbers from the manual counter. If headquarters planned to plunk down seventy-five thousand to renovate a new location of MoonBurst Coffee, they needed to determine if it would bring in enough revenue to turn a profit.

Dropping the counter on the passenger seat, she slid the tablet into her handbag and turned off the car.

"Okay," she said, releasing a heavy breath. "Time to check out the logistics."

Stepping out of her Chevy—the one her father detested because it was a "poor-man's car"—she tugged the collar of the wool coat her parents gave her last Christmas tightly around her neck. The price tag for the ridiculously expensive garment had been obscene, but at least it kept her warm.

After an hour, two at most, her job would be complete and she'd be on her way back to the city. With the fall weather sending a brisk wind biting her face, it was the perfect time to remind herself what was on the line: her home.

As she came within twenty feet of the Bean & Brew door, her heavy intake of breath forced a string of nerves through her. It always happened just before she met the faces of the people she possibly could be putting out of business. Up until this point, they were merely numbers on a chart. She reminded herself, as she always did, this was how business worked. Businesses were susceptible to three outcomes: they thrived, went belly up, or got acquired. And when you worked for the tyrannosaurus of businesses, smaller businesses got gobbled up. Just the natural order of things, she often convinced herself to soften the blow and ease the guilt of her job. It was a good job, one she'd jumped into right out of college so she wouldn't be forced to the pressures of working at her father's company. Working for MoonBurst was a means to an end, not only for her finances, but for her sanity of keeping her family off her back.

Ten feet closer to the door.

Her heart pumped heavily against her ribs. Like it always did whenever she was about to spy on an unsuspecting business owner.

Five feet away.

The sound of the line of cars that passed turned into a whir of white noise around her. Her palms grew moist then shook as the cold air blasted them. A knot formed deep in her throat, causing her breathing to sputter.

Her feet stopped moving.

This is the last time, she repeated in her head as she sucked in a deep breath and stared at her reflection in the full-paned glass door, reminding herself that living her own life and continuing to support herself would remain within her grasp.

With her hand on the metal handle of the Bean & Brew Coffee Shop door, she said, "One last time," and bounded in, knowing she was ultimately going to ruin someone's life.

~ ~ ~

Evan Cavanaugh just witnessed the taping of a Super Bowl commercial. Well, not exactly, but it sure felt that way.

The door to his coffee shop flew open with a gust of wind and in blew the most irresistible woman he'd seen in his thirty-two years. His hands stopped midway lifting a case of coffee and he stared at the long waves of black hair tumbling around her shoulders. As he put the case down, he noticed an even longer pair of legs ending in a pair of black, patent leather heels. A pale-gray, tight-fitting skirt snuck out from between the bottom of her coat's opening revealing a portion of thigh that drew his attention away from his task.

The woman brushed a few scraps of leaves off of her shoulders and slowly unbuttoned the coat's shiny black buttons, releasing its bulk to showcase a tight-fitting suit jacket that matched that incredibly short skirt. As she made her way to the counter, Evan swallowed hard. His gaze followed the deep slit of her white blouse, teasing him to peek inside.

Then their eyes met. An involuntary jolt hit him from out of nowhere. She had the most beautiful eyes he'd ever seen. Not quite blue, not quite purple. When he focused on her glossy, deep pink-colored lips, Evan felt like a dumbstruck teenager again.

"Well, this is a nice change," his mother said as she bumped his arm, snapping him back to reality. "You haven't looked at a woman like that in years."

Shaking his head to clear his vision, he ignored his mother's comment and focused on filling his friend Todd's order. Evan reached toward one of the mugs hanging from the hand-crafted wooden mug holder secured to the wall, took hold of Todd's personal *World's Greatest Dad* mug, and automatically filled it. He forced his glance from drifting toward the new woman standing in line and concentrated on the coffee grinder when he heard a low hum of the machine instead of the popping sound of pulverizing beans.

Evan took off the cover of the old machine, quickly cleared the accumulated gunk inside, and made a mental note to thoroughly clean the grinder at the end of the day. As soon as the store was financially in the black, he'd order a newer, modern grinder. But for now, he banged on the top to loosen all the other crap clogging the machine.

"Easy," his mother, Arlene, warned as she brought in a tray of danish that had been delivered from the bakery. "Breaking it isn't going to help."

"This thing's been acting up the past few days. I'm going to have to call the company. And you know what that means."

His mother laid a hand on his arm. "If it has to be fixed, we fix it."

"Yeah, but—"

"But nothing. I told you, we take the money out of the store account. We're not going to use *your* money to support this business."

She was right. Repairs and supplies needed to come from the store account. But with the new changes he'd made to the place, the store's account was on the low side, so he felt obligated to personally kick in the cash to keep everything running smoothly.

Yeah, the shop needed to pay for itself, but he didn't want their account to fall into the red zone. It had taken him four years after his father's death to bring the coffee shop into the 21st century. Falling behind would be counterproductive. The way he figured it, in a few weeks the shop account could reimburse him. He banged the top of the machine one more time.

Evan's gaze traveled back to the customers on line, past Todd Ellison, toward the second customer. *Man, she is good looking.* But even as his body slowly hummed with awareness, he reminded himself that good looking came with expectations and demands, neither of which he'd ever deal with again.

"You need to get out," Mom insisted, "and socialize."

Socialize? Code word—dating. *That* wasn't going to happen, either. "I get plenty of socialization here."

"Maybe you could go on a date," she said, just before she made her way toward the basement doorway with an arm load of towels and aprons.

"Your mom's got a point," Todd prodded, giving Arlene a choirboy smile.

"Don't you start, too."

"Hey, I'm just saying, looks like you need something like that in your life." Todd motioned his head in the direction of the mystery woman and raised his eyebrows. "Someone to give you a more *active* social life. Get you outta this place. You're here 24/7."

"I'm fine just the way I am. I don't need another woman messing up my life. My life's exactly where I want it."

"Todd," Arlene interrupted again, sidling up to the counter to address his friend. "Why don't you and Evan get together one night and go out?"

"Uh, Mrs. Cavanaugh, I haven't been out in ages." Todd rubbed the side of his neck. "The kids kind of slow me down, if you know what I mean."

"Exactly! You and Evan are both mother and father to your kids. All work and no play is making old men out of the two of you."

"Ma, let it go." Evan slid the filled coffee mug across the counter to Todd, ignoring his meddling mother.

Todd was finally getting over his wife's death, trying to make a new normal for his two kids. He didn't need a woman muddling up his life, too. Mom meant well, but the only person Evan needed in his life right now was his daughter. When his ex walked out on him and Julie the day after his father's funeral, Evan's world crashed around him. Miranda had a major fit when he told her he wanted to quit his job and move from Manhattan to Cedar Ridge. Raising Julie in the same small town he grew up in would be a much better environment where she could be surrounded by people who cared about her. In the city, she was just another kid living in an apartment building. But his ex wanted no part of it. Went back to the city, alone, and never looked back. From then on, he focused all his love and attention on his daughter. His mother knew that, but kept at him anyway to find someone. The way he figured it, sometimes it's just better to be left alone.

Todd handed him the money for his order. "You know, Mrs. C., maybe you and my mom can get together sometime. You know, a ladies' night out." He lifted his chin in an upward nod to Evan.

"Yeah, Ma," Evan said, picking up on Todd's direction. "That's a great idea. Go catch a movie or dinner in Newton."

His mom slid a glare at both of them. "Okay, I get the hint. I'll back off." She grabbed a tray to clear the empty customer tables and walked away from them.

Evan reached and high-fived Todd across the counter. "Thanks, man. I owe you one."

"No thanks necessary. My mother's just as pushy. They just don't get it." Todd stepped away from the counter as he headed for the door and said over his shoulder, "Later."

"See ya, buddy." Evan saluted a goodbye, then focused on the mystery woman.

"Good morning," she said in a deep, bedroom voice.

"It is now." He gave her his most-charming smile. Even though he'd sworn off women, he still appreciated the view. "What can I get for you?"

"You have such a nice menu, simple."

"We do coffee, and a few specialty drinks. And danish and pastries, to go with the coffee."

"I can see that. I guess it goes with the *quaintness* of your little store."

"Quaintness of your little store?" Uneasiness inched across his shoulders. Was that a putdown or a compliment? Four years ago, he'd taken the Bean & Brew from a two-table coffee shop to a full-fledged coffee house with several tables and an extended menu. His hard work not only gave the locals a place to meet and greet, but it also kept his father's dream alive.

Despite this woman's good looks, her condescending attitude suddenly became a complete turnoff.

"Yep. We're a quaint little store in a quaint little village. Just the way people like it." He wiped the counter again, this time counting to ten until he could give her what she wanted and she'd be on her way. Damn. All that beauty on the outside, but black coal on the inside. "So, what will it be?"

"I'll have a grande light-mocha decaf cappuccino."

"Don't serve cappuccino. Coffee or tea, decaf or regular, with flavored syrups. Cream or milk. What we have is listed on the board." He pointed to the chalk board that hung on the brick-covered side wall. "How about a Caramel Explosion? Regular coffee with caramel syrup and cream."

When she quickly turned her head to read the menu, Evan took note of the elegant slope of her nose as it gave way to full, plump lips. He swallowed hard, but when she tucked her thick, dark hair behind a delicate ear, a huge diamond-studded earring sparkled under the shine from the store's fluorescent lights.

Yeah, high maintenance, for sure.

"Okay, since there isn't much choice, I'll go with decaf mocha."

Humph. Not much choice, aye? Where did she think this was, MoonBurst?

When he worked in the city, there'd been a MoonBurst Coffee in every neighborhood. There, he had little choice but to fork over five dollars for a cup of their burned brew. So when he came home to run the Bean & Brew, he vowed to carry on his father's tradition of serving a great cup at a great price.

He clicked his tongue. "A light decaf with mocha syrup it is. For here or to go?"

"For here."

He yanked a Bean & Brew ceramic mug from the lazy Susan wondering why she wanted to stay in his store if it was too small and too ordinary. All her beauty lost its luster. She just proved his point, that women didn't have a place in his life.

The bean grinder came through this time, and he slid

the filled coffee mug and a napkin across the counter to her. "That'll be one dollar."

"That's all?" Her perfectly formed eyebrows wrinkled together in question, which was kinda cute, but that obnoxious tone turned him right off. "How do you stay in business?"

"We're doing just fine. Gotta keep the regulars happy." He aimed a purposeful smile at her to drive his point home.

"Is that where you keep all the regulars' coffee mugs?" She pointed a long, slender finger towards the mug holder on the wall.

"Sure is." Pride filled him at the mention of the wooden mug holder his father had lovingly handcrafted some twenty years ago.

"Quaint. Just like the rest of the place," she said.

Right then, if she'd been a guy, he wouldn't have a problem showing her the door. Too much attitude for his blood. With any luck, she'd drink her coffee, get out, and never return.

"Enjoy your coffee," he said with a smile, because the customer is always right, no matter how obnoxious they are.

As he turned away from Miss High and Mighty, he went to make sure the grinder still worked. Any woman who made fun of his mug holder wasn't worth his time or anger. His gaze landed on the wooden fixture. Right next to it—out of sight from the customers—he re-focused on a picture of a man holding the first Bean & Brew mug.

"Dad, no matter what people say about this place, I swear it's gonna work. I'll make you proud. I promise."

~ ~ ~

"Don't pay any attention to Evan, he's harmless," an older woman said as she stood with a glass coffee pot in one hand wiping a table next to where Nora stood. "He's had a lot of stress lately." She waved a hand for Nora to sit at a clean table.

Nora's free hand went to her face. The blush that heated her fingertips was a sure sign to the woman that Nora had been caught trying to hide her attraction to her employee. The last thing she needed right now was to get involved with a guy, but she was afraid that a smidgen of the harsh attitude she'd learned from her mother had sneaked out as a defense so the man wouldn't suspect she found him attractive. She may have offended him, and right now, she was ashamed of how she'd acted.

Taking the woman's lead, Nora headed toward the table that rested next to the picture window facing Elm Street. It was a perfect spot not only to monitor sales in the store, but take note of the tourist traffic outside. She'd known she was going to visit a Mom and Pop store, but she'd never expected to actually see *Mom* in the flesh. Although, her boss had said the business was registered to Arlene and Thomas Cavanaugh, so she shouldn't have been surprised.

Mom—dressed in a pair of jeans, a beige turtleneck under a hunter-green corduroy button-down shirt—had a white apron tied around her waist. With graying brown hair, she looked like the predictable small-town innkeeper in a Hallmark Christmas movie—the one everyone came to with their problems.

Nora glanced around to see if *Pop* was anywhere in sight. It seemed the woman and her employee, Evan, were the only people working. The woman's smile seemed genuine, kind of like Mary Claire's mom. But Nora didn't know how to read Evan. They'd definitely gotten off on the wrong foot. Between her attraction to him, and trying hard to check out the store, her curt manners evidently caused his attitude shift.

She couldn't blame him. But, oh, boy, if Mary Claire could see him. Nora couldn't wait to tell her about him. That exciting, country-boy type her mother warned her about. All looks, no ambition. But there was something welcoming in his hazel-colored eyes that'd had her staring moments ago, had her thoughts drifting toward possibilities of how his strong set of shoulders would do nicely at keeping her warm at night. But then reality checked in once the sparkle in his eyes had vanished, even though he tried to hide it behind a smile.

Well, it didn't matter. A guy, especially the wrong guy, didn't fit into her life's plan right now.

Feeling a set of eyes on her, Nora turned her attention back to the smiling woman standing next to her.

"Is there anything else I can get you?" the woman asked.

Nora blew out a slow, frustrated breath, pushing a wayward strand of hair out of her face, hooking it behind her ear as she tried not to be too negative. "There doesn't seem to be much on the menu."

"We've got more than we used to." The woman's green eyes bracketed with deep-set wrinkles glimmered with pride. "We don't have all kinds of exotic sandwiches and desserts like those chain stores, but we've got enough to keep everyone happy." She narrowed her eyes. "I guess it's not what you're used?"

Why would she assume that?

The *ah-hah* moment immediately popped into Nora's thoughts. It was a natural assumption since her clothes screamed NYC power exec.

So much for slipping in unnoticed.

She ran her gaze around the store again. No one in suits or casual Friday clothes. Locals all informally dressed, regular people living regular lives, rushing off to work. She pulled her coat tighter to hide her designer suit. Darn. She should have closely studied the demographic report.

Three older men sat at separate tables lining the far brick wall, nursing what appeared to be different mugs. Probably part of the "regulars'" with their mugs hanging on that hand-made mug holder behind the counter.

The charm of the village buildings outside, and the smiles on all the people's faces here in the store, confirmed Nora's impression that Cedar Ridge was the type of town that appeared in the old-fashioned Christmas cards, the kind where everyone is happy and caring. The total opposite of her life. No matter where the Bainbridges lived, no matter how many prayers or hopes she counted on, her family would *never* be the family on a Christmas card.

Pushing that old wish aside, she retrieved her tablet from her oversized purse and keyed in the number of people and the limited menu selections.

Customers came and went, laughing and chatting as if they knew each other. They probably did.

The place definitely held a homey, small-town charm, nothing at all like MoonBurst's successful, contemporary chains.

Turning to get a better view of the counter area, she concentrated her thoughts on data collection instead of focusing on that guy Evan's ruggedness and back-home style.

As each customer approached the counter, none of them gave him their order. He simply reached for that mug holder, snatched individual mugs off of their pegs, and proceeded to get exactly what each customer wanted.

She watched a genuine smile flash across his face, how his eyes lit with a touch of mischief. She wondered how much fun it would be to just let go and play along with the game of not taking life serious, but quickly dismissed it. Life *was* serious, especially if she didn't concentrate on completing her job. The thought of having to find another place to live truly frightened her.

She couldn't help but notice how Evan's attention honed in on a conversation with each customer while he deftly hustled orders without missing a beat. Every few seconds, his wide shoulders stretched as he lifted a hand to grasp mug after unique mug from its perch while turning out orders in record time. Impressive. Both his efficiency and his muscles. But being nice to *some* of the customers wasn't enough. MoonBurst employees were trained to be nice to *all* customers. And all company cups were standard issue, logoed and trademarked, not like the hodgepodge going on here.

It appeared the shop owners collected the mismatched mugs at yard sales or flea markets, probably to save money. Although, they did seem to add a comfy feel to the place.

She inspected her own mug. Brand-new Bean & Brew logo on it. Scanning the other patrons, no one had the same. Most likely, a free mug sent from a promotional company trying to get the owners to buy their products.

The various mugs used by the three elderly gentlemen sitting by the far wall gave Nora a chuckle. They couldn't actually belong to those men, not with sayings like . . .

Honk if you like bingo!

A hot mug for a hot Grandpa.

Looking for love!

Well, maybe the bingo mug could. It was kind of cute seeing the old men sipping from them, though.

Sampling the coffee from her free mug, the taste of a perfectly brewed beverage confused her taste buds. She stared at the beige liquid. The aroma filling her nostrils embodied a rich bouquet that accompanied a deep, satisfying flavor.

Pushing from her seat, she made her way to the counter. "Excuse me."

Evan barely acknowledged her as he played with one of the machines. The genuine smile he had radiated a few minutes ago must have been reserved for his regular customers because he certainly didn't shine it on her. "Can I help you?"

The man didn't make eye contact, maintaining his attention on his task. Maybe that was a good thing so she could keep her wits about her. Nora squared her shoulders and used her corporate presentation voice to mask the school-girl stutter she was trying to hold back. "There's been a mistake. You gave me regular instead of decaf."

"What makes you say that?" He finally glanced at her over his shoulder.

"Because it tastes like regular."

"Coffee is coffee," he said as he fiddled with an obviously antiquated machine. "It tastes the same whether it's regular or decaf."

Nora shook her head. "Not where I come from."

He dropped his hand from his chore, his broad chest releasing a heavy sigh, then he moved to meet her on the other side of the counter, an annoyed scowl plastered on his face. "Then you're at a disadvantage. Coffee in my *quaint little shop* tastes the same."

"Your shop?" She scoffed. Good. The man was delusional. Made him seem less attractive. "I highly doubt it. You're using the same coffee even though you're telling customers they're getting decaf. Do you realize you can hurt someone that way?" If he were a MoonBurst employee, he'd be written up immediately.

Bracing both hands on the counter, he snorted then smirked as if she were an idiot. "Do you really think I'd do that to *my* customers? Look around. They're all my friends."

Yes, she had been on point earlier that he had been trying to hide his annoyance at her. Instead of staying calm, there was just something that made her all the more confrontational. She couldn't believe she was actually attracted to a guy like him. "Maybe *your* friends don't require decaf, but some people do."

"Short of having you come around to see the difference

in the color of my regular grounds versus decaf, I don't care if you believe me or not."

"Is that any way to treat a paying customer? I think Mrs. Cavanaugh would have a problem with your decorum." God, she sounded like her mother, but the guy needed to be put in his place.

"Do you now?" He lowered his gaze to the counter and slowly shook his head of wavy dark hair. When he lifted it, his hazel eyes blazed, making him even more attractive than when she first walked in. "You're *not* a customer. You're just someone passing through. So, here's what I'm gonna do. I'll refund your money and you can go back into the city to get a cup of decaf mocha cappuccino if you'd like." He punched a button on the cash register and at the sound of the bell, the cash drawer popped out. Scooping a dollar bill from its place holder, he pitched it on the counter in front of her. A plastic smile stretched his lips.

"Have a *delightful* day."

Chapter 2

If she didn't get her act together and submit her report ASAP, Nora could kiss her promotion goodbye.

She'd blown it yesterday. Big time.

Bruce expected it on his desk this morning by 9 a.m. sharp, and she hadn't completed it yet. Hadn't even returned to the city.

Instead of flying under the radar at the Bean & Brew yesterday, she had just about announced herself and ruined any chance of getting the rest of the info she needed. And, she also suffered the slight humiliation of being kicked out of the meager coffee shop. At the same time, her blasted heart had raced like a 13-year-old at the sight of Evan. She knew better than to let a good-looking guy get in the way of her job.

So careless. Everything had been riding on this expansion project. Not only her apartment, but losing it would fall perfectly into her mother's theory that she couldn't take care of herself and, therefore, needed to marry a rich man—pushing her to marry Harrison, the man of her mother's dreams.

Oh, why couldn't she have a normal family?

The money, the corner office—correction, the 23rd floor office—symbolized a corner office-type position. Enough to keep Joan Miller Langston Bainbridge from insisting her daughter needed a rich man to make her happy. The Langston money—Mother's money—had funded Nora's father's business. Even though Daddy had turned it into one of the *Forbe's* Top Ten List, Mother had always thrown it in his face that he'd be nothing without her money.

Nora didn't view marriage as a business deal. Love was more important than money, something Mother couldn't grasp.

And the corner office status on the 23rd floor didn't mean anything to Nora either, another thing Mother couldn't grasp.

But right now, she had to concentrate on her more pressing dilemma. Since she wasn't able to gather all the data yesterday because she left the coffee shop so soon, Nora realized she'd have to come up with a different plan. She had no intention of running back to the city last night without presenting a full report.

She had found a motel room for the night with the idea of trying a different approach to the situation. This morning, by the time she keyed in the preliminary data and had gone clothes shopping, the day had quickly morphed into early afternoon. She straightened a new sweatshirt over the jeans she just purchased, opened the door to the Bean & Brew and casually walked up to the counter just like everyone else. No corporate image, just one of the locals coming in for a cup of java.

"Hi, there. What can I do for you?" Evan, the same infuriatingly handsome guy, greeted her as she stepped up to the counter.

With her gaze trained away from his, Nora politely asked, "A cup of decaf mo-French vanilla decaf, please." She turned her head to the side, pretending to read one of the posters positioned on a bulletin board for the Cedar Ridge Pumpkin Festival.

"Do you want that black?"

She snapped her head toward the guy. Oh, no. Did he recognize her? "Excuse me?"

"Your coffee, how do you take it?"

Careful, don't order what you did yesterday. "Sweet, with a drop of cream, please."

"You got it."

While he quickly went to the orange-handled coffee pot, Nora noticed he didn't pay much attention to her. Yesterday, when she'd first walked in, his tongue practically hit the floor. His eyes had barely left her. It had been a compliment she hadn't enjoyed in a long time since Manhattan was filled with attractive thirty-somethings, one better looking than the next.

Now, dressed as one of the locals, or at least a tourist, he hadn't given her a second glance. It seems forgoing contacts for her glasses, eliminating make up, and pulling her hair into a ponytail had done the trick.

Although, maybe her mother had been right after all. Maybe men only cared about how a woman represented them on their arm, the trophy wife syndrome. Wouldn't give you the time of day if they thought you didn't fit the bill.

Evan slid the finished coffee and a napkin to her.

"How much?" she asked.

"One dollar" He studied her for a second, then cocked his chin to the side drawing his eyebrows together. "You've been here before, haven't you?"

Nora plunged her hand into the front pocket of her new jeans. As she feigned a struggle with the bill, she wondered whether to come clean or deny. When she handed him the dollar and mistakenly made eye contact, she relived that same connective spark their gazes held when she arrived yesterday. Quickly, she looked away and pushed the plastic-framed glasses a smidge higher on her nose. "Uh. yes, I was."

"But you didn't look like this, right?" He stepped back a moment, crossed his arms over his solid chest, and eyed her. "You were dressed differently."

"I came in just before work."

He quirked his eyebrows together, and when he finally seemed to make the connection, his left eyebrow arched. "I didn't expect to see you here again. Thought you were passing through."

She finally met his gaze. "Not exactly."

"Judging by that suit you wore, I'm guessing you work in that new office building."

"Uh, yes, exactly. The new office building." Oh how she hated lying. Unfortunately, she just couldn't say that her reason for being there was to possibly open a nationally-known coffee chain that would eventually put this shop out of business. As much as she was uncomfortable with it, the lie helped her stay anonymous. No use raising red flags if she found the village wasn't a viable option for MoonBurst.

The guy kept staring. His laser-sharp gaze sent a tingle down her spine. Her hand shook, and coffee sloshed over the side of her generic Bean & Brew mug. She swallowed hard to get herself back in control and wiped the side of the mug with her napkin.

"Thanks," she managed. "I'll take it over here."

"Enjoy," he said, but she noticed that his smile didn't quite reach his eyes.

Making her way to an empty table, Nora felt him watching her from across the store. Keeping her eyes averted, she scanned the shop, taking mental inventory of everything about it. After a few sips of coffee, which she still swore wasn't decaf, an odd prickling of her skin caused her to glance toward the counter. She jumped when she found it empty and Evan standing three feet to her left.

"How's the coffee?" he asked, motioning his chin toward her as he wiped down an empty table.

"Good." Nora sipped, trying not to gawk at the way the muscles in his arm flexed as his hand glided over the tabletop. "Just as good as yesterday."

His lips inched up to the left. "We aim to please."

Finishing the table, he moved toward the side of the counter area, reached an arm around the back, and retrieved a newspaper. Carefully, he placed the paper on an empty table where one of those three elderly gentlemen sat yesterday. She darted her eyes away, embarrassed that he caught her staring.

"Are you staying in town," he asked, "or did you move in?"

Oh, boy, another opportunity for another lie. But maybe not. "I'm staying at the motel on Route 15."

Okay, it was half a lie. She was staying at that No Tell Motel, the only place with a vacancy. She barely slept for fear something would bite her, and she had to stop her mind from conjuring images of things that had happened in that bed in the past. The one and only Cedar Ridge bed and breakfast was full and wouldn't have an opening in two days, which didn't do her any good. She was forced to endure the night in motel hell. With any luck, she'd be home by dinner, never needing to step foot in the place again.

"Oooh, the motel, huh?" A grimace accompanied an outward shiver of his wide shoulders. "Is that until you find a permanent place to live?"

With him standing a few feet away, she became fully aware of his presence as he held her gaze for a brief moment. She forced her gaze away. Being tempted by this guy was a total distraction. She had a job to do. But *his* gaze never left her, and the heat of it had her glancing back again, only this time, she focused on his hair so she wouldn't be drawn into the intensity of those hazel eyes. The soft mix of dark-brown and maple-colored waves made her want to run her hands through its thickness. She sharply jerked her eyes away, focusing on the floor. The embarrassment of him knowing she'd been staring caused heat to flush her cheeks. Evan *definitely* was the kind of guy her mother warned her about.

But she could also hear her mother's words as if the woman was sitting next to her.

He may be gorgeous, but what kind of life would he provide?

Nora shook her head. No matter how hard she tried, that same tired lecture always resurfaced. She'd done her darnedest to break that line of thinking, change her first impressions, but it seemed her mother's words were stuck in her head for eternity.

She snapped her thoughts out of the nightmare images that always appeared when thinking about her mother and realized he'd asked her a question. "Uh, a permanent place?" she asked.

"Yeah, since you're working in the office building. You looking for an apartment?"

Darn. The office building thing. "Um, that would be the plan." Ugh. Lie number three. But what harm could come of it? She'd be out of Cedar Ridge in a few hours, so this place and this guy would be a distant memory. Whatever he wanted to believe was necessary to make sure she got the job done.

She noticed Evan's head turn toward the opened door, and she sighed in relief that his attention was on something else, giving her time to cool down and think straight.

A customer entered the store, along with a brisk wind of swirling leaves scattering onto the Bean & Brew tiled floor.

"Hey, George, how ya doin' today?" Evan slapped the elderly man on the shoulder after he shuffled near them.

"Same as yesterday and the day before that," the elderly man said.

Nora recognized him from her previous visit. She took out her cell taking note of the time. Two p.m. The door opened again and another man hobbled in, a magazine under one arm and a cane in the opposite hand as he laboriously slid into the chair of the middle table next to the man named George.

Both men nodded toward one another.

"Howard."

"George."

Howard unrolled his magazine and began reading. By the time he had the first page turned, Evan appeared with two coffee mugs. The same mugs from yesterday with the cute sayings.

"Everything okay?" Evan asked, when he noticed her watching.

Nora nodded. "Can I ask a question?"

"Shoot."

"Does everyone have their own mug in this place?"

With a quick nod, he answered, "Yep."

"And you know how everyone takes their coffee?"

"That's two questions, but yeah, I do."

"And you store all their mugs on that mug holder you've got hanging in the back?"

"That's three questions, but yeah, that's where they go."

"Wouldn't it be easier to store them on a turntable than on those hooks?"

"That's question number four. And no, it wouldn't."

"Why?" When she realized what she'd done, she held up a staying hand. "I know, that's question five."

"Exactly," he said, his eyes danced with amusement. "But I'll answer it anyway. People feel comfortable knowing their personal mugs are parked in the same spot all the time. Important that they're part of the community."

Nora never heard anything like that before. And Evan said it as if it truly mattered to him that the customers felt at home.

How odd that a place of business held such a personal commitment to their customers. No wonder the coffee shop was small. While it was a considerate ideal, the old-fashioned practice left no room for growth, creating a clear path for MoonBurst to open and prosper.

She glanced out the store's large picture window, noticing all the foot traffic milling about on the street. When her boss read that the village of Cedar Ridge had been making a big splash in the tourist business, he was right in sending her to assess the location. All indications showed a big enough draw for their nationally-known coffee chain to open and thrive. Name recognition. And an extensive menu. Something the Bean & Brew sorely lacked.

Okay, so she'd messed up yesterday. But it wouldn't stop her now. Fortunately, from what she learned so far, success was imminent. Her stomach twisted into a knot.

Unfortunately, she was more than likely going to bring the Bean & Brew down.

~ ~ ~

"He's married." Arlene, the owner of the Bean & Brew, the same woman who told her yesterday to ignore Evan's bad attitude, stood near her again with an orange-handled coffee pot in hand.

Nora felt her cheeks heat. Again. Just like yesterday. She'd been caught gawking at a man standing in line.

"What a shame," she mumbled as she turned her view to her coffee mug. That's the second time in two hours that she couldn't take her eyes off a good-looking guy. First Evan, now this guy. She needed to get a grip. Spending time with MC this weekend should help clear her head and help her think straight.

"The shame is," Arlene broke in, "that this place is loaded with single women and not enough men to go around." She refilled Nora's mug.

"That one—" She pointed her chin toward the guy on line, the one that Nora couldn't help but notice when he walked in with his golden tan and his jet-black hair floating across his forehead. "—that's Adam, one of Evan's best friends. He's loyal as a puppy. Wouldn't think of looking at another woman."

Really. "That's noble," Nora said. Not many guys in her social circle held that trait. Sure, they all had the perfect family scenario—one-point-two beautiful children, pristine house, pristine wife at their side, trampy girlfriend in the shadows. Even many of her co-workers were guilty of that same lifestyle.

That wasn't for her. And neither was she interested in "acquiring" a man as her mother had un-delicately declared more times than she could count. While Nora enjoyed looking—she was, after all, a normal woman with needs—she'd been so focused on getting ahead in her job that those needs had to be squashed. Still, admiring such a great-looking guy did heat her face and other parts of her body.

Thank goodness Mary Claire's brothers showed her that good, decent guys still existed. It gave her hope that in years to come, she'd eventually find one and have a normal life.

"Grandma!" A little girl, no more than six, ran through the front door of the store and flung her arms around Arlene.

"Sweet pea!" The woman wrapped one arm around the child's back, struggling to balance the coffee pot in the other hand. "Did you have a good day at school?"

"Uh-huh." A dark-brown, curly ponytail bobbed up and down as the little girl nodded. "We made, uh, a giant track, all around the room, and raced marbles down it!"

The older woman suspiciously eyed her granddaughter. "A giant track, in the entire classroom?"

"Yep, we learned about grav, grav— I can't remember what the teacher called it. It was science."

"Gravity?"

"That's it!" the girl squealed. "How did you know?"

"I was in first grade once. A long, long time ago." Arlene laughed and ruffled her granddaughter's hair. The woman placed the coffee pot on an empty table and squatted to eye level with the child, unbuttoned the little girl's coat, and gave her a hug. "I missed you a whole bunch today."

"I missed you, too!" The child was gone before the words were out of her mouth.

"Get yourself settled to do your homework," Arlene yelled and slowly stood, securing one hand to her lower back as she adjusted to a stand, her smile stretching from ear to ear. "I love that kid."

"She obviously loves you, too," Nora heard herself say, not paying attention to where the little girl had gone. It was evident the two held a special bond. A pang of loneliness knocked on the door to Nora's heart. Her own grandmother on her father's side had died before Nora was born. She imagined she would have been just like this woman: warm, loving, and caring, the way a grandmother should be.

Her grandmother on her mother's side was a different story. A carbon copy of Nora's mother, or rather, her mother had been a duplicate of her grandmother.

Never show emotion, never let your guard down. Don't let people truly know who you are, and for heaven's sake, DO NOT CRY.

Crying had been strictly forbidden in the Langston family. It caused wrinkles and ruined make up. And *"How in the world do you expect to get a husband, Eleanor, if you don't look perfect?"*

"Hey, sweetie. You okay?" Arlene asked.

Nora stopped breathing for a minute and glanced at the woman. Had she gone to that lonely place she'd always gotten sucked into when recalling her childhood? And had it been that obvious that this woman noticed?

"I-I'm fine."

As if not hearing Nora's words, the woman sat in the chair across from her. "I don't want to pry, but you look like someone ran over your puppy."

Nora rotated the coffee mug in between both her hands. It was presumptuous of this woman to think she'd share her inner thoughts, let alone share something as private as emotional turmoil from her childhood. But it was also comforting, like some of the talks she had with Mary Claire's mother. "I'm fine, really. But it's kind of you to ask."

Tilting her head to one side, the woman narrowed her eyes. "Weren't you in here yesterday?"

Nora nodded. "Yes."

"You know what?" Arlene nodded several times and clucked her tongue. A knowing gleam formed in her eyes as she tapped a pointed finger in the air toward Nora. "I like this version better."

"Seriously? I don't have on a stitch of makeup, and I didn't fix my hair." Nora ran a hand down the length of her ponytail. Her brown-rimmed, plastic-framed glasses hid her eyes, the one thing she considered the best part of her average face.

"You don't need all that. You're beautiful just the way you are. Sounds like you bought into all that crap those magazines tout."

The woman's bluntness surprised Nora, yet it was refreshing. It was honest, and obviously not intended to hurt her feelings. In fact, it added a little oomph to her ego. And what girl's ego couldn't use a little boost.

When Arlene stretched her hand in the air across the table, Nora hesitantly took hold of it and the woman shook back. "I'm Arlene Cavanaugh, part owner of the Bean & Brew. Welcome."

"I'm El—" While Nora took an instant liking to this woman, she also reminded herself that she had a job to do. If the woman Googled her real name, she'd learn Eleanor was the heir to the Bainbridge fortune who just happened to work for MoonBurst Coffee. Quickly thinking, she said, "Nora. Nora Langston."

Pairing the nickname with her middle name kept things simple. No use complicating the situation by giving her real name. Besides, she loved when her father and Mary Claire called her Nora, especially since Dad disliked the name Eleanor. In Nora's mind, a person with the name Nora was a free spirit, not bogged down with the rigors expected of an Eleanor. Nora was vibrant and loving, while Eleanor was uptight and proper. Maybe this was her chance to momentarily live as Nora, see if her image of Nora was all she thought it was.

"Glad to meet you, Nora," Arlene said. "Now, if I don't get my fanny back to work, I'm likely to get fired." She motioned her chin toward the counter where Evan was taking care of a family. "Looks like tourists who need a little assistance and a Cedar Ridge welcome."

"Thanks," Nora said. "You've been really helpful."

What began as an annoyance, pleasantly turned into something she'd rarely experienced. She liked hearing the woman call her Nora, gave her a little excitement that she could have a secret identity. Even though she liked it, she still had to keep her distance, needed to close off the part of her emotions that could easily fall prey to the warm welcome Arlene offered.

As Arlene walked away, Nora retrieved her cell from her purse and began typing with her thumbs—under the guise of texting—punching in a few notes about the Bean & Brew without anyone in the store realizing. She needed her work to bring her back to reality even though she was having fun with her new name. Staying emotionally detached was necessary for her to do her job efficiently. Besides, there was no room for emotion in her life. Her parents had made sure of that.

~ ~ ~

That same opinion Evan had of that good-looking brunette when he first met her slammed to the front of his mind. Yeah, he'd found her sexy and his body hummed at the sight of her. But once she opened her mouth and all that high-maintenance crap came spilling out, it stopped him cold.

But now, as she sat across the store—minus the corporate raider outfit—she looked innocent sipping her coffee and talking to his mother like she'd known her all her life.

Yep, that in itself was a red light to stay far away from the woman, especially since she was going to be living in Cedar Ridge. Once his mother got it in her head that there was an available woman within 100 feet of him, she'd be on him to ask her out.

Nope. Not gonna happen. Doesn't matter what kind of knockout she was yesterday, or how cute and approachable she looked and acted today, two personalities meant drama and dishonesty. He had no intention of putting himself through that, and he certainly wasn't going to let his daughter live through that kind of crap again.

As his mother left the woman and joined him behind the counter, Evan glanced at the glint in his mother's eyes.

"I was just getting to know our new customer," she defended.

"Mm-hmm."

"Her name is Nora. Isn't that a pretty name?"

"Whatever." Definitely didn't like where this was going.

"I was telling her I think she's much prettier without all that makeup she had on yesterday, don't you think?"

Evan stopped checking the temperature of the milk and looked his mother straight in the eye. "I'm not going there."

Yeah, he noticed how Nora kept checking him out. How it gave him a little more pep in his step as he did his job. But-

"She's new in town, and I'm sure she'd like someone to go out with. Maybe grab a cup of coffee."

"You're kidding, right?" He went back to reading the thermometer that he had just plunged into the cream container. "Why would I go out to get a cup of coffee when I own a coffee shop? And why would I go out with her? She's obviously a MoonBurst kind of person."

"How can you say that? She seems to be enjoying your coffee right now."

"You know our coffee is excellent. We brew the best around, thanks to Dad."

"I know, but she looks lonely. There's a kind of sadness about her."

"Maybe it's because she's not a nice person. She came in here yesterday all high and mighty and made fun of the place."

"She did? How?"

"She called it quaint and small, not much on the menu."

"Well, we are quaint and small. I did tell her we increased the menu. I'm sure she'll get used to us in a few days."

"Really?" He scrubbed his hand around the back of his neck. He knew the kind of person she was. City girl, wealthy, or at least looking for someone to keep her wealthy. Theater seats. Fine dining. Lavish weekend getaways to the Hamptons. He knew the type all too well. She was just like the rest of them. Just like Miranda.

How could his mother forget the demeaning way Miranda had talked about the Bean & Brew? How she thought that Dad's childish woodworking belonged in the garbage and not on display for everyone to see?

If his mother wasn't getting it, maybe she'd get this. "She made fun of Dad's mug holder."

Evan watched surprise register on his mother's face, and then her eyes narrowed as her lips puckered. "You mean she's like your ex-wife?"

Chapter 3

After Nora called Mary Claire to let her know she'd have to postpone the trip to help her with her parents' horses, Nora spent the rest of Saturday afternoon scouting the village's beverage competition.

Jenkinsen's Corner Store on Main and Oak Ridge sold bottled water and soft drinks as did the Quick Mart at the gas station. The only places in Cedar Ridge that sold coffee were the Acropolis Diner, The Cookie Cottage, and the Bean & Brew.

As far as she was concerned, no real competition existed for MoonBurst. There was a *donut* chain on Rt. 15 to contend with, but everyone in the coffee business knew they catered to a less-discerning clientele. MoonBurst chose to view their customers as having a gourmet palate, and as the latest demographics indicated, the untapped tourist revenue source in this area of Sussex County would welcome their coffee franchise with open arms.

To prove it, Nora decided to take an impromptu survey of the tourists. It made sense that the locals were loyal to the Bean & Brew, but she was sure the tourists would appreciate a cup of their favorite MoonBurst designer beverages on their weekend getaways.

Making her way on the sidewalks of the bustling village, her step became lighter. She realized it was sort of liberating to do her job without the confinement of heels. Sneakers, jeans, sweat shirt, and a ponytail were a pleasant change from her usual business suit. Yes, being a Nora definitely had advantages over being an Eleanor.

Oh, her mother would freak if she saw her now.

What has gotten into you, Eleanor?

Satisfaction lifted the corners of her lips as her insides jumped with giddy anticipation.

She turned the corner onto Main Street and noticed a family studying a glossy Cedar Ridge pamphlet. She recognized the brochure from one she had picked up at Jenkinsen's Corner Store. Setting her sights on the family, she headed straight for them.

"Excuse me?" Perfect. The dad had a Bean & Brew take-out cup in his hand. "I'm taking a survey. I notice you visited the local coffee shop."

"Yes, we did," the man answered. "Great little place."

"I wonder if you would have preferred a MoonBurst Coffee instead."

The man looked up and down the street, his wife imitating the action. "MoonBurst? Where?"

"There isn't one, yet, but if you had a choice, wouldn't you love your favorite MoonBurst flavored coffee instead of the local coffee?" Nora motioned an opened hand to his cup.

"Nah. This coffee is great and has a great price, too."

"Don't listen to him," his wife said. "He's cheap."

"Yes, it is a good price. But you know the old saying, 'You get what you pay for,'" Nora said. At a dollar a cup, she knew the economy sometimes dictated people's purchases, good or bad.

"I would love a Praline Latte right now," the wife said.

"Not me," the husband said. "MoonBurst is too strong. I don't like going there. Too many choices. Never did know what half those things were." The man shrugged at his wife. "Bean & Brew is just right. Good coffee, nice people, a taste of the local flavor."

Nora didn't know what to say for a moment. Her company didn't get to be number one in the country with bad coffee. Sure, it was a darker, stronger brew that many enjoyed. Evidently, this guy never tried their lighter Platinum Blend.

"Thank you very much for your time," Nora said, and with a quick wave continued, "Enjoy the rest of your trip."

She walked a few blocks then zeroed in on a group of people on Oak Ridge Road, all middle-aged, listening intently to what appeared to be a tour guide pointing to one of the restored Victorians.

As she drew closer, the tour guide described the decorative, textured shingles gracing the front-facing gables on the Cedar Ridge Library. She appreciated the tender loving care that obviously went into the restoration of what the guide said was a Queen Anne Victorian. She also admired the Village Improvement District for providing guided tours to help visitors discover the village's amenities.

When the tour guide finished, Nora trailed behind the crowd, blending in. She didn't want to be obvious and out right ask anyone about MoonBurst just in case the tour guide overheard. A premature leak that the company planned to open a store in the village would hinder her from gaining the data she needed. She also didn't want to think about how Arlene at the Bean & Brew would feel learning that kind of news, either. The expansion wasn't set in stone yet, so no use getting everyone upset.

"I could really use a good cup of coffee right now," she said aloud, trying to engage the people around her.

"Two blocks away, there's a coffee shop. Nice little place," a woman said, waving a finger toward Elm Street.

"Is it a MoonBurst?" Nora asked.

"No, it's the Bean & Brew. I guess Cedar Ridge isn't populated enough for MoonBurst," another woman said. "The local coffee shop is pretty good."

"Would you like it if MoonBurst was here?" Nora asked.

The second woman shook her head. "Doesn't have the same charm as the Bean & Brew."

"And MoonBurst doesn't have the guy who works at the Bean & Brew. He's so cute," gushed the first woman. "If I were a few years younger—"

"You mean a few decades younger," the second interrupted.

"Speak for yourself."

"I am. We're the same age."

Oh, boy. Nora didn't mean to start an argument. And so far, her survey wasn't going as anticipated. But hearing the two older women talk about Evan did cause her mind to wander.

Evan. Seemed his country-boy charm even turned the heads of women old enough to be his mother. Nora doubted there'd be a woman alive who wouldn't be attracted to a guy who gave his undivided attention, whose easy smile cast a lazy, come-hither spell on whomever he set it upon. But there seemed to be more to it. Something about him piqued her curiosity. His dedication to the customers, almost as if he owned the business himself. If he hadn't exhibited such an attitude with her the first day she met him, she would have recommended him for a position in her company's new location.

Although, earlier today, when he hadn't realized who she was, he was cordial, kind of sexy in a fun way.

But what about his ambition? Her mother's words swam in her head.

At his age, working at a store couldn't yield a high enough salary for a comfortable living. If—and that was a very strong *if*—Nora decided to get involved with someone, he'd have to be her equal in drive and motivation. While she didn't want a man to take care of her, she certainly had no desire to take care of a man.

And judging his age, maybe he was the type to bounce from job to job. Probably never stayed in one place long enough to work his way up, gain a higher salary or advance.

Although, that couldn't be right. Especially watching the way he handled himself with the customers, knowing what they wanted and providing it with ease.

Maybe he'd been working at the Bean & Brew since he graduated high school. The type of guy who never ventured out of his comfort zone, who only wore flannel shirts and denim. Probably still dated his high school sweetheart. But with those killer eyes, Nora imagined women flocked to him, no matter their age.

Uh, oh. Killer eyes? Strong shoulders, sexy crooked smile?

The quicker she got out of Cedar Ridge the better. She didn't want to fall for Evan whatever-his-last-name-was. All his tempting good looks made it harder to remember a man would distract her from her goal.

And, when she did *want* a guy, it certainly wouldn't be someone like him.

She steered her thoughts back to the task at hand, gently stepping away from the tour group. Problem was, the harder she tried to put Evan out of her mind, the more it seemed his presence kept throwing her off track.

~ ~ ~

"What are you doing?" Arlene asked her son as she walked into the back of the store late Saturday afternoon.

Evan handed the repairman a check for fixing the grinder machine, hoping the guy would have been gone by the time his mother returned from the park with Julie.

"Sorry about not picking you up," he said, quietly slipping the receipt into the back pocket of his jeans. When he realized it was four p.m., he quickly called in a favor. Once his mother saw he was late, he knew she and Julie would walk home. With the fall evenings getting darker at an earlier time, he called Todd.

His mother glared at him. "I knew something was up

when you texted that you couldn't come. When Todd showed up, he said you were busy. You're busted, mister."

Yeah, he was, but he did what was needed to repair the old machine.

He bent down and scooped Julie into his arms. "Hey, kiddo, how's my favorite girl?"

Julie wound her petite arms around his neck. At her young age, he was the most important person in his daughter's life, and he *loved* it. He hoped like hell she'd still love him the same when she became a teenager.

"I missed you, Daddy." She rubbed her cold nose on his cheek, then kissed him.

"Oooh, and I missed you, too." He snuggled her neck. "Did you and Grandma have fun at the park today?"

"Uh-huh. Gramma let me run around the pond!" Her toothless grin always beamed right into his heart.

"She did?" He arched an eyebrow at his mother.

"Don't worry." Arlene swatted him with one of her gloves. "I let her run on the grass, not the sidewalk."

"Ahh, that was nice," he said to his daughter. His mother wouldn't let Julie do anything that would put her in danger, but you can never be too careful. "Did you see any geese?"

"Yep, they squawked at me." Her tiny lips pouted as she shook her head. "I don't like them."

Evan leaned his forehead against his daughter's. "You know what, pumpkin, neither do I." He gave her one more hug, then she squirmed downward and he released her to the floor.

Arlene shot her 'disapproving Mom glare' at him, causing him to take a deep breath in anticipation of a small confrontation about the grinder. "I thought we discussed this already? You are *not* paying for this repair."

"Jules, why don't you get started on your snack." He ruffled her ponytail so she wouldn't think there was a problem. "I'll be there in a minute."

"Okay." Her crop of dark-brown, curly hair bounced as she scampered to the back table in the dining area where he had a glass of milk and a pumpkin-shaped cookie waiting for her.

"Evan, you're stalling."

"Ma, not now. The machine is fixed. We'll work out the details later."

Arlene glanced at his daughter then trained her eyes back on him. "You can't keep bailing out the store," she said in a lowered voice. "If we're not making enough money, maybe we should think about selling."

Evan resolutely shook his head. "No way. I promised Dad. The only reason we're a little short right now is because of all the improvements. In a few weeks, when the holiday crowds start coming, we'll catch up."

"Have you taken a paycheck or are you still living on your savings?" she asked.

"We've been over this already. I have more than enough in savings, so don't worry. I'll do what I have to to keep this place going." The Bean & Brew meant more to him than just a job or a pay check. It had changed his life, grounded him, given him an appreciation of what's important. He and Julie now lived in a great town surrounded by people who care about them. No amount of money could give him that.

But his mother continued that I-don't-believe-you look.

"I promise." He held up his hand as if citing an oath. "After all the Halloween events are done in two weeks, everything will work out."

"And?"

He placed both his hands on her shoulders and gave her his most convincing smile. "I'll make sure to take a paycheck."

~ ~ ~

Oh, darn. Nora rolled over on the lumpy bed in the horrid motel and glanced at her vibrating cell resting on the night stand. This trip was turning into a nightmare. First, she had to cancel her weekend at the horse farm with Mary Claire. And now, the continual vibrating of her phone reminded her of how she'd come up short for work.

"Bruce," she groaned.

He surely wanted an update of the results of her trip. Trouble was, she didn't have them yet.

With the Bean & Brew privately owned, their records weren't public. In order for her to get more in-depth numbers, she'd have to speak to Arlene or Thomas Cavanaugh and she doubted either of them would be forthcoming on the financial status of their business. Besides, she still hadn't met Thomas, so she'd have to see if she could get something out of Arlene. She didn't feel at all comfortable prying into the woman's business, even though Arlene appeared approachable and friendly.

She grimaced as she swiped the cell screen to direct the call to voicemail. It was the third time she'd done the same over the past 24 hours. Bruce was going to be furious with her, but she didn't have a choice.

Her findings suggested Cedar Ridge was ideal for a new MoonBurst location. Problem was that few wanted it.

Okay, it made sense that the locals didn't want it, all that loyalty and such to the Bean & Brew and their community. She even began to understand how they felt. It was kind of refreshing in a time when no one really felt strongly enough about their neighbors to foster that kind of loyalty.

But the tourists had surprised her. They were mixed on her company. Some wanted it desperately; others didn't care. As they put it, they could get MoonBurst anywhere. They liked how quaint Cedar Ridge was. Their opinion: MoonBurst was too modern and would spoil the atmosphere and charm of the village.

On one level, she did agree with them. The place was *charming*, and if she hadn't agreed, she'd probably hate that word right now since she had heard it over and over.

And now, as her phone vibrated again, she put the pillow over her head to block out the muted noise. Bruce would have to wait.

The motel's neon sign flashed outside her window while the rumble of police cruisers dashed by, echoing along the highway. She needed to get out of this place. But the thought of going back without a full report guaranteed no chance of getting that promotion, so she had taken another trip to Target for another outfit and a heavy, hooded jacket and gloves, and sucked up the need for one more night.

As Mary Claire had reminded her, Eleanor Langston Bainbridge never failed at anything. It wasn't allowed. And she certainly wasn't going to start now even if she was masquerading as Nora. She just needed more time. But would it be enough time to save her home?

~ ~ ~

"There she is! Good morning, Nora."

For a second, Nora didn't realize she was being greeted as she entered the Bean & Brew. Slowly she turned her gaze toward the voice. An old man with stark white hair, who sat at the middle table along the brick wall, warmly saluted her with his index finger.

Another older gentleman looked up from his newspaper and said, "Oh, hi there, Nora."

"Good morning," she mumbled, wondering how they knew her name and why they felt the need for the salutation.

"It's a beautiful Sunday morning, don't ya think?" one of them asked, but she didn't turn her gaze back to figure out which one.

"Morning." Evan nodded from behind the counter. "Somehow, I had you as an early riser. Guess I was wrong."

She scurried toward him, only to be met by a mug of steaming coffee and the sexy playfulness of Evan's hazel eyes which today mirrored the deep royal blue of his tee shirt. She nearly whimpered with delight, noticing his trademark flannel gone showcasing the bulk of bicep muscles etched under his tee.

"I decided to sleep in," she said. He was right, though. She was an early riser. After not sleeping well, her body finally ignored the light show outside her motel window and she slept straight through until eight this morning, something Eleanor would never do.

"Good. Every once in a while, it's important to sleep in." The wistful tone of his voice gave her pause.

"When was the last time you did?" she asked.

"Me?" He pointed to his well-sculpted chest. "I don't require a lot of sleep."

"Where's Mrs. Cavanaugh?" Nora glanced around, noting the woman's absence. "Are you manning the store alone?"

"Yeah, she's a churchgoer."

"And I take it, you're not?"

"Let's just say there were times in my life when I needed divine intervention, but none came." He leaned one hip against the counter, arms crossed over his broad chest.

The pull of the material across his skin caused her to swallow hard as awareness streamed through her. She liked it better when he wore the heavy flannel shirt. The tee left nothing to her imagination and all those muscles left her totally distracted. Whatever he lacked in ambition, he certainly compensated in the strength of a solid body.

"So, how come you're not in church?" He seemed less curious, but almost as if he wanted to make conversation.

Nora hesitated and took hold of the end of her pony tail, stroking it with one hand. "To tell you the truth, I never really gave it a thought."

"That's probably because you're busy getting settled with the new job. Any luck finding a place to live? I heard Amanda Russell might have an apartment for rent by the end of the month."

Great. Getting trapped in the lie she wove seemed to be getting tighter each day. "I'm fine where I am for now, thanks."

"In the motel?" His eyes widened in surprise. "Are you kidding? I wouldn't put my worst enemy in that place."

If all went well today, her association with that motel would be history. "I really had no other choice. The bed and breakfast on Primrose Lane didn't have an opening until Sunday night."

He snickered. "I see your point."

"What's so funny?"

"That place is the last place I'd picture *you* in."

It was her turn to cross her arms over her chest. "What do you mean?"

"When you came in here on Friday, if I was a bettin' man, I would have lost my shirt that you'd stay in that place."

The thought of him shirtless made her mouth dry. What was it about him that had her mind thinking such tempting thoughts?

Friday. He's talking about Friday.

She remembered the silk suit she had on two days ago. The one that now lay carefully folded in the back seat of her Chevy, waiting patiently to go to the dry cleaners for its usual routine. "Yes, I guess you would have. I don't dress like that all the time."

"Really?" He cast a discerning eye on her.

Coming to town in her work clothes definitely had been the wrong choice. "I'm not dressed like that now, am I?" She pushed her glasses higher on her nose.

"No, but somehow, I'm thinking this—" His finger circled several times toward her. "—isn't the real you."

How did he do that? First he nailed her on being an early riser. Now he was able to tell she didn't normally dress in sweats. Well, she did, but only at night when she was cold and needed the snuggle of fleece to keep warm. Being alone in her apartment usually lent itself to being temperature cold as well as companionship cold.

"I love wearing jeans and sneakers." It wasn't a lie. Over the past two days, she'd grown accustomed to the fit and feel. The darn things were extremely comfortable.

"So what's up with you?" He uncrossed his arms and leaned a capable hand on the counter. "What's your thing?"

"My thing?" She swallowed hard, thinking that her thing right now was to concentrate on not reaching across the counter to touch the veined contours of his strong hand. To feel his smooth skin and run her finger up the textured hair on his arm to biceps that expanded at the edge of the short sleeve of his tee shirt. Terror coursed through her at the thought that the few times she'd been near him, she seemed to lose control of her normal rational thinking.

"Yeah, you know, your story. Why are you here on a Sunday morning?"

She quickly took hold of her mug, held it to her lips, and gulped a generous sip. "I'm here for coffee."

"Don't you have something more important to do than hang out here?"

A blush ran over her face. Was he reading her again? Was it her attraction to him that he sensed, or was it her *real* reason for being there? Darn, but she was a poor liar.

"Um . . ." She needed an excuse. Now! She couldn't tell him she had a list of questions that needed to be answered by the owner. Wasn't about to tell him her company considered building one of their locations a few blocks away from the Bean & Brew. As it was, he knew she was hiding something, her clothes had been a dead giveaway. He hadn't thought highly of her since she waltzed in here on Friday with her "city" attitude. *Wait. That's it!*

She glanced at the tables of the semi-empty coffee shop to make sure she wouldn't be heard. It was a long shot, but she had to give it a try. "I'd like to apologize for my behavior on Friday."

Evan's eyes opened wide. "You what?"

Nora lowered her head and drew in a deep breath. She met his gaze. "I want to apologize for coming in on Friday and making fun of this place."

Evan edged away from the counter and stared at her as if unsure of what he'd just heard. "Wow. I never saw *that* coming."

Neither did she. But it was the only response that popped into her head.

She turned her back to him, trying to survey the store with an objective eye this time. No modern, upscale furnishings. No graphic art on the walls. Well-used, odd chairs sat beneath mismatched tables.

When she had first arrived on Friday, she had discounted the relevance of the place. Now, as she focused her full attention, she observed it from a customer's perspective. Each unique piece of furniture was a work of art, antiques that were lovingly cared for. A layer of protective glass covered all the table tops for easy cleanup, allowing the richness of the wood patterns to be visible.

She walked from the counter and ran a fingertip over a ladder-back chair, noticing the pristine condition of its cane seat. "This place does hold a certain charm," she said aloud. "It's not at all like the chains that dot the country. It's different—" *Dare I say . . .?* "—special."

"It's about time you came 'round. People usually love this place the minute they walk in. How many visits did it take for you to appreciate the eclectic welcome?"

Nora thought a minute. "Only three, counting this one." And it probably would have taken more to open her eyes had it not been for her failed survey. But she needed to get back on track, and even though Arlene Cavanaugh wasn't working today, she'd have to make due and get as much info from him. The sooner she got what she needed, the sooner she could say goodbye to Cedar Ridge, and Evan, the hot coffee guy.

She slipped a dollar across the counter for her beverage, and as he retrieved it, she flinched at the excitement flittering through her when his hand brushed hers. That kind of reaction was *not* supposed to happen.

"Mrs. Cavanaugh has a nice business here." She changed tactics in order to get her head back in the game, trying not to dwell on the heat he suddenly triggered. She also didn't want to think about her job actions resulting in a nice woman being put out of business.

"Yeah, she does." He snorted.

"Are you her only employee?"

This time, a hearty laugh burst from his mouth. "Yep. Just the two of us." He backed away from the counter and busied himself with some new sleeves of disposable cups.

"Does she ever hire extra help, you know, during the village's busy seasons?"

He stopped with the cups and directed his attention back to her. "Are you looking for a part-time job?"

"No-No. Not at all. It just seems like a lot of work for two people."

He shrugged and resumed his task. "We manage."

"I'm sure you do." She'd seen him at his best, filling order after order. While she wouldn't consider him a trained barista, he sure knew his way around the cozy shop. More importantly, he knew his customers.

"The place seems like it makes a nice profit with all the tourist traffic."

Evan stopped stacking the new cups again, the playfulness vanishing from his eyes as he stared at her before replying. "We do all right."

Nora knew when to back off. "Good. I'm terrible with numbers, so I admire anyone who understands all that stuff. I'm more a creative type."

"R-e-a-l-l-y?" The arch of his eyebrow coupled with his suspicious glare caused a weave of paranoia to creep through her. "I wouldn't have taken you as a *crafty* person, creatively speaking."

Ouch. Okay, he *didn't* trust her. Probably ready to warn his boss about her. But why would he? She gave him no reason for suspicion. Neither Evan nor Arlene knew who she was or why she was there. She pushed her paranoia aside and forced herself to relax.

"Oh, no. I'm not crafty. Glue guns and I don't get along. I'm more of a high-concept, idea person."

His shoulders seemed to slacken some after her comment. "Idea person? Is that what you do for your job?"

Oh, boy, time for another lie. "Sort of. I'm more of a gopher."

He smiled. "Hard to picture you as a gopher."

An unladylike snicker crept out of her throat. "Not the mammal, silly. I do a little of this and that."

"So, you're an administrative assistant?"

"Kind of." Offering nothing further, she aimed to get him off the uncomfortable subject. "Can I ask you something?"

He shrugged again. "Shoot."

"Those three men over there, do they do anything but sit here all day?" Three elderly gentlemen, each taking up a full table all day long was bad for business. "And, why do they each sit at a different table?"

Evan came from behind the counter and when he leaned close, an unexpected thrill surprised her. "They're all best friends, but they like their personal space. Especially

Howard. He likes his own table so people can speak to him without interrupting the other two." He extended a hand to follow him. "Come on."

It had been a while since Nora held hands with a man. Evan's hold was gentle, yet strong, something that oddly comforted her.

"Gentlemen, I'd like to formally introduce you to Cedar Ridge's newest resident. This is Noraaaa . . ." He waited for her to fill in the last name.

"L-Langston." The experiment of living a secret life had her cringe inwardly. Maybe this wasn't such a good idea.

Each man rose from his seat and nodded toward her.

"This is George Statler. George retired from the electric plant a few years ago."

"Really?" She took care to not hurt his fragile, boney hand as he extended it to her and she gently shook it.

"Yes siree." The man nodded, pride shining over his wrinkled face. "Gave the company forty-nine years. Started with them right after I got out of the service."

"That's impressive," she said. No one worked that long for a company anymore. "Thank you for your service to our country."

As George saluted her, Evan made eye contact with her, taking her by the elbow and leading her a few inches to the next table. The warmth of his hand felt different, more intimate, than the countless men who had touched her with the same cordial gesture in the past. Again, the loss of her emotional control around him percolated to a simmer, making it difficult to pay attention.

"This is Howard Waldorf."

"Pleasure is all mine." The tallest of the three, with a full head of white hair, winked as he took her hand in both of his in a kind, grandfatherly way. That alone softened Nora's heart since she hadn't known either of her grandfathers.

"Nice to meet you," she said, noticing the whimsy dancing in his eyes.

"Howard's a former Bud man. Worked at the Budweiser plant in Newark." Evan leaned in close again and the smell of fresh-roasted coffee surrounded her nostrils as the aroma of hazelnut coffee drifted from his lips and she nearly swooned, but somehow held it together. "If you ever need to know about stocks and investments, Howard's your guy."

"He's not kidding," George said. "He's worth more than all of us put together."

"Shhh!" Howard swiped a hand at George. "You want me to get kidnapped or mugged?"

"By who?" George asked, looking around the store. "There's no one here but us?"

Luckily, the shop was empty at the moment. But Howard was right. As an elderly gentleman, he would be ripe for a mugging if word got out that he was wealthy. At least he would if he were in the city. Nora didn't think he needed to worry in Cedar Ridge.

"Don't worry, Mr. Waldorf, I'll keep your secret." Just as she said his name, she immediately thought of the famous hotel in the city. She looked at him again. No. He couldn't be one of the originals, could he? No. Not if he worked at the beer plant.

The man winked at her again. "Thank you." He switched his gaze from her to Evan and said, "This one seems *really* nice."

"Knock it off, Howard," Evan said. "She's just a customer."

"I didn't mean for you," Howard said with a laugh. "I meant for me!"

Nora caught the smile on Evan's face as he said, "I don't think Muriel would appreciate that."

"You're married?" Nora asked and sputtered out a laugh.

"Sure am. Goin' on sixty-two years in April."

"Congratulations."

As the man winked at her again and slowly settled back into his chair, she took note of the amount of years these gentlemen spent in committed relationships. That small-town loyalty thing more prominent than ever.

A gentle push of her elbow by Evan again—and another flutter of her heart—had her standing in front of the third man's table. "This is Walter Buchanan."

The softness in the man's dark-brown eyes verged on tears. "I haven't seen a pretty girl like you since I first laid eyes on my sweet Dolores." He wiped the corner of one eye and blinked several times.

"Walter lost his wife a few months ago. But we're all here for you, Walter." Evan moved between Howard and Walter's tables and placed a hand on Walter's shoulder. "You got all that food I sent over, right?"

"Sure did. That cornbread was pretty good. Not as tasty as my Dolores', but pretty good," he said in a quivering voice.

"No one's cornbread was as good as Dolores', or her sweet potato pie," Evan said as he gently patted the elderly man's shoulder.

Nora held out her hand and extended it farther as the man's mocha-toned hand shook, trying to connect with hers. "It's a pleasure to meet you, Mr. Buchanan." She glanced at the booklet on the table in front of him. "I see you like to work on crossword puzzles."

"I try, but my eyes aren't as good as they used to be. Dolores used to help me with them."

She didn't know how to react to that. Studying the sadness of the man's expression, she said the first thing that came to mind. "Would you mind if I tried to help?"

His eyes then fully clouded with tears. "I'd be honored, young lady."

Nora realized Evan's introduction of these men impacted their importance. They may have looked irrelevant to the community, but she now knew nothing could be farther from the truth. Not only that, but they were important to Evan.

For once, she felt compelled to let down her guard, let emotions she wasn't comfortable exposing dictate her actions. It felt foreign, but it also felt right. She sensed that helping Mr. Buchanan would garnish so much satisfaction, her insides were bubbling with pride that she'd be able to help someone in need.

So much for not getting involved. Whatever happened to her 'get in and get out' routine? This was so against all she practiced when it came to business. She was so far behind in compiling her report, the longer she delayed, the slimmer her chances would be for that promotion.

She directed her attention away from Mr. Buchanan when the warmth of Evan's hand on her elbow comforted her. A glimmer of satisfaction and pride shown in his eyes as he connected with her gaze. Suddenly, her job, the report, her life in the city seemed a world away. How, in such a short time had this man, and these elderly men, broken down the emotional barriers she had shielded herself in for most of her life?

She wanted to snap out of it, to wake up, run back to her rational life, but the connection that welded her and Evan together proved greater than her resolve.

What in the world was she doing?

Chapter 4

Nora helping Walter with his crossword puzzle surprised the hell out of Evan. Not a pleasant surprise, more like a cautious one. His first impression of her was not as a person who'd selflessly volunteer to help a senior citizen. It was a good trait, but he warned himself not to be sucked in by her generosity, or by the kindly way she spoke to Walter, or by the lilt of her laugh as Howard flirted with her.

No. He refused to be drawn in by all that stuff. So he concentrated on her odd behavior when she had arrived an hour ago. She had been civil, not snooty, almost pleasant as if she didn't want to leave. And she had complimented his business.

What was she up to?

Was it as simple as she was attracted to him?

She showed no signs of interest other than the blush that turned her face bright red when their hands touched as she had paid him. Damn lucky for him. Women were off limits. Especially women like her who demanded and expected a lot. Hurt lasted long and deep, and he wasn't about to get his heart broken again. More importantly, he had to protect his daughter. No one would penetrate the fortress he built around his precious little girl.

But, as hard as he tried, there was something drawing him to Nora. Maybe his mother had been right. It was probably sexual frustration.

He remembered how Nora looked when she initially walked into their lives two days ago. Yeah, he was definitely interested at first, but he brushed that aside. Instead, he concentrated on the patronizing attitude that permeated all that beauty and polish.

The Nora he spied now was fresh, vibrant, approachable. Real. And it scared the hell out of him.

Which one was the real woman?

"A seven-letter word for extinguish," he heard Nora recite to Walter.

Evan's attention snapped toward the table where Walter pushed up his silver-rimmed glasses as he thought a minute, then yelled, "Smother!"

Evan hadn't seen his old friend this happy since before Dolores had gotten sick. At least Nora brought a glimmer of sunshine back into Walter's eyes which made Evan glad she had stopped by.

But why had she asked him those questions about his business just before he introduced her to the guys.

"Are you her only employee?"

"Does she hire extra help during the busy seasons?"

"This place seems to make a nice profit."

Why the pointed questions and comments?

Her sudden interest didn't make sense since she didn't seem the type to want to work in a place like his. Maybe she was asking for someone else, a friend, relative, or someone unemployed. He should probably ask before jumping to conclusions.

And then she questioned him about George and the guys. No way would he let her insult them. They had helped his father when things got tough and were now part of the harmony of the store, adding a certain character to the place. Had been since before he'd graduated college.

Nora still didn't know he was part owner, and he didn't intend to tell her. She assumed he was an employee. Assumed his mother was the sole owner. In his former life, he found that line of thinking typical of an ambitious woman who discounted any man who didn't bring in a six-figure income. The situation gnawed at him. Which woman was she?

Did she work for the bank?

No. She said she wasn't good with numbers. Besides, his personal accounts were flush. And he had purposely left enough in the Bean & Brew account so his mother wouldn't worry.

Had his mother taken out a loan, suspecting he was fronting the store account with his own money?

Nah, she wouldn't do that without talking it over with him.

Nope. Probably the inadequacy of falling slightly behind this month had his paranoia flying around like the fall leaves outside with the wind.

He had taken a huge risk coming home to run his parents' business. But it had been worth it. For him *and* Julie. He was keeping the business alive. Keeping his father's memory alive.

Once again, Nora's voice broke through his thoughts. "What's a four-letter word for cloudy air?"

"Haze!" Walter yelled out, pride beamed on his face.

Evan's stomach suddenly lurched when Nora glanced his way with a sparkle in her eyes he couldn't ignore. Definite heat between them. Better not get sucked in. She was just being generous toward his friends.

Just before he was able to shift his gaze from hers, she broke the connection and turned her eyes back on Walter.

"You're a wiz at this," she said to his old friend. "You just need some help to read the small print. Maybe a magnifying glass might work?"

Evan watched as Walter laid his dark hand over the pale brightness of Nora's. "I don't need one of those things when I've got you."

A lump formed in Evan's throat. The joy on the older man's face had him rethinking his suspicions about Nora.

If anyone could detect insincerity it was Walter. His 35 years on the police force gave him a keen sense of whether a person had something to hide or not. If Walter approved of Nora, Evan thought maybe he shouldn't be so mistrusting. As much as he didn't want to, he'd give her a break, and worry about the attraction later.

~ ~ ~

Now what? Nora's life suddenly became muddled and unclear. Everything seemed off kilter, causing her to do things she normally wouldn't do. Staying in Cedar Ridge, getting involved with the locals, and neglecting her job wasn't how she normally operated.

She definitely was losing her touch.

Evan hadn't been much help, which shouldn't have surprised her. Employees weren't privy to the knowledge of their bosses.

And spending the afternoon around Evan distracted her from doing her job. The effect he had on her merely indicated she was craving much needed physical intimacy. She and the man clearly didn't like each other, so her physical reaction to him when their hands touched was all in her head, or deep within her belly where sparks began to awaken. But those few times when he had been staring and their gazes met, she almost heard the crackle of electricity bouncing around the room. *That* wasn't all in her head.

Her body reacted to a guy who clearly wasn't her type. Some kind of weird proof that this place had some kind of control over her. Her overreaction to Evan, her endearment to George, Howard, and Walter clearly wasn't in the plan. She let her emotions involuntarily slip into her world. But helping a dear, old man who had recently lost his wife filled Nora with a sense of purpose no promotion could satisfy. Her inner Eleanor wouldn't see it that way though.

These unusual emotions and actions had her asking what kind of spell Cedar Ridge wove around her?

While she wasn't completely content with her life in the city—and had longed to live in a place similar to where Mary Claire had grown up—this place cast a blanket of confusion over her normally rational thoughts. Impulsivity had her abandoning the mission of doing her job to aid a kind, old man with a useless puzzle. But the puzzle wasn't useless. The pastime he shared with his wife meant a lot to Walter Buchanan. By doing so, Nora helped keep his wife's memory alive while it filled her with an unexpected sense of gratification.

Unfortunately, she hadn't gotten any work done, so she needed to substitute the thought of Evan as a desirable man with Evan as Arlene's employee and ask him one more question.

She marched up to the counter with conviction. "Can you tell me when would be a good time to speak with Arlene?"

"She's here tomorrow bright and early. Anything I can help you with?"

Nora forced her eyes on the counter, then at the pastry display shelves, anywhere but on Evan's eyes or the solid bulk of his biceps. "I wanted to thank her for being so nice to me since I arrived in Cedar Ridge." It wasn't entirely a lie. She appreciated how the woman had taken the time and interest in her the first day they met. And then again yesterday, when Arlene told her she liked this stripped-down version better than her corporate image.

"No thanks are necessary. That's just the way *Arlene* is." He snickered for some odd reason. "I'm sure she'd love to see you again," he continued. "She likes to take lost souls under her wing."

"Lost soul?" Nora didn't know how to react to that. "Is that your impression of me?"

Evan's hands went up in the air in surrender mode. "Hey, not me. *Arlene* thinks you're lonely because you're new in town. She's just being friendly."

Well, lonely and a lost soul were two different things. She was far from a lost soul. She had goals, and dreams. She had people back home who counted on her to do her job.

But other than Mary Claire, was there anyone in the city *she* counted on?

Darn, but the man made her think and feel things she didn't want to think and feel.

"I'll stop in tomorrow to see her." Nora waved goodbye to him over her shoulder—another strange involuntary action—and headed for the door.

A few hours later, she made her way back to the hotel, retrieved her clothes, placed them in a new suitcase and headed for her car.

As her cell phone rang for the thousandth time, she decided to man up and answer the call, providing her with extra reason to leave the Bean & Brew. And Evan.

"Hi, Bruce," she said, driving into the last empty space in the parking lot of The Comfy Quilt Bed & Breakfast.

"Where the hell are you?"

"Excuse me?" In all the years she'd worked for him, he'd never spoken to her in that highly unprofessional tone.

"I'm sorry, but I've been calling you for two days. Didn't you get my messages?"

"No," she lied. "I've been having problems getting a signal out here. I'm standing in the street right now just to catch one." Wow. What was in the air that enabled a lie to slip out so easily?

"What kind of place is it without cell service?"

"It's a cute little town—" She stopped herself. Cute and homey and welcoming. Definitely *not* what Bruce wanted to hear. "A lot of tourists, good earnings' potential—" She purposely left out the unsettling detail that those same tourists did *not* care if MoonBurst was in the village. "I'm not finished gaining all the data," she continued, walking from the parking lot, turning the corner to Primrose Lane to the front entrance of her destination. "I'll need one more day, then I'll be back."

"One more day? You've been there for three already."

"I know. There's been a few glitches. By tomorrow I'll have everything I need."

She ended the call just as she arrived at the white-gated walkway of sandstone-colored pavers leading toward the inn's porch. The cornflower-blue Victorian with the welcoming spindled-lined, wrap-around porch had potted yellow mums on the edges of each step inviting her to see if the inside was as charming as the outside.

Charm didn't begin to describe the spacious parlor. As she registered at the well-polished mahogany counter, Sarah, the inn keeper asked, "Are you sure you only need the room for one night?"

Nora glanced at the fireplace, its glowing warmth made her hesitate. Finally, she said, "Yes. One night, thank you."

After that, she thought sadly, she'd be on her way home.

She signed in, gathered her small, rolling suitcase, retrieved the old skeleton-type key from the woman and headed up the stairway to the second floor. Each step creaked under the carpet runner. She found her way down the long hallway to Room #6. Ceramic trinkets and knickknacks rested on lace doilies covering antique furniture. She pressed the old, round buttons on the wall near the doorway, and one by one, different lamps lit the room well enough to notice all the intricate carvings in the furniture. She busied herself unpacking the few items she had purchased, then changed into the long-sleeved pajama set she'd given in and purchased due to Cedar Ridge's cold mountain temperatures. Even though it was still too early to go to sleep, she turned in early so she could be refreshed and ready to go as soon as the Bean & Brew opened in the morning.

Her body sank into the clean, fluffy mattress, so different than that lumpy bed she'd been forced to sleep in the past two nights. Two plush blankets assisted a down comforter in keeping her snug and toasty. The plump, down pillows relaxed her neck, aiding all the tension in her body to melt away. She could have drifted off sooner, but the stretch of Evan's tee shirt kept flashing into to her mind, delaying sleep a little longer than she hoped. Images of his capable hands had her overheating, and when she pictured the sexy curve of his lips that bowed upward when he smiled, she kicked away the covers in search of cool air.

She needed to switch her thoughts away from Evan, so she glanced around at the shadows in the cozy room, appreciating how safe and at home it felt. Then she remembered how she had hesitated when Sarah asked if she'd be spending more nights at the inn. That question had left her feeling an odd sadness that she'd be home tomorrow—the home she'd been fighting so hard to keep. Why had she suddenly wanted to stay in a place where she clearly didn't fit in?

~ ~ ~

As the morning sun peeked through the cellular-blinds the next morning, Nora's eyes opened with a snap. She slowly dragged herself out of bed and stretched her muscles that finally relaxed after a restful sleep. "This place is wonderful," she said as her hands slid open the wooden louvers covering the large picture window at the back of the room. The view of the pond and blast of reds, oranges, and golds from the trees took her breath away.

As she made her way down the floral-papered hallway, the restored hardwood-planked floor creaked under her feet. In the bathroom, happiness bounced through her when she saw the porcelain, claw-foot tub. A long, luxurious bath would settle her mind, maybe give her the answers she'd struggled with last night. As she turned the cross-handled chrome and white porcelain knobs to fill the tub, her gaze fell on an array of bath crystals lining a glass shelf over the white pedestal sink. Fresh fall flowers were delicately placed in a ceramic water pitcher with a card that read, 'Compliments of The Laurel Wreath Florist.'

Minutes later, she lowered her body into the warmth of the lavender fragrance. "Oh," she moaned. "I needed this sooo bad."

The silkiness of the bath eased the tension in her shoulders, leaving Bruce and the Bean & Brew miles from her thoughts. The only nagging concern was how she was going to keep her mind in check if she ran into Evan again.

When the smell of fresh-brewed coffee wafted under the bathroom door, Nora knew she had soaked long enough. She grudgingly withdrew her prune-wrinkled body from the warmth of the tub and dressed for the day.

Her nose guided her downstairs to the dining room where hot french toast, homemade cranberry muffins, and bacon simmered in steam trays. Carafes of flavored coffees waited nearby which was great for the inn's guests, but Nora realized it would also be bad because the need to grab coffee at the local coffee shop—or the soon-to-be newest location of MoonBurst—wouldn't be necessary.

"Good morning!" Sarah, the owner, greeted as she entered from the kitchen with a platter of scrambled eggs in hand. "Did you sleep well?"

"Like a baby!" Nora fibbed, but couldn't stop the smile stretching across her face as she realized it had been months since she felt this good.

"I don't know about you," Sarah said, "but my babies never slept. Now if you're talking about my husband, his eyes close as soon as his butt hits the couch cushions!"

Nora chuckled. One thing about Cedar Ridge: the people were real. Nothing held back, nothing phony. And they gave out *waaay* too much information.

Although, it was strange that she was beginning to like that honesty.

Sarah motioned her chin toward the antique server. "Help yourself. There's hot syrup in the pitcher and softened butter on the warming plate. Oh, and there's hot water for tea in the water urn."

As much as the aroma of hot coffee conjured up warm and cozy images, she'd had more than enough over the past few days. The assortment of herbal teas lined neatly in a wicker basket called to her.

Stacked at the outside corner of the server, mismatched china plates and real silverware waited for guests. Nora fetched the top dish from the stack—a delicate pattern of purple Lilies of the Valley edged with a gold rim—and loaded it with a slice of french toast drowning in hot syrup, topped with two scoops of scrambled eggs.

After placing her plate at one of the three, lace-covered tables in the dining room, she poured herself cup of Chai tea. When Sarah came back into the room, Nora asked, "Am I the first person up?"

"I think I heard some movement in Number 4. Everyone's probably sleeping in because they were out so late last night."

"I took a nice, long bath and no one knocked, so I thought the place was empty."

"Empty?" Sarah took a seat across from Nora. "Not a chance. We're booked solid because of the pumpkin festival."

"But it's Monday, a workday."

"Not around here, it's not, if you're competing," Sarah said in all seriousness. "The baking contests start today. Local residents compete in the pumpkin bake-off: pies, breads, soups, and cookies."

"All made of pumpkin?"

Sarah smoothed the lace tablecloth with her fingertips. "Right down to the pumpkin bread croutons for the soup. Visitors sample all the entries and vote along with the judges."

"So it's an interactive contest."

"Hadn't thought about it that way. I guess it is."

"Do the winners earn a 1st Place Ribbon?" Seemed like a big ordeal for just a piece of satin.

"Absolutely! The ribbon and a $500 prize, plus bragging rights."

Bragging rights? Only in rural towns did that make sense. In the city, unless you owned a famous restaurant or bakery, won a challenge on the Food Network, or had your own cable TV baking show, there was little to brag about for baking. Cedar Ridge sure did take their pumpkins seriously.

"Sounds like fun," Nora surprised herself by saying. A few days ago, she never would have made a comment like that.

"Are you going to come?"

"No, I can't." Nora cut into her french toast. "I'll be leaving today."

"You're leaving already? Sure you can't stay another night?"

She swallowed and the deliciously syrupy toast slid down her throat. "Sorry, I have to be back at work. Although, I *am* going to miss the room here. I especially love the view."

"Number 6 is one of my favorites." Sarah sat back, crossed her legs, resting her hands in her lap. "People don't like it because it's in the back of the house, but that's where all the colors are this time of year."

Nora nodded as she sipped her tea. "The fall leaves mixed in between all those giant evergreens is beautiful. I love how the colors are reflected in the pond back there."

"Yep, it's a beauty."

"And that tub in the hallway bathroom was lovely." Nora briefly closed her eyes as she recalled the hot water covering her body.

"Most people don't like sharing the bathroom. That's why 6 isn't a favorite. Hopefully, it will be vacant the next time you visit."

The next time. No chance of that anytime soon. But Nora would keep the inn in mind for the future. It was a lovely place for a getaway. "I thought the touch of flowers in the bathroom was charming." Oooh, she used *that* word, but it *was* charming. Everything about Cedar Ridge was. And she liked Sarah. She seemed like the kind of person Nora would like to get to know better.

"Those were Laurel's idea. She owns the flower shop. She and her husband are expecting."

Nora thought a minute. "I don't think I've met her."

"I'm sure you met her husband at the Bean & Brew."

Husband?

Oh, no! I've been mooning over someone's husband!

No wonder Evan didn't need a more lucrative job. His wife owned a business.

"You look confused," Sarah said. "I'm sure Adam's been there. He and Evan are good friends."

"Adam?" A sliver of knowledge relieved her.

"Yeah, tall, dark, and handsome," Sarah said. "Not the kind of guy you'd forget. But don't let looks fool you, he's a great guy, too."

All at once, that description sounded familiar. "Is he the one who's totally devoted to his wife?"

"That's the one! He used to play the field, but once he and Laurel got together, he only has eyes for her. It's sweet."

"I'd say so." Well, at least Laurel wasn't married to Evan. Nora definitely noticed Adam when he had come to the Bean

& Brew. That's when Arlene had caught her gawking at him and mentioned he was married.

Up to this point, Nora pretty successfully blocked Evan from her mind, but now that Sarah mentioned him in a roundabout way, he was front and center once again.

She took the last bite of her breakfast and finished the rest of her tea in one gulp. "I better be going. Thank you for the delicious breakfast."

"You're quite welcome."

"I have a few errands to run, but I'll be back by eleven to check out."

Nora stepped down the blue-painted wooden stairs of the Victorian's front porch and nodded at the yellow mums lining each step, inhaling the clear, crisp autumn air. The two-block walk along Primrose and Elm was colorful as the leaves on the trees began their turn into a palate of fall tones. Nothing at all like the gray of the New York City streets.

She loved how the atmosphere brought a spring to her step and wished she could bottle it and bring it with her back home. She opened the door to the Bean & Brew, hopefully for the last time, to finally talk with Arlene, only to find the shop owner swamped with customers.

She glanced over at the three empty tables where George and the guys usually sat. She truly enjoyed spending time them and was disappointed they weren't there yet. She'd hoped to at least get a chance to thank them and say goodbye.

As she waited for a break in the customer flow, she decided to wander the street for one more try that her survey might garner different results. After all, different people flooded the village today, so she was hopeful.

She came upon a group of senior citizens, then two sets of families. She asked the same questions as yesterday's survey, and the same frustrations brewed. Unfortunately, both days yielded the same results. She found only a group of college students who wanted MoonBurst.

By the time she arrived back for her third trip to the Bean & Brew, the customer traffic slowed to a manageable crawl.

"Nora, I'm so sorry we couldn't talk earlier," Arlene said, finishing the last customer on line.

"Not a problem. Where's your able-bodied assistant?" *Able-bodied*? She needed to keep her head about her and forget about Evan's body.

"Mondays are his day off. He works the other six days."

The man worked six days a week? Seemed Nora totally misjudged him. Why did a guy with his management talents chose to work in this type of shop? He obviously loved his job. Anyone could see that by the way he interacted and served every customer. She had noticed a strong drive in his eyes that his job was important to him. Too bad all MoonBurst's employees didn't have that much dedication.

"What can I get you?" the coffee shop owner asked.

The thought of more coffee turned her stomach, so Nora studied the menu. "A cup of chamomile tea, please."

As Arlene busied herself with the order, Nora ran questions in her head that she needed Arlene to answer, but tried to think of something casual to start the conversation. When the woman returned with her steaming mug of hot water, Nora said, "I see you've got a lot of customers coming in with the pumpkin festival."

"Yes, we do. It's like that every time the Village Improvement District runs an event. I tell ya, it's a lot of work, but really worth it."

"So, it's profitable?"

"Oh, yes. And then some. In fact, the sales we make these next two weeks should take care of things nicely."

"Take care of things nicely." Was the Bean & Brew in financial trouble?

"That's good." Nora kept her tone casual. "It's great when you have enough to pay off some bills."

Arlene made her way to the rack of pastries and danish. With a bakery pick-up tissue, she grabbed a cinnamon roll from the display shelf and placed it on a heavy-weight paper plate, then added a packaged tea bag and presented it to Nora.

"There you go. Hot tea on a cold day." Arlene leaned forward over the counter toward Nora and whispered, "Cinnamon rolls are my favorite. It's on the house." Arlene's hint of playfulness in sharing the secret tickled Nora's insides. A true, I-feel-it-down-to-my-feet grin stretched her lips.

"Gramma?" Julie asked from the far table at the back of the store. "Can you help me with this math problem?"

"Excuse me, Nora," Arlene said, whipping her hands on a towel. "She's home from school with the sniffles, but the homework has to get done!" Arlene quickly sprinted from behind the counter to join her granddaughter. When she reached the child, she encased her in a giant bear hug. "Of course, I can help you. Just remember, this new math isn't what I learned, so be patient with me."

"I will," Julie responded.

Arlene was the kind of mom Nora had always wished her mother had been. So many nights she had prayed that God would tell her mother it would be alright to relax and have fun with her. But each morning, Nora awoke to Joan warning her daughter not to touch her face or hair or her clothes for fear Nora would mess them. She just wanted a hug. Was that too much to ask?

"Oh, dear. I'm not sure I know how to do that," Arlene said as Nora settled herself at an empty table near the large, plate-glass window. "Howard," the woman yelled across the store. "Do you think you'd be able to help Julie with this problem?"

Nora hadn't seen Howard come into the store, but now she noticed the grimace on his face as he hoisted his body from his chair. Grabbing his cane, he limped toward Julie's table. He raised the cane in salute to Nora, topping it off with his patented wink and slowly made his way to the child and her grandmother.

Arlene offered him her seat next to her granddaughter and made her way back to the counter, just in time to greet a group of people entering the store.

Nora watched as Arlene took care of the orders, noting her lack of proficiency compared to Evan. His six days a week, versus Arlene's Monday, showed that the woman was out of practice and flustered when she got an order wrong. Where was her husband, Thomas? Nora had yet to meet him or hear mention of him.

Maybe this place was too much for Arlene to handle. Maybe the responsibility of the job exacerbated the financial problems she alluded to earlier. Maybe MoonBurst would give her a reason to close, affording her more time to spend with her granddaughter.

Come to think of it, the few times Nora talked with the woman, she spoke with pride about her granddaughter, but never about any children. Was she raising Julie? A huge undertaking for a woman in her fifties. Not impossible, but truly difficult.

"Oh, little kins, I'm not sure about that," Howard said to the child. "Let me think about that for a minute."

Nora's heart tightened in her chest. The people in this village were so in tune with each other, just like Mary Claire's family. The caring they showed one another was as foreign to Nora as a visit to outer space. The image of Howard and Julie, grandfather and granddaughter-like, yanked her emotions to the surface, yearning for that security and tenderness only an older, respected family member could provide. Unfortunately, since both of her grandfathers had passed before she was born, the image of Howard and Julie brought to light what she missed in her life. A strain of longing tightened Nora's throat as she stared at the two.

A puzzled frown came to Howard's face and when he made eye contact with Nora, it was replaced by a surprised smile.

"Nora!" His eyes lit like a Christmas tree. "You're a lot younger than me. Maybe you can figure this out."

"Me?" She pointed a finger to her chest then wiped at her eyes. "I-I-I don't know anything about elementary school math."

"Yes, but you graduated college in the same millennium as Julie. You're more equipped to handle this than I am."

Helping out a kid with homework?

She'd never dealt with kids, let alone helped one with something that two other adults already had trouble with. But seeing Julie's pout sent a pang of sympathy through Nora. It was the same look she must have had on her face each time an adult in her own life had disappointed her.

"Please, Nora?" Julie asked in a scratchy voice. "I'll be the only kid who doesn't get a sticker if I don't do my homework."

With a strange twist in her chest, Nora's heart softened. "Well, we can't have that now, can we?" She took hold of her tea mug and plate with the cinnamon roll and made her way to Julie's table. Another impulsive action.

What is it with this place?

She settled in the seat Howard offered next to the little girl.

Julie's bright smile eased Nora's fears, but she still had no clue how to deal with a child.

Okay, it couldn't be that hard. *Just talk to her like you would any other person.*

"I haven't seen one of these in a *long* time," Nora said, leaning closer to the child as she glanced through the math workbook.

"You're pretty," Julie said, staring at her.

"Why, thank you." Nora tapped the tip of Julie's nose. "So are you." *What made me do that?*

Julie giggled, then coughed. "Are you gonna help me?"

"I'm going to try," Nora said, moving her head slightly away from the coughing child. "Where are you stuck?"

"Right here." The girl's stubby finger pointed to a workbook page of fractions.

"What grade are you in?" Nora asked, pursing her lips.

Julie sniffed hard and coughed again. "First."

Even though she wasn't a germ-a-phobe, Nora hoped the kid only had allergies and not the flu. She turned her attention back to the math book and flipped back a few pages to get the idea of what they had learned so far.

"There's a parents' message at the beginning of the chapter, if you need help," Arlene yelled from behind the counter.

"Thanks." Nora flipped to that section. At first she scanned it, but that wasn't working. Then she read each word, trying to understand what Julie needed to do.

She hadn't learned fractions until she was in fourth or fifth grade. How did they expect these little ones to grasp the concept? They barely knew how to print their names correctly. Now she understood why Arlene and Howard kept referring to it as "new math." The parents' message confused her until the last paragraph. "Why didn't they say that in the first place!"

She gathered the workbook and a separate piece of scrap paper, then turned to the child. "Okay, Julie, here we go."

Nora sensed that Julie craved female attention even though her grandmother treated her so well. She noticed how the child hung on her every word. They talked about fractions, talked about school, and Nora's family. But when she asked the child about her mother, Julie matter-of-factly stated, "I don't have one," and Nora's heart ached for Julie. She wanted to wrap her in her arms.

Not knowing where that reaction came from, she quickly gained her composure and turned the girl's attention back to the colored pie chart indicating the different fractions. But it was hard to concentrate. How could Julie *not* have a mother?

If her mother died, she would have said so. If her parents were divorced, she would have said so, too.

What happened that this adorable little girl didn't live with her mother?

"My daddy is bringing me to the pumpkin festival on Saturday."

"W-What?" Nora's thoughts of the girl's absent mother kept her from paying attention. "I'm sorry, sweetie. What did you say?"

Julie pushed her bangs out of her eyes, then held her hands palm up near her shoulders. "I'm going to the festival with Daddy on Saturday."

Daddy?

In four days, Nora hadn't seen a father around Julie. And Arlene never mentioned a son or son-in-law. She wondered if the father had visitation on certain days, maybe every other weekend.

Julie slammed her tiny hands to the table top as she squealed with glee. "Are you going?"

Oh, right. Saturday. The pumpkin festival.

With any luck, Nora would be on her way home within the next hour. "I don't think so."

Although, the pumpkin festival might be advantageous to the company. If they had known about it sooner, they could have set up a temporary coffee bar to promote the opening of their new store. But that was too forward thinking at this point.

The decision to actually open in Cedar Ridge was under consideration, still in the exploratory stage. If headquarters decided to proceed, it would benefit the company to obtain a list of village events where they could tie in promotional enterprises. Nora asked, "What kind of things do they have at the festival?"

"There's a pumpkin contest!" Julie said, her eyes growing the size of small pumpkins. "People bring pumpkins to see who has the biggest."

Cute. Everyone getting excited over a few large pumpkins.

"They even throw them!" The little girl's brown eyes lit with excitement.

"Throw them?"

"Uh-huh." Julie's nodding had her disheveled ponytail bobbing up and down.

"Aren't they too heavy to throw?"

"No, they use those things."

"What things?"

"Wait. Gramma knows." She leaned across Nora's chest and yelled, "Gramma, what are those things that throw the pumpkins?"

"Catapults," Arlene yelled back.

"Really?" Nora was surprised by the answer. But then something clicked.

"Yep," Arlene answered. "Some of the pumpkins get chunked over two thousand feet."

Pumpkin chunking. Right. Bruce had mentioned something about them in the preliminary report of Cedar Ridge events. Said they hurled pumpkins across one of the farm fields, but failed to mention there was an entire festival to go with it. She'd have to include that info in her report so MoonBurst could add it to their marketing strategies.

"That's some catapult," Nora responded, drawing her attention back to the child.

"They're this big!" Julie stretched her pint-sized arms toward the ceiling.

Nora found herself caught up in the child's delight. Shooting a pumpkin over 2,000 feet meant the catapult had to be enormous, but to a kid, her arms could only reach so high. What amazed Nora most was that this little person, all full of life and energy, showered happiness on everyone around her.

Nora remembered her own solemn childhood. Bainbridge children had a polite image to uphold, fun wasn't permitted. Since that line of conditioning carried through as an adult, she had shielded herself from any situation where she'd let her guard down. Her career had become her only focus. Fun would eventually come when all her goals were achieved. Yet, it felt odd now letting Julie's exuberance incite her with true enjoyment. It was kind of liberating.

"I'm gonna enter the pumpkin decorating contest," Julie said.

"You are?" The thought of it was kind of cute.

"Uh-huh. I'm gonna make it a fairy princess."

A round, orange pumpkin…princess? Well, at least the kid had a good imagination.

"If you come to the festival, you can see her."

Her? Oh, right. The pumpkin princess.

Not wanting to squash Julie's enthusiasm, Nora thought before she answered. "I'll have to see if I'm not too busy on Saturday." Another lie. And to a child, no less. But she didn't actually say she'd be there.

This conversation was getting too personal for Nora's comfort. Needing to bring the kid back on track, she pointed a finger toward the fraction chart.

"Okay, back to work. Let's pretend this round chart is a pumpkin."

Julie giggled and her cough came back. It took several seconds before she trained her gaze on the graphic.

"If you wanted to share the pumpkin with me, what would you do to the pumpkin?"

Julie thought a minute. "I cut it here." She pointed to the middle of the circle. "I get one side, you get the other."

"Right. I get one half and you get one half."

The girl nodded as if she already knew the answer.

"Now. If you have a whole pumpkin and you want to share it with your grandmother, Mr. Waldorf, and me, how would you cut it?"

When the light bulb moment had Julie's eyes shining like stars, Nora, too, had been struck by a lightning moment. It was the same fulfillment she felt yesterday helping Walter Buchannan with his crossword puzzle, but amplified tenfold. Helping Julie felt right.

Suddenly, just like that, as her heart opened, a warm, fuzzy feeling overcame her.

Nora found she actually enjoyed spending time with this little girl, and at that moment, her job was the farthest thing from her mind.

The magic of Cedar Ridge was at it again, pushing her promotion far from her thoughts, even though, in a few weeks, she more than likely was going to lose her home.

Chapter 5

If Evan heard Nora's name one more time, he was going to hurl.

Normally, he picked up Julie from school on Mondays so they could spend time together on his day off. But she hadn't gone to school, and since he had an appointment with his accountant, Julie stayed at the store with his mother.

Later in the afternoon when he went to the store to get her, she went on and on about how Nora had helped with her homework. How Nora explained it, how she was going to be the smartest kid in math because of Nora, how pretty Nora was, how nice she smelled. Nora, Nora, Nora.

Okay, so she helped his daughter, and in turn, bailed out his mother and Howard who tutored Julie when he wasn't around. And then Saint Nora helped Walter the day before with his crossword puzzles. And Howard wished he was a few years younger because he thought Nora was a real catch.

It seemed the mysterious Nora Langston, the creative idea person who wasn't good with numbers, was a goddess in his daughter's eyes, not to mention the rest of those around him.

But as much as it irritated him, he realized his daughter's constant repeating of the woman's name was more than a childish annoyance. It was a sign that Julie missed having a woman in her life. A mother.

The constant fear of his ex-wife, Miranda, coming back into their lives—demanding full custody—haunted him each night before he went to sleep. She was the one who didn't want to be a mother, who didn't want her own child to interfere with her social life. Didn't want to be married any longer. Even though he had full custody, all the legal documents in the world didn't clear his mind that if a mother wanted her child back, the courts would oblige. He'd seen it many times.

For four years he hadn't mentioned Miranda to Julie, hadn't acknowledged the woman's existence, hoping she wouldn't suddenly materialize. Yeah, it was lame. But it was the only way he knew to protect himself from losing his mind. The threat of having his daughter ripped out of his life constantly hung over his head.

As he sat on the side of Julie's bed, he tucked the blankets under her chin. "Did you brush your teeth?"

"Uh-huh." Julie nodded. "And I said my prayers, too."

"Good girl." He smoothed her hair from her face and leaned to place a kiss on her forehead, holding back tears at the thought of his little girl hurting because she didn't have her mother.

"Daddy?" Julie asked. "Can Nora come to the pumpkin festival with us on Saturday?"

Evan stopped just as his lips were about to plant one on her forehead. He eased away and wiped the corner of his eye with the back of his hand. "Why?"

"Because she's nice and fun and I like her and—"

He put his finger on her cupid lips to halt her. "I got it. You like her."

"Uh-huh." Julie giggled.

How could he say no to the most important person in his life? How could he disappoint his daughter when he vowed four years ago to do everything in his power to counteract what her mother had done?

He needed to give his daughter's innocent request some thought. Since Nora had been nice enough to help Julie, the least he could do was thank her. But asking her to join them for a full afternoon together?

He didn't want to risk his daughter getting attached. As it was, she had been asking a lot of questions about her mother lately. Every kid at school had a mother. Every kid but her, and Todd's two kids. But they knew their mother, knew she was in heaven. Julie never knew Miranda. Each time she got sad about it, or asked a difficult question, it broke his heart all over again. No kid wants to hear her own mother didn't want to stay around to raise her. No kid wants to think she's not good enough for her mother to love her.

He desperately needed to protect his daughter from that heartache. But as time marched on, and she grew more aware of the world around her, it became increasing difficult to protect her from the impending truth.

If he allowed Julie to spend time with Nora, it would only set his precious daughter up for disappointment. Besides, he didn't know anything about the woman, where she came from, what she really did for a living, what kind of family she had, whether she was seeing anyone.

Whoa, that last question stopped him cold.

What difference did it make to Jules if Nora had a guy in her life?

It didn't.

So why had it surfaced in *his* mind?

He didn't need a woman mucking up his life, especially one he hardly knew.

"Pl-lease, Daddy?" Julie tugged on his arm. "Please can we ask Nora to come to the festival with us?"

Evan scrubbed the back of his neck with his hand.

Damn. How can I get out of this?

He did have to thank her for helping Julie. And it was just one afternoon.

How attached could his daughter get in just a few hours?

And if he did ask her, what happened if she said no? Julie would be disappointed.

But—

What happened if she said yes?

~ ~ ~

Nora walked into her apartment and dropped her belongings next to the sofa. The new suitcase filled with the clothing she had purchased in Cedar Ridge reminded her of the four-day adventure that left her exhausted.

When she arrived at her apartment building, the doorman almost didn't recognize her without her contacts. And with her dark-brown glasses, pulled-back hair, and faded-denim jeans, he had questioned her as to whom she was visiting. Once she removed her glasses, he realized it was her. She felt like she had been living two lives, and for four days, she had been. She had discarded Eleanor and savored the opportunity to live as Nora which gave her pause to compare how different her life could be.

Collapsing into her favorite white leather chair, she stared at the city lights shining through the row of floor-to-ceiling windows.

The brutal ride in from Cedar Ridge tired her more than she realized. Eastbound Route 80 was a bear. The bridge traffic into the city equaled a parking lot, taking forty minutes to go twenty blocks to her apartment building. Leaving Cedar Ridge at four in the afternoon had been a bad choice.

In between stop-and-go traffic, musings of Julie's bubbly behavior warmed Nora. She couldn't erase the image of the child's satisfaction when Julie finally grasped the concept of fractions. Why had someone thought it a good idea to introduce fractions to six-year-old first graders?

And why was it that *she*, the consummate professional, now had her head wrapped around the crazy notion that she'd eventually like to have a child. She shook her head, closed her eyes tightly, sank deeper into the chair, and soaked in being at home.

After several seconds, she opened her eyes, and her gaze landed on a few of the things that were most precious to her. Her *Light Iris* Georgia O'Keefe print, the porcelain floor vase her parents brought back from Japan, the hand-crafted toucan from Belize, the starburst wall art she bought in Santa Fe: a hammered-copper array that reminded her of glistening sunsets.

Her home. Modern, clutter free, the low-pile white carpet under her feet cleanly blended with the cream-colored furnishings. A few deliberate accents of bold royal blue popped just as her mother's decorator had envisioned, but Nora had been indifferent to. It wasn't as homey as she wanted, but since the house she grew up in was just as sterile, she hadn't put up a fight. Her mother insisted on paying for it. Everything in place and orderly.

She retrieved her cell from her bag and tapped the contact for her best friend.

"MC, it's me."

"It's about time you called me. What's going on?" Mary Claire asked. "Are you home?"

"Yes, I just got here."

"Good. Now that you're done with field work, we'll be able to spend more time together."

"You know, that's the only reason I'm happy about this promotion. And I can keep my apartment." Nora glanced around the room again, but instead of feeling content, she felt empty.

"Yeah, and you'll be able to get your mother off your back. Is she still insisting you marry Harrison?"

Nora sighed into her words. "Y-Y-Yes. The raise will help me keep this place, but it's still not enough to convince her that I won't marry him. I'm going to marry whomever

I want, not who she picks out for me." And with that, Evan popped into her mind, and she momentarily got lost in comparing him to Harrison.

"Nora, are you still there?"

"Ah, yes. Sorry."

"Okay. What happened? Why'd you zone out like that?"

Leave it to Mary Claire to know her so well. "Just comparing what my life could be . . ." She explained how she lived as Nora for the past few days, and how liberating it felt. How she felt in control of her life. "Coming back home woke me up to reality," she said. "What's it like to live in the burbs? Do you feel like you're missing out on something?"

"Uh, no. You know how I feel about it. Living in the city isn't for me. In fact, the burbs get to be a bit much every once in a while, that's why I love going back to my family's farm. You're not thinking of moving, are you?"

"I don't know what I'm thinking or feeling. I'm really confused."

"Ah, ha!" Mary Claire said with a bounce. "You met someone, didn't you?"

Nora squeezed her eyes tight and cringed. "W-Why? What makes you say that?"

"Because, before you left, you were hell bent on finishing this project and getting that promo. Now, you're questioning everything you wanted. I want details."

With her feelings in flux, Nora wasn't sure if she should tell Mary Claire about Evan. And if she told her about Julie, Mary Claire would surely insist she see a doctor.

"It's not one person, it's a few. The people in Cedar Ridge are special."

"And???" Mary Claire prodded.

"And my life is about to become everything I've wanted."

"And???"

Evan, Julie, Arlene, the guys tugged at her heartstrings and muddled her brain. Especially Evan. Why was she sorry to be home?

And who was she really? Eleanor? Or Nora?

~ ~ ~

"Ah, the elusive Ms. Bainbridge." Harrison fell in step with Nora as she walked the long hallway to her MoonBurst office. "You're harder to find than a 2009 Petrus Merlot at a fundraiser."

"Just doing my job," she said without glancing his way. She doubted the man looked any different from the last thousand times she'd seen him.

His good looks resembled those of that polished weather guy on the morning news. Perfectly-styled blond hair with a gentle swoop falling across his forehead that gave a natural, soft, free-flowing appearance. The one time she tripped and fell into him, her hand aimed for the wall, but missed and landed on his forehead. Nearly broke a nail from the helmet of hairspray applied to his head. He had been more worried about messing his hair than her twisted ankle.

Now, as he grabbed her arm, she slowed to an annoying pace, then stopped. "Harrison" she warned and yanked her arm from his grasp.

"You wouldn't have to do your job if you'd just say *yes*."

Nora turned her head away from him, inhaled deeply while closing her eyes, and took stock of her slow, simmering frustration.

"One little word, and all your problems will vanish like—" He snapped his fingers. "—that."

He was right. One little word and her problems would be gone. Except, he refused to listen to *her* one little word.

Opening her eyes, she peered right, then left, making sure the corridor was clear. "Harrison, I've told you countless times, I'm not interested in your *offer*. I never have, nor will I ever be, in the future."

"Yes, you've made that clear for several months now." He crossed his arms over his designer suit jacket and spread his feet apart in a cocky stance. "My offer works out nicely for both of us. We give our notice here, you become a lady of leisure, and I go to work for your father. Perfect."

Perfect for a guy who's driven to advance his career by marrying the daughter of one of Manhattan's richest moguls, yes. But dreadful for the daughter.

Nora wanted no part of being a woman of leisure, living off of her husband's money while being a part of that undesirable socialite scene. Besides, it was *her* family's fortune Harrison planned to live off of. She wanted a real life with a career that fulfilled her, where people were important. One that didn't involve a rich husband taking care of her. She was capable of taking care of herself, and soon, after she presented her report, she'd be more than capable.

"I already have *my* career," she said. "My life's perfect the way it is."

"Okay, I'll give in to you having a career. You can work for your father, too. He'd love to have both of us at Bainbridge Enterprises."

Harrison *was* right on that one. Daddy would gladly have her on his team, but he also knew she wanted to make it on her own, and she was grateful that he hadn't pressured her the way Harrison and her mother had. Especially Mother.

But having Harrison intertwined in their personal lives was a different story. Both her parents thought he was the perfect fit for her, no matter how hard she stressed otherwise.

"My father would like to have you work for him. But I'm not part of the package. Never was. Never will be." Bowing her head, she pinched the bridge of her nose and squeezed her eyes tightly, hoping to end this tedious conversation.

What a waste of time. The guy refused to listen to anyone who told him "no." He'd been the all-around athlete, voted most likely to succeed. He'd gained her admiration a few years ago because he'd built an impressive reputation all on his own. No coattails of a wealthy family to glide on, just hard work and that damn glinting charm that made people do as he wished. Even her father had been prey to it.

But after a while, Nora saw through the charade. The arrogant way he played people to get whatever he wanted had been sickening to watch. He'd simply flash that tens-of-thousands-of-dollars veneer smile and whatever he asked was given. That was the problem with Harrison. Nothing was ever sincere.

He suffered from New Money Syndrome—the need to impress people by throwing around money. As a part of the one percent, Nora knew keeping a low profile not only helped one keep their own money, it also kept you humble, better able to relate to everyone, rich or poor. Something Harrison couldn't and wouldn't do. He definitely wouldn't fit in her world, no matter how convinced her parents were that he was perfect.

Harrison took her by the shoulders, turning her to face him, then switched on that 75-watt smile. "You're tired. This job has been stressing you for far too long. You need time to rejuvenate and recharge your mind. Go to the spa, get pampered. Then you'll see that my offer is the best you can get."

She sucked in her bottom lip to keep from screaming at him, the pompous ass. He sounded like a TV infomercial.

Raising her gaze to his, Nora stared him straight in the eye. "Please, please listen to my words," she said softly, then strengthen her tone. "I'm not interested in a marriage business deal. I'm not hard-wired for that. Please don't ask me again, and for the love of God, please refrain from speaking to my parents about it again. She extended her hand toward him in an effort to show good faith. Deal?"

~ ~ ~

Harrison stared down at her hand with a look that said if she thought this was over, she was sadly mistaken. He hadn't worked his ass off to align her father in his corner and have her blow it for him.

He took hold of her hand and, instead of shaking it, he tenderly held it, closely watching as the surprise on her face turn to annoyance. "Eleanor Langston Bainbridge, I could no sooner agree to a deal like that then cut off my arm. We belong together."

"Harrison, this is done." She dropped his hand and the satisfaction that he'd gotten to her slid through him like the smoky heat of a shot of Glenfiddich 21. They weren't done until he said they were. And that wouldn't be until he was in line to receive some of that Bainbridge money. Correction, Langston money. And he knew exactly how to get it.

~ ~ ~

For the past two days, Julie had bugged him to talk to Nora.

Evan hadn't been avoiding the woman. She just seemed to have vanished.

Yesterday afternoon, when he fetched Julie and his mother from their weekly trip to the park, he scanned the sidewalks and streets for signs of Nora. A lot of good that did. He didn't know what kind of car she drove. Even rode past the new office building where she worked and did a once-around the parking lot in hopes that he could spot her.

He intended to fulfill his daughter's request to ask Nora to come to the pumpkin festival with them. But he also racked his brain for a tactful way to tell her that even though he was extending the invitation, he didn't want her encouraging a relationship with his daughter.

Yeah, it was kind of harsh. But he was only going along with Julie's crazy invitation so he could thank Nora for helping his daughter. Further involvement would hurt Julie, whose motherless vulnerability was at an all-time high right now. The pediatrician said it was normal at Julie's age to be curious. All the more, Evan couldn't risk his daughter forming an attachment to Nora that wouldn't be reciprocated—or worse—reciprocated and then broken in a few weeks or even a few months.

The way he figured it, if adults got attached to one another, and something went down, they eventually got over it. But kids took things to heart. In their narrow worlds, there was no reason why relationships couldn't work, and he didn't want Julie thinking it was her fault if it didn't.

No, he needed to dissuade Nora from any kind of relationship with Julie. Needed to be upfront and honest from the start. This "date" was going to be a one-time deal. He'd make sure Nora knew that. After all, people could get hurt.

~ ~ ~

The next morning, Nora stepped out of the elevator, a hardcopy of her report tucked under her arm, the electronic copy already e-mailed to Bruce and the regional director.

Her meeting with the "team of three" in charge of the Sussex County Expansion Project had her up on the infamous 23rd floor. It also gave her a sneak peek of what her life would be like after her promotion. As she walked the hallway to the conference room, the quiet clicking of keyboards broke the silence of the stodgy executive floor. Passing each office door, she wondered which one she'd inhabit once her promotion went through. As a few employees hurried past, they politely greeted her in hushed voices, just barely glancing her way. No eye contact, no smiles, no jovial bantering. The welcome felt as cold as the wind whipping through the concrete canyons of the buildings outside.

What did she expect? This was the executive floor of the world's largest coffee company where people weren't afforded the luxury to stop and chat. Even though she had been caught up in that high-achieving rat race only a week ago, it seemed foreign now. Maybe some of that laid-back Cedar Ridge mentality had worn off on her.

Everything in her normal world didn't seem so normal any longer. This morning when she donned her suit and stepped into her heels, she noticed her posture and attitude changed. Eleanor was back. Gone was the sneaker comfort she had quickly adopted. Walking into the office definitely changed the relaxed mindset she had during her visit with Arlene and Julie.

She had a job to do now, and she needed to squelch those happy memories that were merely a vacation from reality. Her focus had to remain on her goal. But a pang of guilt shimmied its way through, influencing her emotions, the same emotions she had skillfully turned off when it came to business. And the same skill she had forgotten when she was in Cedar Ridge. The thought of taking away Arlene's business didn't sit well, even though it was the typical outcome of most field studies. Just as she suspected upon her arrival in Cedar Ridge, this time had been different. She let those emotions her father warned her about interfere with her judgment.

Get your head in the game. She could practically hear her father's words blaring in her head.

She stepped into the conference room to present her findings, hoping everything would be accepted, and she'd be on her way to a new, more beneficial position. But the bulk of guilt intensified, having her question if this promotion was worth it. Yes, she desperately needed it, but at what costs to others?

~ ~ ~

Nora finally settled back behind the desk in her postage stamp-sized, but comfortable office with a ping-pong game pounding in her head. The two narrow windows didn't provide a panoramic view of the city, but they did let in enough light to brighten the cold, fall day which seemed to make her head hurt more.

She stared at the expansion project file folder lying in front of her, realizing she made the unfortunate mistake of getting to know the cast of characters. The emotional attachment blossoming for Arlene and her granddaughter made presenting Nora's findings to the team all the more difficult especially since unearthing a critical piece of information.

The Google search she did yesterday found that Thomas Cavanaugh, Arlene's husband, had died four years ago. That fact entwined itself around Nora's heart, now understanding how difficult it was for the woman to run her business alone.

Bruce's preliminary data on the Bean & Brew missed that important information. If that fact was missing, what others had he neglected to include? Surely the county records listed the Bean & Brew's owners. Why had Bruce been sloppy with something that a simple Internet search provided? He made sure to tell her the inconsequential fact about the pumpkin chunking catapults, but failed to mention that Thomas was dead.

The pounding in Nora's head throbbed deeper as she realized her report made the opening of a MoonBurst location a reality, surely putting Arlene out of business. She thought about a woman Arlene's age running the store while also raising her granddaughter. That struggle had been evident as she noticed signs of strain every time Arlene rubbed her lower back whenever she had to bend, how she became frazzled when she had to work the store alone.

Maybe a MoonBurst location in Cedar Ridge would help Arlene? Nora tried to convince herself that if Arlene sold her business, she'd have time to focus her attention on Julie. But who would buy a coffee shop with MoonBurst a few blocks away?

The idea of ruining a woman's only source of income riddled her mind with even more guilt. Arlene, Julie's, and even Evan's lives would be upended.

Evan.

He wasn't such a bad guy once she got to know him. But she hadn't gone to the town to make friends, even though it seemed like everyone she met enveloped her into the village culture of friendship and acceptance.

She knew if Arlene closed the Bean & Brew, Evan would lose his job. With his looks and talent for serving customers, Nora was certain he'd be able to find employment.

Yes, Evan would be okay, but she wasn't as sure about Arlene and Julie.

Julie, such a happy kid. Oh, Nora thought, she needed to put the wonderful people of Cedar Ridge out of her mind and focus on doing her job. Not only did the promotion of Director of Field Operations on the 23rd floor come with a view, it also promised a handsome pay increase—all the elements needed to continue living in her apartment with the added bonus of putting an end to her mother's archaic delusion that she needed a man to provide for her.

She reached into the top drawer of her desk for the acetaminophen bottle when a knock on her office door startled her. She spun in her chair to see the one and only Colin Bainbridge standing in the doorway.

"Daddy?"

"You look like you've seen a ghost." His tall, broad body filled the doorway, blocking the light from the hallway.

"I didn't expect you." She uncapped the bottle, secured two pills in her hand, and rose from her seat. She walked to the side console table to fetch a glass of water wondering the reason for his visit. She learned long ago that even if it had been weeks since she'd seen him, hugs or kisses were inappropriate. Signs of affection and emotions signaled weakness, even within the family. She popped the headache pills into her mouth and gulped a half glass of water. Turning to him, she said, "You didn't call."

"Do I need an appointment to see my only daughter?" His gray-blue eyes radiated an arrogance that accompanied a man who owned half of Manhattan.

"No, of course not," she said as she faced him, gripping the chair top opposite her desk with both hands, waiting for him to drop an unexpected bomb. "But you usually do in case I'm in a meeting or out in the field."

"I happened to be in the area and thought I'd just drop in."

Drop in?

Her father *never* acted on impulse. Was he feeling well? He looked fit as usual. Although, his hair seemed to have turned a brighter shade of white in contrast to his deep, year-round tan.

"Is something wrong?" she asked.

"No. Not at all." He helped himself to the other matching chair and just before he sat, unbuttoned his custom-made suit jacket. "I heard through the grapevine there may be a promotion in your future."

Nora remained standing, gripping the chair top tighter. *Don't sit. Always stay higher than your opponent.* One of Daddy's strategies. She didn't let on her surprise that he knew about the impending promotion. She hadn't planned to tell anyone until it actually happened. "Where did you hear that?"

"From Harrison." He inspected his manicured nails and didn't look at her. "We played on Saturday."

Harrison. Why wasn't she surprised? "Isn't it a little cold to be walking a golf course this time of year?"

"Nonsense." Her father let out a clipped, condescending tone, then gave her his patented Colin Bainbridge stare. "The cold air is invigorating. Gets the blood pumping faster and super charges the adrenaline." He puffed out his chest like a preening peacock. "Many a deal have been cultivated on the links."

"Yes, I know." During her entire life, her father always returned victorious from a rousing round of golf. If he won, it meant he got exactly what he wanted from his opponent. If he lost, even better. That meant he threw the game in order to seal an almost impossible deal. The man was a master at the game.

"What's riding on this promotion?"

Didn't waste any time, did he?

She stopped herself from saying, "none of your business." After all, he was her father. Not only would it be disrespectful, he also didn't understand the meaning of the phrase unless it uttered from his lips.

Don't get into it. Keep it simple. "Just doing my job."

"Nora, this job has you traveling a lot. If you work for me, you could stay in one place. Your mother would love for you to get married and raise a family."

"Yes, but that's not what *I* want. I'm good at my job." Well, at least she had been before the Cedar Ridge trip. "We agreed that working for your company wasn't a good idea." So much for keeping it simple.

"You agreed. I merely respected your decision."

"I'm thankful for that respect." She relaxed her grip and moved to lean against the front of her desk and remained standing, certain he wouldn't give up. She crossed her arms for good measure. "Getting married and raising a family is *not* in my plans." Evan's face sprung to mind and Nora quickly focused on her father's deep tan to dispel the image.

"From what Harrison said, this new position doesn't require travel."

"It sounds like Harrison has the lowdown on this supposed job. Maybe he's the one you should talk to." If the guy was any farther up her father's butt, he'd be in her office right now as a seat cushion.

"Harrison is a good man. I should have gobbled him up when I had the chance. Unfortunately, he said he'd only work for me under *one* condition."

"That one condition is *not* going to happen." Nora huffed as she thought of a change in topic. "How's Mother?"

Her father stared at her for a few seconds. "Your mother is your mother. Nothing more to say. It's been a while since you called her."

"Yes, I know." Nora couldn't help comparing her ice queen of a mother to the caring warmth of Arlene. "I just can't deal with another 'You need a man' lecture."

"We both want you to be happy."

"By happy, you mean married to a healthy investment portfolio. I've already got one of my own."

"No. *I* want you to do what makes *you* happy. If that means this new promotion, take it. If it means leaving this job for something that fulfills your heart, do it." He crossed one long leg over the other and resting his elbow on the armrest, positioned his chin in his hand. "If it's one thing I've learned after all these years, it's that the safe, expected road is not always the right one. There's a saying, 'Success is right over the edge of your comfort zone.'"

He was right. She'd always done what had been expected. Working for MoonBurst had been her first attempt at rebellion. Her second was refusing to marry Harrison.

Her parents may have had their hearts set on her marrying him, but that was *their* dream, a dream that would be *her* nightmare. Only she knew what was best for her.

"Thanks for understanding, Dad. I don't want what Mother wants. I want to marry who I want, when I want."

A sarcastic snicker rumbled from her father's lips. "No one understands that more than I."

Chapter 6

Damn.

Julie had been looking forward to today, and now Evan had to disappoint her.

Halfway into the Saturday morning rush—when the grinder and all the coffee machines refused to work—it took a few seconds for Evan to determine an electrical problem, especially after the breakers tripped. Twice.

He was forced to close the Bean & Brew for the day until the building landlord arranged the repair. And right now, at the beginning of the pumpkin decorating competition, he received a text that the electrician was on his way. Evan didn't have a choice; he had to meet the man. Today's sales netted zero, and he couldn't afford to be closed tomorrow, too.

Walking away from his daughter at the pumpkin festival was one of the hardest things he had to do. Armed with a plastic shopping bag filled with girly stuff, Julie stood at the table under the contest tent revved and ready to transform a plain orange pumpkin into a bedazzled fairy princess. He never understood why little girls loved shiny, gaudy stuff. But thinking about it, big girls did, too. Except, their shiny stuff came with a higher price tag.

He kissed Julie on the top of her head, squeezed in a quick bear hug for luck, and left her in the capable hands of his mother.

As he made his way across the Pembrook Farm's Fairgrounds, he turned his gaze to the clear, blue sky peppered with a few, scant wispy clouds hoping there was a Heaven up there.

"Dad, I'm trying to keep things going," he said aloud, "but every time we make progress, something else goes wrong. The Universe is not cooperating."

He wove his way through a cluster of people down the dirt and gravel walkway toward the exit gate. Just before he entered the exit's roped aisle, his friend, Adam, and his wife, Laurel, greeted him.

Shaking Adam's hand, then giving his pregnant wife a hug and asking how she was feeling, Evan turned his attention back to his friend. "How's the re-election campaign going?"

"Pretty good. Running un-opposed has its advantages," Adam said with a chuckle.

"I'm glad you decided to run again for the council. You've been helping the village on the sidelines for too long. At least now you'll be able to have more of an impact on what goes on around here."

"I'll try, but they still consider me the new guy, so they're not apt to listen to my suggestions," Adam said as he put his arm around his wife's back. "It won't be easy. A lot of them are set in their ways."

"You can say that again. At least you're going to lower the average age of the village council down to the fifties," Evan joked with a fist pump to his friend's arm.

"See," Laurel added, "you're helping already."

Evan was drawn to the sun's rays that bounced off a set of sunglasses several feet away.

"Whoa!" He patted Adam's shoulder. "Adam, you gotta excuse me, buddy."

"Sure," Adam said.

Evan yelled over his shoulder, "I'll catch up with you soon," as he headed in the direction of the sunglasses.

"Hey." He stood in front of Nora, purposely blocking her.

"Hey, yourself." She moved around him, side-stepping the roped-off aisle to let the people behind her pass.

Evan followed her lead. "Where ya been?"

He watched her perfectly formed eyebrows rise above the top line of the darkened sunglasses as if she was surprised. "Busy. Working."

"I tried to find you this week, but you weren't around." He purposely put on his biggest smile to lighten the mood because she seemed hesitant. "Don't you like my coffee anymore?"

She lowered her gaze to the ground and murmured, "Your coffee's fine. Like I said, I've been working." She looked up at him. "Is there something wrong?"

"No. It, um, it's Julie."

"Julie?" Her hand flew to her glasses, pulling them off, revealing frightened concern in her eyes. "Is she okay?"

"Yeah, yeah. She's fine." He never expected that reaction, so he patted her shoulder to reassure her. In the sunlight, he noticed tiny freckles lining the bridge of her nose. Noticed how fresh and vibrant her cream-colored skin shined. She radiated grace like the women on those TV commercials touting natural beauty without any makeup. An overwhelming need to keep his hand on her shoulder hit him, so he immediately withdrew it. "Julie wanted to know if you could come today."

"Oh," she said as if she was trying to calm herself, then, "Oh?" Another surprised expression showed on her face and then she grinned. "Is she here?"

When her lush lips rose into a full smile, his first reaction was to put his arm across her shoulders and walk her over to his daughter. The thought of holding her right now overpowered any concerns he had moments ago about touching her.

And then he remembered why he was here and not with Julie. The electrician. As much as he wanted to hang with Nora right now, his business took priority. "Yeah, she's in the pumpkin decorating tent." Needing to put some distance between them, he started to back away. "Look, I gotta run. Could you stop over and just say hello to her. It would really mean a lot."

"Sure. She's the reason I came today."

He stopped for a minute. "She is?"

"It's not every day I get to see a pumpkin fairy princess."

How did she know Julie's plan for that poor gourd? And she was here to see Julie? He hadn't had a chance to ask her to come. She came on her own to see his daughter?

"I'd love to stay and talk, but I've got to meet the electrician. No power at the store. Gotta run." With that, he hopped a few steps to turn away and left her standing alone. She'd come to see his little girl because she knew how much Julie's creation meant. Not too many women would do such a thing.

With each passing day, a different Nora than he first met made him take a second look. And not just physically. A caring personality began to emerge, giving him a glimpse of who she really was. He also figured she probably didn't share that part of herself too often because if she had, it would have been evident the first day he met her.

He considered the facts. He and Nora hadn't hit if off at the beginning. He enjoyed letting her think he was a lowly employee. Never bothered to correct her on that one. Never bothered to tell her he was Arlene's son, either. At least now they could hold a casual conversation without barbs volleying between them. Maybe she wasn't at all like his ex. Maybe she wasn't a high-maintenance, selfish person that he thought she was. She seemed to care a lot about Julie.

But . . .

Would she still care about Julie if she knew Julie was *his* daughter?

~ ~ ~

Okay. That was odd.

Nora made her way across the grassy fairground, passing tents as she followed the brightly colored signs for the pumpkin decorating contest.

She didn't understand why Evan had been so worried about his boss's granddaughter. She marveled at how everyone in the village looked after one another. While it was considerate, it could also be somewhat smothering, too.

Yesterday, as she sat at her desk and stared at yet another acquisition report, an uncontrollable urge to come back to Cedar Ridge overcame her. She wanted to see Julie. She fought it for several hours, but the child's giggles kept echoing in her head.

If she were being honest, it wasn't just Julie. Arlene had also been on her mind. And there was Mr. Buchanan, whose comment about not needing a magnifying glass because he had Nora to read his crossword puzzles had her wanting to come back. There were George's jokes and how she reveled in Howard's harmless flirting.

And if she were honest with herself, she had even looked forward to seeing Evan. When he spotted her a few minutes ago, the pleasure on his face made her heart skip. While he was a good-looking guy, he shouldn't have given her that type of visceral reaction.

When he mentioned Julie, it reinforced her desire to come back to share in the child's endeavor. She hoped she hadn't arrived too late. She'd be disappointed if she missed the masterpiece in production.

Finding the decorating tent, she scanned the tops of the contestants' heads all lowered in deep concentration as the girls and boys created their designs. Then she spotted the top of Julie's head, her dark-brown hair in its usual pony tail. Nora chuckled at the two miniature, plastic pumpkins secured to her ponytail holder, loving how Julie really got into the pumpkin theme.

A hand waving behind Julie drew Nora's attention. Arlene stood with other spectators behind the roped-off area. Nora waved back and strode toward her. After weaving her way through the crowd, she stood next to Arlene at the front of the viewing area. The air of excitement crackled, filling her with nervous anticipation. When Arlene wrapped her in a welcome-back hug, Nora didn't know what to do. Her arms went to Arlene's sides, but she didn't hug back. All the years of practiced emotional restraint kept her from responding to Arlene's generous show of affection. The woman was genuinely happy to see her, filling Nora with honest-to-goodness acceptance.

"Where have you been?" Arlene asked. "We haven't seen you in days."

Nora shrugged one shoulder. "I've been busy at work."

"Oh, good. As long as you're okay." She pointed to the contestants. "Julie's going to be so happy to see you. She's done nothing but talk about you ever since you helped with her homework on Monday."

Really? Nora couldn't think of a time when someone was honestly happy to see her without an agenda. It made her day that Julie thought so highly of her. Evidently, so did Arlene, judging by that greeting she just offered.

For the next few minutes, they talked about how seriously Julie executed her pumpkin princess. The child didn't even bother to check out the other contestants' creations; she stayed focused on painting, gluing, and poking the poor pumpkin with all kinds of feathery, dazzling accessories.

When she placed the finishing touch of a plastic tiara atop the pumpkin, she proudly turned to show her grandmother. That's when she spotted Nora, and she squealed and ran to the rope line. As she flung her pint-size arms around Nora's waist, Nora held back a small tear forming at the corner of her left eye. Arlene and Julie's warm welcome sent sentimental swells across her chest. She knew she made the right choice to come back. This time, she hugged Julie back and it felt good.

There was something magical drawing her to Cedar Ridge and its people. The laid-back lifestyle. The refreshing, slower, non-competitive pace of old-fashioned support and encouragement. Their acceptance of her, an outsider, showed Nora that the cynical attitude of city life wasn't the only way to live. If her parents were to see her right now with Julie's arms wrapped around her, and her hugging the girl back, they'd think she lost her mind.

An odd touch of heat startled her, and then she sensed Arlene's hand placing a gentle squeeze on her shoulder. The woman's eyes radiated such approval, Nora knew Arlene was truly glad she was there for her granddaughter, too.

"Oh, look," Arlene said. "They're getting ready to announce the winner!"

"Good luck," Nora yelled as Julie ran back to her princess. She felt a surprising tug of pride as she watched Julie's courage as they announced the third prize winner. It was as if the kid was a relative. Both she and Julie had a case of hero worship for each other, filling Nora with such gladness, she could hardly control herself.

Second prize was announced. Julie pressed out her bottom lip. She looked at Nora and Arlene with pleading eyes.

"It's okay, baby," Arlene yelled to her.

Nora didn't know what to do, so she gave her two thumbs-up and a smile, but already plotted in her head what she'd do if Julie lost.

First prize was announced, and the blue ribbon awarded.

But not to Julie.

Nora's heart broke for the little girl who ran into her grandmother's open arms.

"I tried so hard," Julie gulped between tears.

"I know you did. And that's what's important." Arlene loosened her hold, surveying Julie's tear-streamed face. "Look around. There are only three winners, but there's about twenty of the rest."

Julie tried to look brave and listen to her grandmother, but Nora saw the child's heart wasn't in it. She doubted the kid saw anything through all those tears. An overwhelming urge surged through her to wrap the girl in her arms, but this was time for her to be comforted by her grandmother. Something Nora herself had longed for all her life.

"Now." Arlene knelt to eye level with Julie. "I'm so proud that you tried. You don't need a ribbon to let you know you did a good job. Yeah, a ribbon would be nice, but sometimes you win, sometimes you don't. If you didn't try, we wouldn't have this pretty pumpkin to put in the store for everyone to see."

"Really?" Julie asked with a hesitant smile.

"You betcha." The woman wiped Julie's tears with her thumbs. "Now, you go get her, and be careful not to hurt her."

Julie nodded, wiped the rest of her tears with her glitter-pasted fingertips, and ran to get her pumpkin.

"The poor kid," Nora said. "I wish I could do something."

"You already have. You're here. That's more than enough. Besides, everyone's gotta learn they can't win at everything. Better she learns it now. She's a Cavanaugh. We're tough. She'll be all right."

A Cavanaugh.

Arlene said it like it was a prize in itself. And, by the way she was raising Julie, Nora guessed it was a prize. She wished she felt that kind of pride in being a Bainbridge. But she needed to keep that name quiet. As far as Arlene knew, Nora was a Langston. That thought had Nora cringing.

Langston was her mother.

Nora did a quick mental comparison of the two families. Right now, she would give anything to be a Cavanaugh.

~ ~ ~

What a day.

Nora couldn't remember the last time she'd had fun without spending a fortune.

The fresh air, good company, and relaxing environment cleared her head and filled her heart.

She hated saying goodbye to Julie and Arlene, but she didn't have a choice. Her last-minute decision to go to the pumpkin festival had her wanting to stay longer. Unfortunately, when she called The Cozy Quilt Bed & Breakfast, they were all booked. A cancellation for next weekend had her impulsively reserving it.

Even though she was now on her way back to the city, at least she knew she could come back to Cedar Ridge in a week for the last weekend of the festival. An odd sadness of disappointment seeped into her gut. She was beginning to love living as a woman named Nora, and was hesitant to return to her life as Eleanor. Even though she needed to leave, a strange optimism flooded over her at seeing her new friends again.

As she aimed her car for the onramp for Route 80, Nora remembered how Julie's eyes lit with joy when she suggested Arlene watch over the pumpkin princess so she and Julie could ride the giant Ferris wheel. Then they reveled in cotton candy and the largest mugs of root beer Nora had ever seen. She glanced over at the stainless-steel mug sitting on the passenger seat next to her handbag. Silly souvenir had afforded them free refills, but by night fall, she had had enough of the beverage to last a lifetime. Eyeing the mug brought a smile to her face. From now on, every time she looked at that mug, she'd remember the ring of Julie's giggles when her upper lip became covered with root beer foam.

The three of them had so much fun together that Nora had given Arlene her cell phone number. She didn't know why, but she was learning that Cedar Ridge had her doing things she wouldn't ordinarily do.

As she began her lonely drive home, she thought of her lonely apartment waiting for her. No one knew she had left the city. No one cared. Now she'd count down the next six days until she could leave work on Friday and head back to Cedar Ridge. Back, she realized, to the place where she really mattered.

~ ~ ~

"Son of a—"

Evan Cavanaugh stifled his reaction and swallowed the last word so he wouldn't offend his customers.

There had to be a mistake.

"See, it says it right here," George said, holding up the newspaper.

Evan grabbed *The Star-Ledger* from George's hands, his gaze followed the old man's arm as it reached across Evan's chest to point a gnarled finger at the blurb buried in bottom corner of the *Business* page.

MoonBurst intended to open a store right in the heart of Cedar Ridge, along with another just outside of town on Rt. 15 as part of the Sussex County Expansion Project.

He slowly glanced around the place that he'd worked his butt off to modernize and listened to the hum of conversations from his friends and customers who stuck with him over the past four years. He couldn't believe all his hard work could be wiped out so quickly.

George tapped him on the shoulder. "What are you going to do, Evan?"

"Give him time to think," Howard interrupted. "The boy's had the rug pulled out from under him."

"You got that right," Evan mumbled, harnessing the impulse to kick a few chairs.

How could he stop it from happening? The article had to be wrong. He scanned the words again just to be sure. More than a few expletives jumped through his mind.

What kind of a cruel joke was this?

His eyes met despair staring back at him in his mother's gaze as she stood behind the counter, her arms tightly hugging her waist. The two of them had been through hell, but were finally able to overcome it with hard work, determination, and a lot of love. Now, this had to intrude and screw up all his plans and dreams?

How was he going to tell his daughter there might be a possibility he'd have to close the store, maybe move again? He'd uprooted her four years ago, had earnestly transformed his family's floundering business, only now to get pummeled by the nation's largest coffee company. Okay, so the Bean & Brew wasn't in the same league as MoonBurst, but it worked and thrived, had become the meeting place of the town he loved and now called home again.

As word spread to the customers, everyone mingled around him, encasing him in a claustrophobic cocoon. Yeah, that's what Cedar Ridge citizens did in a crisis: rally around the one in need. But right now, he needed room to breathe, to think, to calm his racing heart, and figure out how he would save his business.

"Folks, I appreciate your concern, but right now, there's no need to worry." The eyes trained on him clearly weren't buying the smile he forced at his lips. "It'll all work out."

As the crowd slowly withdrew, he stood rooted in the spot next to George's table, watching Julie hold on to his mother's arm, her face in a state of confusion. He handed the newspaper back to his friend, then extended his hand in appreciation. "George, thanks for looking out for me."

"That's what I'm here for. You always look out for us, it's the least I can do." George returned the shake while his other boney hand patted Evan on the shoulder.

"Evan, let me know if there's something I can do." Howard leaned forward, grabbing him into a manly hug.

Evan didn't back off as quickly as he normally would. Even though Howard was two decades older than Evan's father would have been, it felt good to have a heart-felt embrace from a man who truly cared about him. He didn't realize until now how much he missed that gesture.

With a few hearty pats on the back, he broke free from the man's hold. "Thanks, Howard, I appreciate it."

"Howard! Are you giving out free hugs today?"

Evan glanced past Howard's slumped shoulders and head of white hair to see Nora's smiling face as she strode through the entrance door.

"Sure am." Howard placed an arm across her petite shoulders and planted a kiss on her head. "It's that kind of day. We all need a little reassurance."

"Why's that?" Her eyes sparkled as her hand wove itself around the back of Howard's waist.

"MoonBurst. Weren't you paying attention?"

Nora's eyes narrowed as her brows knit together. "No, I just got here. M-MoonBurst?"

Evan watched her suddenly draw away from Howard, as if burned by the sound of the company's name.

"They're coming to Cedar Ridge," Howard explained. "Probably put Evan out of business."

The tension of those words spoken aloud hit Evan like a bulldozer. His gaze found its way to Nora's. Even though he'd only known her for a short time, she'd quickly become a regular customer who truly enjoyed hanging out at the Bean & Brew. Somehow, spending time with her felt comfortable, and right now, with this impending problem looming over his business, he needed a little comfort.

But the look of horror on Nora's face was reason for concern. "Hey, easy there," Evan said. "Don't worry. I'll figure something out." It was his business, no sense having their new friend worrying about something that wasn't her problem.

"H-How do you know about MoonBurst?" Her voice was barely above a whisper as she grabbed the back of a chair like she needed to steady herself.

Her hands trembled. In fact, her shaking body reminded him of the coffee beans in his grinder, bouncing and jumping all around. He reached forward, taking hold of her hand to calm her. "Are you all right?"

The soft warmth of her flesh against his palm brought back memories of how it felt to be with a woman. Wanting to jump far away from that feeling, but not wanting to insult his friend, he carefully dropped her hand and patted her shoulder. Even though Nora was worlds apart from his ex, getting involved with a woman was the last thing he needed, especially now that MoonBurst's decision turned his world upside down.

"Have a seat." He led her to an empty chair at Howard's table. "I'll get you a cup."

Striding behind the counter, Evan poured fresh decaf beans into the grinder and pushed the button. As the beans did their dance inside the machine, he spat out a curse, then looked around to make sure none of his customers heard.

What the hell was he going to do?

Everything he worked for would be wiped out the minute MoonBurst opened its doors. It didn't matter that he spent four years enlarging the store, slowly expanding the menu, and adding extra tables and chairs so customers could lounge for a few minutes to enjoy their stay. If the national chain made a grand entrance, he could kiss this place goodbye.

He pulled his gaze toward the ceiling and puffed out a heavy breath. Shaking his head, he turned his eyes to the picture on the wall of his father holding the first Bean & Brew mug. The place had changed since he came back four years ago. *He* had changed, finally finding what made him whole and happy, making his daughter whole and happy, something he didn't think possible. But it was.

A tear filled his eye, and he swiped it away with the back of his hand.

His world was unraveling. The Universe was once again on its mission to ruin him. He was about to lose everything.

Chapter 7

Nora sat stiff, frozen in her seat. Who in the world had leaked the news that the company planned to open in Cedar Ridge?

The decision to open the store was still under consideration, and without her final report, which she hadn't submitted yet, that decision couldn't be made. And even after they received the go-ahead, the entire project had to be kept under wraps until the deal was approved by the Cedar Ridge Village Planning Board. Who had jumped the gun and allowed *The Star Ledger* to print the blurb?

Oh, no. Terror plummeted in the pit of her stomach. Was it sent out on the wire or did someone at headquarters give the newspaper the scoop?

Her hands trembled again and she grasped them in her lap, hidden under the table. Darn it all. She knew immersing herself in this community would backfire. The last thing she wanted to witness was the effect the news had on the owner. This was *not* in the plan.

Emotions and business don't mix. *Emotions make you weak, give the opponent the upper hand.* How many times had she heard her father expound those words just before acquiring another company?

Ugh! This entire situation had gotten completely out of control. The people here had been so welcoming, she was afraid she'd put herself in too deep. That blurb in the *Ledger* was as good as giving up her identity, especially if the company's head brass decided to show up.

God, she hated this part of her job.

Just thinking about how messed up this had become had her heart pounding.

"Here you go." Evan placed a mug of coffee in front of her.

Light mocha decaf. Perfect each time he handed it to her over the past eleven days. When he settled in the seat across from her, next to Howard, Nora couldn't look either man in the eye. Not after they embraced her into their world, just as everyone else in Cedar Ridge had done. Not when they'd eventually find out she was the one sent here to research MoonBurst's potential.

"Little lady, you need to settle yourself." Howard reached across the table and took hold of her shaking arm. "Don't worry your pretty little head. We'll all help Evan figure out what to do." His focus turned to Evan. "Won't we, son?"

Nora froze in place. Evan *owned* the Bean & Brew?

Wasn't Arlene the sole owner? How had Bruce gotten that wrong, too?

Nora focused on Arlene from across the store; saw the pain in her eyes. Just then, Julie walked to her grandmother and tugged on the edge of Arlene's sweater. "Grandma, are we gonna lose the store?"

"Don't worry, Julie," she heard Arlene say. "Everything is going to be all right."

"Yes, it is," Evan announced over his shoulder. "This store has been in business for over forty years. It's not going to close because some corporate bigwig decides to keep his shareholders happy."

The vibrant hazel of Evan's eyes dulled as his gaze landed on her. Then they opened wide.

"Nora!" He took hold of her hands from across the table. "We need your help."

"Me?" A shot of heat sizzled through her veins then throbbed with panic. "W-Why would you think I could help?"

"Seriously, you're the type to frequent a place like MoonBurst, what do you think we can do here to compete with a place like that?"

Are you kidding???

She gently eased her hands from his grasp and placed them back in her lap, although, there was something comforting in his touch, it didn't keep them from shaking uncontrollably. She shook her head furiously as her pulse accelerated. "I-I'm not the one to be giving advice on this matter."

"Sure you are. You're the Cappuccino-type. You're obviously a successful business woman. Got any ideas?"

This was worse than she thought possible.

Why would he ask her? He barely knew her. If he was taking advice on how to run his business from strangers, then he didn't have a clue as to how to be successful. MoonBurst would blow him out of the water within a month. It was truly pathetic.

Quickly coming up with a story, Nora explained, "I write copy for a medical newsletter." She shrugged. "I'm not good with numbers."

Graduating with a master's degree in economics clearly qualified her as being good with numbers, but they didn't have to know that.

"Doesn't matter." Evan shook his head with what looked like renewed determination. "We're not going down without a fight."

But as quickly as she saw it, that spark of determination evaporated from his eyes, the drive bolting through them dulled to a blank stare. Worry etched on his face. A few wrinkles she hadn't noticed before became evident around his eyes and mouth. The man who seemed to have the world at his feet a few days ago, now had his zest for life deflated.

Of course he did. The great and powerful MoonBurst was coming.

Nora couldn't handle this. Her emotions weren't supposed to be involved, yet a pang of worry and sympathy sprinted through her mind as a rumble of queasiness overpowered her insides.

Picking up the mug, she feigned a sip, unable to stomach anything at the moment, but not wanting to tip off Evan that all this was terribly, terribly wrong. She glanced around the crowded store, watched customers approach Evan to offer condolences. It was like a damn funeral.

Suddenly the room began to spin, the air cut off from her lungs, a whir of white noise filled her head. She clutched the mug, then the edge of the table.

Her mind was a jumble of unanswered questions, with one jumping to the forefront.

What on earth am I going to do?

~ ~ ~

How the hell am I going to fight MoonBurst?

Staring at the ceiling with only the glow of the digital alarm clock casting shadows in his bedroom, Evan realized that if he didn't come up with a plan, all he had worked for would be lost. And the death-bed promise he made to his father would have been made in vain.

Rolling to his side, he pulled the sheets with him, wrapping his body in a protective bubble. Taking on the responsibility of his parents' business, losing his wife because of it, and raising his daughter alone all seemed like monumental tasks. But all those combined didn't compare with saving his business.

This was David against Goliath.

But at least David had had a slingshot. The only thing Evan had going for him was a coffee pot. It was going to take more than a pot of regular and decaf, even if they *were* pretty damn good, to take down a national coffee chain.

Rolling over again onto his back, several shadows on the walls and ceiling seemed like ghosts taunting and teasing him. His father's face, gaunt and sallow, appeared on one shadow. The face of his former boss's shocked expression when Evan had told him he was resigning to run a coffee shop was on another. And the last ghost, the one that had given him nightmares even when he was awake, was that of his ex-wife. The self-indulgent smirk on Miranda's face when she told him she was leaving him and Julie still haunted him, returning with the impending fear that she'd show up to claim his daughter.

He'd never set out to be a quitter. Never intended to not finish what he had started. Life handed him a number of choices, none of which were part of his plan, but he had always ignored what was best for him and chose to do what was best for others.

Now fate once again dealt him an undesirable hand.

He rolled over to his other side, kicked the sheets from his body, slammed his fists in the pillow to position it under his head and closed his eyes. Hopefully, by the time he woke up in the morning, he'd have a solution. If not, he was about to lose everything.

~ ~ ~

After ignoring all the voice messages Bruce left on her cell last night, and earlier this morning, Nora needed to contact him *now*.

She punched in his cell number so that she'd be sure to catch him, unsure if he'd be at the office, on the subway, at home with his family, or in the arms of his girlfriend. She needed to find out who leaked the Cedar Ridge Expansion Project location to the press.

"Hell-o!"

"Bruce, it's me."

"Where the hell have you been? You were supposed to let me know last night how things went. I left you seven messa—"

"I know," she cut him off, not wanting to go into how she had failed at the field study, wanting to focus on getting answers of her own. "What could possibly tempt headquarters to leak the building of the two New Jersey locations?"

"A stroke of genius, if I do say so myself. Whoever did it told them about the three locations in Delaware, too. Before that, we had been losing confidence. Our stock went down three points. The announcement gave a much-needed boost to our shareholders. Stock rose 4.3 percent! They're loving it."

Nora pinched the bridge of her nose. "That's great," she said, lacking enthusiasm. Sure, the stocks were tied to her retirement plan—and that was a boon for her—but she felt as if she'd taken the money right out of Arlene and Evan's pockets. And that left her feeling selfish and empty. When had her company's mission statement changed from providing the best customer service and products to keeping the stockholders happy? When did people stop being important?

Nora felt her heart shifting, her loyalties in flux. The worry and concern on the faces of Arlene and Evan played on her emotions. The show of overwhelming support thrust upon them earlier by the community left her yearning. What kind of people were they to instill that type of help and encouragement by everyone around them?

Suddenly, she felt all alone. Bruce's constant babble about how well the company was doing turned into a mist of words, evaporating into the air as she wallowed in her own thoughts. Was this promotion and promise of a new economic life what she truly wanted? Her entire life, all she wanted was to be accepted, to feel she truly belonged. The magic of Cedar Ridge seemed to encompass that while the cold, corporate world she was setting herself up for seemed sterile, void of feelings, of emotions. But wasn't that how she lived her life?

So, why did it seem that right now, her goal was exactly what she *didn't* want?

~ ~ ~

Could it get any worse?

There, on the flat screen above the table area of the Bean & Brew, the five-p.m. edition of the local news showed the Cedar Ridge Planning Board Chair shaking hands with the CEO of MoonBurst. It looked like a done deal.

Evan's insides scrambled. His world was about to change as soon as the mega giant broke ground. Probably take them only a few months to be up and running.

Yeah, he had decided to fight them, thought long and hard on how to approach the village planning board, too. But, for now, his thoughts had to be on something more important. In the next few weeks, all his time and energy would be spent fighting for his business. Right now, he needed to prepare Julie for what might happen. That poor kid had been through enough in her short life. Evan didn't want to think about uprooting her again.

Lately it seemed he kept screwing things up, kept disappointing his daughter. He angled his gaze to the ceiling to his father. "I could use a little guidance right now, if you don't mind."

He waited a minute—always waited a minute—for a sign to see if his father was listening. With that, a gust of brisk air swung the door open and in walked his sign.

He wasn't sure how he felt about it, but if his father sent it, so be it.

Nora.

Since Julie liked Nora so much, maybe Nora could help him break the news to her. Maybe having Nora there would soften the blow, bring a nurturing side to the situation that he wasn't so great at. It was worth the shot.

The way his thoughts and feelings kept bouncing back and forth about Nora drove him crazy. If he didn't admit it out loud, he had to at least be man enough to admit it to himself.

He liked her.

A lot.

Yeah, at first she seemed far from his type, but any woman who cared about his daughter the way Nora did had to be worth exploring.

But Nora didn't know Julie was his. When he asked his mother about it, she said the subject of him being Julie's father never came up. Which probably led Nora to think that Julie was orphaned or abandoned by Arlene's deadbeat son or daughter.

Since today was his day of honesty with his daughter, he might as well come clean with Nora, too. If he wanted to pursue the interest he had for her, she had to know about Julie. If she was gonna run, better she run now before his feelings got further involved.

Unfortunately, Julie's feelings already were.

"You're here early for a Tuesday," he said, trying to keep his tone upbeat.

"Took a few days off. Mental health days."

"Lucky you. We don't have that option here."

"No. I supposed you don't."

"Um. I was wondering, if you're not busy right now, would you do me a favor?"

She eyed him suspiciously. "Me?"

"There's something I need to do, and I think you're just the right person to help."

"Ooo-kay."

She didn't look comfortable at all, but he guessed he'd

feel the same without any details. "Hey, George, can you man the fort for me?" he yelled across the coffee shop.

"You betcha!" George put down his newspaper and looked up. "Is it Tuesday already?"

"Yep."

George took his place behind the counter as Evan scooted toward Nora. Jacket in hand, Evan swung it onto his shoulders and as he drew both arms in, escorted Nora to the door at the back of the shop. "My truck's out here," he said as he opened the back door.

They crossed the small parking lot to his pick-up truck. He didn't know if she'd mind riding in a truck, but since it was his only vehicle, she might as well get used to it, assuming things worked out today. Just another test to see if she was really the down-to-earth woman everyone talked about, or if she was that snob he initially met.

"Here we go." He pushed the electronic transmitter to disengage the door lock.

"This is your truck?" she asked, her eyes brightening as her lips curved into a smile.

"Sure is."

She hopped one foot onto the flat running board and he steadied her with both his hands around her waist. He appreciated the softness of her curves even though her jacket was in the way, but she stopped for a moment and glanced at him over her shoulder, so he quickly retracted his hands, not wanting to scare her off.

"Thanks." She turned her gaze to the truck and swung her foot into the cab as she slid in.

"All set?"

Her head bobbled and she grinned like a kid. "Yes! This is sooo exciting!"

Evan closed her door and a wave of relief filled his gut. He sprinted around the front of the truck, opened the driver's side door and hopped in.

"I've never been in a truck before," she said, the sound of excitement in her voice added to the sparkle in her violet eyes.

"Really?"

"No one I know has one."

He could believe that, never expecting her reaction to be enthusiastic. "Just your basic truck. The only amenity it has is power windows." He couldn't afford the upgrade because his liquid cash had been tied up in the Bean & Brew.

"Does it have heat and air conditioning?"

Odd question. "I think so, last time I looked," he joked.

"That's all you need!"

Really? She wasn't disappointed that the seats weren't leather, or that there was no mega sound system?

He backed the truck out of the spot, maneuvered through the narrow driveway between his store and the building next door and turned the wheel sharply onto Elm toward the park. He was running late because that news report had him temporarily stunned, but he was sure Julie and his mother would understand. Having Nora with him should make up for him not being on time.

The five-minute drive had him wondering if he made the right choice. Whatever smelled good on Nora had his insides jumping around, aching for release. She sat only a few inches away, but right now he wanted to take a fast right turn so she'd slide closer.

Unfortunately, right turns wouldn't get him to the park. And her smelling so good and being so close reinforced what his mother had tried to say the first day Nora stepped foot in his coffee shop: He needed to date.

He swallowed hard thinking about those long legs she showed off that day. The ones he hadn't seen in a while because every day since she hid them in jeans or sweats. Someday he'd have to try to catch her going or coming from work to gain a glimpse of them again.

Like his mother had inferred, he hadn't had sex in forever, and he needed to keep his mind on the difficult task ahead of him, not Nora's luscious limbs.

Nora felt as much exhilaration riding in Evan's truck as she did on the Ferris wheel with Julie. Except, this was so much more tempting, more exciting, and, dare she think, heady.

Everything about Evan screamed male.

His broad shoulders took up a good part of the truck's interior making her feel safe. His hands sliding over the steering wheel had her staring at their strength, and when his right arm casually rested along the back of the seat, his fingertips were almost able to reach her shoulder.

When he asked her to do him a favor, she feared it would have been something concerning his MoonBurst dilemma. Her nerves had been frazzled ever since she learned Evan was one of the owners of the Bean & Brew, and that her cover had almost been blown.

But this truck ride slowly relaxed the tension in her shoulders, releasing all the worry that had built in her mind and body over the past two days since the media leak. Being this close to Evan was the perfect prescription to clear her head, keeping her mind off her job.

But right now, her job would be difficult. Evan smelled of coffee and sweet pastries with a slight touch of male musk that had her practically purring. She inhaled a deep breath, needing to break this seductive spell he wove around her. "We're so high up," she said, trying to lessen her body's reaction to him.

"You like it?"

She shook her head. "No. I love it. It's so powerful, like you rule the world."

"I wouldn't say that. It's only a pick-up. There are plenty of larger trucks out there."

"I bet they aren't as much fun as this."

"Fun?" He glanced at her, and when their eyes connected, sparks ignited throughout her body.

As Evan turned into the parking lot of Grover's Park, Nora was both disappointed and relieved. Not wanting the closeness they shared to end, she knew something had to break the sexual tension swirling in that truck cab.

"What are we doing here?" she asked. The exhilaration from being this close to Evan and the truck ride now diminished, and a hint of worry wormed back to her mind.

"You'll see."

She waited for him, and just like the gentleman she suspected he was, he opened her door to help her down from the truck.

When he placed a hand at the small of her back, the possessive move sent a thrill up her spine. "This way," he said with a nod.

As they walked across the green lawn scattered with picturesque leaves, Nora noticed the playground equipment standing several yards away. The castle-like wooden structure had interconnecting, colorful plastic slides, swings, and tunnels. A soft bed of wood chips broke the fall of the children jumping from it.

"Daddy!"

A little girl came running from inside one of the tubes, a hot pink snowboarding hat with two tassels dangled along both sides of her face. The child ran toward them and out of the corner of her eye, Nora noticed Evan down on one knee. Her gaze shot quickly to him, then back to the little girl.

Julie?

Straight into Evans arms, Julie flew, and his strength kept them from toppling over.

"Hey, Jules, how's my girl?"

"We thought you forgot about us."

"I wouldn't forget about my two best girls," he said as he gave her a bear hug.

Arlene came within a few feet and squeezed Nora's forearm. "Nice to see you, both, *together*." Her smile went from ear to ear. Then she gave Nora a hug.

But instead of the hug bothering Nora, this time she found herself looking forward to it and hugged Arlene back. Not only because she truly liked the woman, but because Nora knew the woman's life was about to become difficult because of something Nora had done. Nora wasn't sure if it was sympathy or guilt that brought out all the emotions bubbling on the inside.

Then suddenly, it hit her.

Evan?

Julie's father?

She withdrew from Arlene and looked the woman in the eye. "Evan is your son?"

"Of course he's my son. Didn't you know that?"

"No. I thought he was just a guy who worked for you." And then a second hit of reality struck her. The first day she met him, he referred to the coffee shop customers as *his*. She turned her attention to him.

"You own the Bean & Brew. Together?"

"Yep. Can't get me fired by Mrs. Cavanaugh like you wanted two weeks ago."

Embarrassment filled her face with a heat that surely colored it red.

Arlene smoothed aside a few strands of hair from Nora's face. "It's okay. We all make mistakes. You know what they say about assuming."

Yes, she knew. And right now, she felt foolish for making that major assumption.

It all made sense now. Evan inherited ownership of the Bean & Brew with his mother after his father's death. That meant he owned it for the past four years.

How had Bruce missed that *huge* detail?

Which also meant, not only was MoonBurst ruining a grandmother and granddaughter, it was ruining three generations of one family. A family that already suffered the death of its patriarch, and suffered the absence of Julie's mother.

Could this get any worse?

Nora glanced at Evan and Julie, watched as he intently listened to the child's story about bringing her princess pumpkin to school for Show and Tell. His gaze never drifted from Julie, and he seemed to delight in his daughter's animated drama.

Nora had been drawn to Evan for some unknown reason. He, just like everyone else in Cedar Ridge, had a magnetism that captivated her, holding her heart hostage. Her brain knew it was nothing more than a few nice people who happened to possess all the qualities she'd been craving, but was unable to find within her own family and friends.

Watching him with his daughter now had her wishing her childhood hadn't been lost to parents who were physically absent and emotionally vacant.

As Evan picked his daughter up and twirled her around, Nora's heart swelled with longing. And when he gently placed her on the ground, the simple act of picking a leaf from Julie's hair had Nora nearly in tears with regret for that missing piece of her childhood.

This man, so tender with his daughter, caring to those around him, responsible for taking care of his mother and their business, also showed determination to fight off MoonBurst.

Could Evan be the one to break her vow of not needing a man?

Chapter 8

As Julie settled her bottom on a chair at the Bean & Brew, Nora joined her at the table.

The child's adoring gaze gave Nora a heartfelt measure of joy. "I like when you're here. I always have to ride in the back seat by myself when Daddy picks me and Gramma up."

"I like when I'm here, too." Nora realized she meant it. Her life in the city seemed a million miles away, and she hadn't thought twice about taking yesterday and today off from work. She had accumulated days since she first started working for MoonBurst nine years ago, but as part of her advancement-driven lifestyle, she never thought to use them. On this last project in the field, she needed to tie up a few loose ends and her promotion would be as good as done. So taking a few days off to reenergize her mind had been a temptation she gave into.

Yet, after speaking to Bruce, she found herself not caring about the promotion any longer. The barren atmosphere of the 23rd floor had been such a turnoff in comparison to the warmth of Cedar Ridge, she slowly felt her goals changing. But jobs were scarce in the village, especially a job that would pay enough to finally get her mother off her back.

So here she was with her third act of rebellion of giving in to the irresponsible impulse of taking days off when she should be working hard to secure her future.

It seemed Cedar Ridge brought out a different side of her. An unnatural, yet comfortable side. Even though it was a bit unusual, Nora couldn't stop herself from loving it.

She was truly living as Nora with nary a thought as to who Eleanor was or what Eleanor wanted in life.

She giggled at the realization and looked across the table at Julie. "You know what? I never rode in a truck before. I loved it!"

"You never did?" Julie's eyes grew wide in amazement.

"No. Never did. Sitting in the back seat with you was a lot of fun!" Of course, Nora insisted Arlene sit in the front with Evan. It was a respect thing. But it also gave her the opportunity to spend some one-on-one time with Julie. Plus, it provided the added bonus of keeping her physical distance from Evan until she could sort through her feelings.

For Evan?

She hadn't even liked him when they first met. There was no flirting, no dating. Why was she thinking about him *that* way?

Just as thoughts of him got carried away, he showed up at the table with a hot chocolate for Julie. A moment later, Arlene placed a napkin with a crystal-sugar covered orange pumpkin cookie in front of her granddaughter.

Oh, what a scene, Nora thought. The kid spent an hour after school at the park with her grandmother, then came back to the coffee shop to spend time with her father with hot chocolate and a cookie. The 1950's perfect life.

Nora's heart skipped a wistful beat. Even though she grew up with all that money could buy, a scene like this never played out for her. Julie had all the security and love a child deserved, even without all that money. Especially love.

Evan and Arlene took seats at the table, while George continued to man the counter. He did surprisingly well handling the tasks, like he'd done it before.

Nora thought of MoonBurst's hiring policy. Ideally, they never accepted anyone over the age of sixty-five. Wasn't acceptable as a draw for younger customers.

But George was a natural. The customers enjoyed his corny jokes and were patient with his slower pace. The Eleanor in her made a mental note to see if they could hire more retirees because George was an excellent example of the value they'd be to any business. The good PR it would bring could raise those stocks Bruce bragged about. But more importantly, it would give the seniors a purpose and some extra money to supplement their retirement.

Directing her wayward thoughts back to this family, she realized Evan's tone had become serious.

"Thanks for hanging around," he said as he leaned closer and whispered so that only she could hear. "I thought you'd be able to help. Jules likes you, and I gotta tell her about MoonBurst."

What?

Was he kidding?

How was she supposed to comfort Julie when it was Nora's fault the family business may close? Couldn't Evan and his mother handle it? Why did they have to bring a stranger into a family matter? Yes, she and Julie had bonded during the pumpkin festival, but that didn't qualify her to be a surrogate family member.

Her wish to be a Cavanaugh just bit her in the butt. Be careful what you wish for. How could she respond to a request like that?

She nodded once and sat quietly as Evan rose and dragged his chair around the table next to his daughter. He didn't waste time explaining the situation to Julie.

Nora's heart pumped even harder.

Dear God, I'm not a regular churchgoer, but if you have it in your heart, please help me do the right thing.

"They're gonna take the store away from us?" Julie asked.

"No. No one's taking it from us." Evan took hold of Julie's hand as he put his other arm around her petite shoulders. "They want to open a store here in Cedar Ridge. They're such a big coffee company, I'm af— I'm sure, a lot of customers will want to go there."

Nora noticed Evan stop himself before using the word *afraid*. Substituting *sure* was a better choice so Julie wouldn't be frightened. Even under this intense pressure, he made sure to take his daughter's feelings into account. Oh, Nora thought, another reason to admire him.

"Does that mean we can't come here anymore?" A pout bowed Julie's lips. "What about Gramma?"

Evan wrapped her in a hug and stroked her hair. "We'll still see Grandma. She only lives a few blocks from us."

"But we won't see her every day."

"Oh, yes you will," Arlene said, holding back tears. "You just try and stop me."

That Cavanaugh strength.

It seemed as if Arlene fought to hold it together, even though Nora knew she was crumbling inside.

Nora's heart broke for her new friends. Why had she gotten involved? She should have stuck to her usual method of get in and get out. This entire situation had her second-guessing everything in her life.

"We're here now," she heard Evan reassure his daughter. "Even if we have to close the store, it won't be for a few months." He glanced at Nora.

She nodded. "Maybe longer. It—" She clamped her mouth to keep from saying it takes anywhere from eight months to a year, if everything is in place.

She held her breath and noticed Evan cock his head as his eyebrows creased together, but then he turned away, and Nora exhaled slowly. She needed to be careful. This poor family was on the edge of unemployment, worse, giving up their lives, because owning a business was a person's life, their purpose.

"Yeah," he began, "it could take longer. But you know what?" He removed his arm from around Julie's shoulders and smacked his thigh. "I'm gonna try to stop them from opening."

"How?" Julie asked.

Nora quickly turned to look at him. *Yeah, how?*

"Well, MoonBurst has to get . . ." It looked as if he struggled for the right word. ". . . permission from Mayor Farley. So I'll tell the mayor that we don't need a MoonBurst."

Julie's eyes lit up as her pout vanished. "Do you think Mr. Farley will listen?"

"I'm not sure. But I can try."

Nora could almost see the wheels in Julie's mind processing her father's words. The child thought a moment then said, "I can try, too."

"You can?" Evan asked.

"Uh-huh. I can write Mr. Farley a letter."

Evan smiled as his eyes glimmered with pent-up tears. Nora couldn't help noticing how choked up he became as he stroked Julie's hair. "That would be nice."

"Yep! I'm gonna ask Mrs. Kramer if my whole class can write letters. She lets us do that for other stuff."

"You know what, Jules? That would be *really* nice." When he kissed the top of her head, he kept his lips against her hair as he struggled with run-away tears escaping from his eyes.

"Hey, Evan, I need change over here," George interrupted.

"No, stay." Arlene put her hand out to halt Evan as she got up from her chair. "I'll get it."

Nora turned away to hide the evidence of a few of her own tears that formed. Evan had wanted her there in case Julie needed her, but there hadn't been a need. Nora wouldn't have known the right things to say if she had to step in to help. Evan had it covered. He was just as much a mother as he was a father to his little girl.

Why did this family have to be so kind to her when she was sent here to ruin them? Why did they feel the need to include her in their lives?

By all rights, they should be broken—a woman who should be enjoying retirement instead of working as a struggling business owner. A man without a wife, trying to hold together the fragments of his family. And a motherless child who had to hang out at a store every day after school because her father worked long, tireless hours.

But they weren't broken. The love they shared held them together, made them whole.

Nora thought of her perfect-looking family. Two highly educated parents and three adult children all living the American dream of profiting from all the stock market could supply. Yet, the Bainbridges weren't anything like the Cavanaughs, because the Bainbridges *were* broken. No amount of money could give them what love had given Evan and his family.

The tears welling in Nora's eyes broke free and she shifted her body in the opposite direction so no one would notice. Carefully, she wiped her eyes with her fingertips.

"Hey." Evan's hand was on her forearm. "You okay?"

Nora turned to face him, no longer caring if he noticed the tears smeared on her cheeks. Sincere concern laced his features. If he was honest with her in revealing Julie was his daughter and honest with his daughter about the coffee shop, Nora felt comfortable to be partially honest about her emotions.

"You're an amazing man," she said as her bottom lip quivered. "You're everything my father wasn't."

~ ~ ~

"Okay, this has gone far enough." Mary Claire's voice came in loud and clear on speaker mode of Nora's cell when she placed it on the dashboard of her Chevy. "You need to get away from that town and those people and your job so you can clear your head."

"I know, but I can't." Nora supported her head in both her hands, her arms resting on the steering wheel. "I've got to fix this. I'm ruining an entire family." Her stomach rolled and her heart pumped in a wild panic.

"You're not ruining a family. Unfortunately, that's the nature of your job. The only thing you've done wrong was get involved. You do have a heart under all that Bainbridge breeding and bloodline, you know."

MC was right. But that didn't help solve this monumental problem of how to stop MoonBurst from destroying the Cavanaughs.

"Come out to the farm. We'll ride, sit on the porch, watch the sunset. I think there's a full moon tonight. It always helped you in the past."

"You're right," Nora agreed. Mary Claire, again, was the voice of reason in Nora's chaotic life. She wondered if MC appreciated that she could be a normal person with a normal family living a simple life. "But I can't do it now. How about we plan it as soon as this mess is over?"

"And which mess are you talking about? The MoonBurst/Bean and Brew mess? Or the mess of you falling in love with Evan?"

~ ~ ~

Evan's insides shook as he waited for the village planning board to open the meeting to the residents. Julie was home—his mother watching her—so he didn't have to worry about her getting to bed late on a school night. With the temperature dipping, he didn't want to have to drag the poor kid out on the cold night. Besides, a boring meeting would be torture for a six-year-old.

As each member of the board settled into their seat up on the dais, he wondered why it took so long for them to start. The anticipation rattled his nerves. He needed to focus on relaxing so he could present his case, but that would be hard with the jumbled cocktail bubbling in is gut.

Hey, is that. . .?

No. It wasn't. A woman with dark-brown hair entered the general meeting room, walked down the aisle separating the residents' seats, and settled herself on the opposite side of the room. From the back, she resembled Nora.

Nora.

Another reason for his insides to be jumpy and his brain confused. When she dropped that bomb of a compliment on him the other day, confusion totally set in. First, she said he was amazing. Man, no one thought that about him. Well, maybe Julie, but his adorable princess didn't count on this one. Why had Nora said that? He hadn't done anything amazing like save someone's life or invent a cure for an incurable disease. No. That comment had to do with his parenting skills, or lack of them. He tried his best to let Julie know that no matter how hard things would get for them, he would always love her and they'd always be together. Nothing amazing about that.

But it seemed, for Nora, it had been.

The same couldn't be said for Julie's mother. And from Nora's last comment, maybe it couldn't be said for her father, either.

You're everything my father wasn't.

After he had time to digest that statement, Evan felt pretty darn good about himself. As far as he knew, it had been a long time since he had the admiration of a woman. He'd just about pushed every woman he knew—minus his mother—out of his life. Nora's comment filled him with hope that maybe he was doing right by his daughter. And maybe, Nora would be just the woman to help him break down that wall he'd built to protect him and Julie from being hurt.

The planning board chair, Ronald Whitmore, banged the gavel plucking Evan from his thoughts as the resident portion of the meeting was about to begin. His nerves kicked in again, but he rationalized that it wouldn't be that bad. Most of the members were Evan's customers. He even made it a point not to mention the MoonBurst problem when they came in for coffee. Didn't want to mix business and politics. Also, didn't want to piss them off before he had a chance to address them all together in public.

A disruption came from the back of the meeting hall causing Evan and everyone else to turn and look. George, Howard, and Walter shuffled their way toward a few seats in the back.

"I want a seat up front," said George out loud.

"There aren't any." Howard pointed his cane. "There's seats over there."

"Excuse me," Walter said as he climbed over the lap of Tom Sweeney, the *Cedar Ridge Sentinel* editor.

Great, Evan thought, he could just imagine this week's headline:

Geriatric Trio Turns into Peanut Gallery at Board Meeting!

"Hey," Todd whispered. "This seat taken?"

"Hey, buddy." Relief shot through Evan at the sight of his friend. "When'd you get here?"

"Just now. I snuck in while everyone was watching Huey, Dewey and Louie get settled."

Evan glanced back at the guys and George gave him a thumbs-up with a huge smile before he sat down. It comforted Evan that the guys came to support him, just like they had supported his father whenever he needed it. But they were slightly hard of hearing, and with their eighty-year-old filters gone, he cringed at what might come out of their mouths. Still, he wouldn't trade them for the world.

"Who's got your kids?" he asked Todd.

"Mom. You, too?"

Evan nodded.

"All right, gentlemen, are we settled?" Chairman Whitmore asked.

"Right as rain," Walter yelled out.

"What did he say?" Howard asked.

"He said to put down your cane!" George replied.

"Oh. Okay." Howard dropped his cane to the tile floor with a clank.

Evan lowered his head, letting out a long sigh as the murmur of laughter subsided from the audience.

"Don't worry." Todd laughed. "They got your back."

Evan fake-punched Todd, glad his friend had a good laugh at his expense. At least he was here for him, and so were the guys. If the situation wasn't so dire, he would have laughed, too.

As Evan waited for his turn at the microphone, he couldn't control the shaking of his leg. Damn nervous tic. He pressed his hand to his knee. Whenever he got nervous, his annoying foot jiggled his leg up and down 60 MPH.

"Okay, next case," Whitmore announced.

Evan left his seat and when he reached the microphone, he adjusted it to his tall height.

"Ah, hi guys." He gave a fleeting wave to the members seated on the dais. "Ah. I'd like to address the new MoonBurst coming into town."

"Before you start—" Whitmore put his hand up. "— nothing has been finalized."

Evan cleared his throat so he wouldn't sound like a frog. "I saw you shaking hands with the CEO on TV the other day."

Whitmore's chest puffed as a huge smile dawned on his face. "Made all the network broadcasts. Great publicity for our village."

"You mean great publicity for you," came from the crowd.

Evan flinched when he recognized George's voice.

Dammit, he didn't want to piss Ronald Whitmore off before he started. As he noticed Whitmore's smile wane, Evan quickly thought of a way to turn it around. "It was great publicity for all of us. Thanks, Ronald, for leading the charge."

"It was my pleasure." The chair's smile beamed back.

"That aside, MoonBurst is a potential problem. You do realize that if they open their doors, I'll be forced to close mine."

Whitmore blotted his forehead with a white handkerchief he plucked from the pocket of his suit jacket, not uttering a reply.

"I realized it," Adam answered from the opposite side of the room. "I told them that when the MoonBurst corporation first showed interest."

"Thanks, Adam," Evan responded, glad his friend, who happened to be on the village council, was there to lend support. "I appreciate that."

"But you don't understand," Whitmore began. "They assured us they won't sell what you sell."

Evan felt his eyes pop open wide. "What?"

"They assured us—"

"They sell coffee, don't they?" George bellowed from the back row.

"Of course they sell coffee," Ronald Whitmore replied, his brow bathed in sweat as he fumbled with his sweat rag.

"So does the Bean & Brew," shouted an unfamiliar male voice from the crowd.

Evan turned briefly to scan the audience, but couldn't figure out who had said it.

"The Bean & Brew has been selling coffee for 40 years." George was on his feet now, and Evan noticed Howard struggling to stand, too. "Tom opened that store back in '74 after he graduated high school."

Oh, no. George wasn't going to tell one of his stories. Not now.

"George, we all remember Tom." Whitmore leaned in closer to his microphone and continued, "And we all love the Bean & Brew. Evan, you've done a great job with it."

He appreciated the compliment, and he appreciated the chair cutting George off. Going along George's trip down memory lane would have been unproductive.

"The point is," Adam continued from the sidelines, "we don't have all the facts. MoonBurst says they won't sell what Evan does, but that's clearly not the case. It also infringes on another business, too."

The crowd mumbled in agreement, and Evan knew Adam truly understood. His mother's cookie business stood to close, too.

"But they indicated they were going to renovate the Baxley property," argued the chair. "Give it a face lift, fix the sidewalks. That end of Main Street was the last area of the village to be completed. If MoonBurst takes over that property, it will be less money we have to pay."

"But at what cost?" Evan asked. "The Baxley property is across the street from The Cookie Cottage. They'll put Molly out of business. My family will also be out of business. What are we all supposed to do?"

"I understand, Evan, but MoonBurst promised a lot of money donated to other projects. It's a hard offer to ignore."

"Money?" He shook his head. "What about people? When did we lose sight that people are more important than money?"

"You tell 'em, Evan."

Evan turned his eyes to the guys in the back. "Thanks, George."

Evan considered what he'd said. People. His customers. An idea percolated for a few seconds before he opened his mouth.

"Evan?" Whitmore prodded.

It was a long shot, but at the moment, it was the only solution he could think of. "Why don't we let the people decide?"

"It's our job as appointed officials to approve such ventures."

"Wait a minute, Ronald," Adam said. "Hear him out. Where you going with this, Evan?"

Get it right before you say it, he warned himself. "How about we have a taste test?"

Ronald Whitmore fidgeted in his seat. "I don't think something as silly as a taste test would be a good gauge for such a crucial financial decision as this."

"No, I think Evan's right," Adam said.

Okay, at least he had Adam's support, even though it was the planning board's decision. "We could have a blind taste test," Evan added, worried his last-ditch effort wouldn't be accepted. "Whichever coffee wins, gets to stay in the village." Great idea, but if he lost, he'd be aiding his business's demise.

After a few moments of awkward silence, Ernie Donaldson, the board's oldest member, chimed in, "That sounds like a great idea!"

"I like it, too," said another.

Phew. The tension in Evan's neck slowly began to relax. This could work. He did make the best coffee around, and he was confident the people of Cedar Ridge thought so, too. He wasn't about to wimp out on this and back down.

All he needed was the approval of the two remaining board members and his unfathomable idea of holding a taste test would be a go.

Time to kick some coffee butt.

~ ~ ~

Nora sat in Meeting Room #2 on the 23rd floor, staring at the suits situated around the conference table. The room held more ass kissing and preening than a person could stand.

Everyone involved in the Sussex County Expansion Project took credit for its impending success, as if each of them personally secured the deal.

"I have to tell you, whoever leaked the expansion to the media is a genius," Bruce said. "At first, the old man got upset, but once he saw the stock go up over four points, he changed his tune. We're swimming in gold right now." The rest of the suited minions murmured in agreement.

Nora glanced at the men, each in their cloned designer suits, white shirts, and various shades of red ties. Yes, red indicated power, and they all sported it proudly. "While you're all celebrating, that leak made my job more difficult. It took some hard work to get those last figures."

"That's why you're on board, Nora." Bruce leaned forward in his chair, directing his eyes toward her. "You're the best at what you do."

Nora found herself squirming in her chair. *The best at what she does?* So much so that she had compromised herself and her job by getting involved with the Cavanaughs. What she and MoonBurst were about to do made her heart ache with regret and her head throb with guilt. And MC's suggestion that she was falling in love with Evan had her head spinning in all directions, making it hard to focus on this almost impossible task.

"Don't sweat it, Nora." Harrison, seated across from her,

grinned from ear to ear. "I figured you'd be able to work around the media coverage."

Talk about the Cheshire Cat.

That arrogant . . .

She knew him well enough to know he had been the snitch, and it turned her stomach.

Why in the world did her parents want her to marry such a snake? His mission was to bring attention to himself, and he never gave a thought on how his actions would sabotage her efforts. Evan never would have done that to a friend, much less someone he wanted to marry. And Harrison had tried endlessly to pressure her into a relationship with the goal of it leading to marriage, guaranteeing him a position at Bainbridge Enterprises.

Thank goodness she saw through him and didn't succumb to his arrogant charms. Although, it surprised her that as a ruthless businessman, her father hadn't been able to see through him, too.

Now, judging the self-serving glare of his eyes, Nora realized that the anti-marriage discussion she had with him had been in vain. He had no intention of backing off from his quest to gain his way into her family's fortune. And this media leak trick to make her job more difficult reinforced her assumption that Harrison would do anything to get what he wanted.

"Right now we're on target to begin construction right after the first of the year," Bruce reported, leading her back to the problem of moving forward with the project. "By then, all the legalities will be finalized."

Panic rose in Nora's throat. "W-Wait!"

"Wait?" Bruce raised a questioning eyebrow.

"Maybe Cedar Ridge isn't the best option. It's a rural village and the numbers don't support—"

"The numbers more than support its development."

"But I don't think this is the right time to begin there," she tried again. "The village revitalization is only in its second year. I'm sure if we give it another year or two—" *or three or four* "—the tourist traffic will have doubled and we'd be poised to pull in higher revenue."

Bruce squinted at her. "You're not going soft on me, are you, Bainbridge?"

Nora scoffed. "No! There's a potential for lower revenue expectations if we act now. We don't want that to reflect in our regional reports, do we?"

She glanced at all eyes aimed on her. When her gaze rested on Harrison, uneasiness flitted through her bones, and she snapped her attention back to Bruce.

"You know, Nora, your father wouldn't do business like that," Bruce warned.

"Like what?" She realized her hands were shaking as they rested in her lap, so she gripped them together.

"Not coming in at the beginning. Jumping in to get the lion's share."

She sat straighter and pressed her back to the chair, her hands no longer shaking as they took hold of the edge of the conference table. "That's the difference between me and my father. Besides, he has nothing to do with this company." Dear old Dad was all about the money, like she used to be. Evan had taught her the valuable lesson that people were most important.

She probably ruined any chance of getting that promotion now, especially since the single-minded executive wing didn't tolerate rogue employees.

Her effort to carve out a life of success also came with a loss of her identity. She was *not* her job. Her job was something she did. She needed to figure out who Nora Bainbridge was, what her real-life goals were, and where her heart lay. The one thing her Cedar Ridge experience taught her was that being true to your heart, and to those you cared about, made you a success, not finally making it to a corporation's 23rd floor.

Corporate life wasn't the be all and end all. And it surely wouldn't keep her warm at night.

Chapter 9

Every time Nora considered an idea to keep MoonBurst from starting the Sussex Expansion Project in Cedar Ridge, she came up dry. A few days later, a possible solution presented itself via a phone call—from Arlene. It seemed Evan conjured up an idea to keep the planning board from a final vote. And while Arlene had explained the plans to her, Nora's mind whirled with ideas of how she could help. And then it came.

Television coverage.

It was a sure way to bring the problem to the forefront of large companies putting Mom and Pop stores out of business.

As Nora drove along Main Street, she noticed signs for the Blind Taste Test everywhere. By the looks of it, Evan held nothing back, making sure this was a serious endeavor.

She steered her car into the last empty spot in the Grover's Park parking lot and walked to the taste test tent set up at the entrance. Evan's friend, Todd, was busy stacking supplies on a few folding tables. "Good morning." His voice wasn't at all cheerful, but she chalked it up to concentrating on his task. "How are those beds over at The Comfy Quilt?"

"They're just fine." She hadn't slept in one in well over a week, but when she had, the beds were like sleeping on a cloud.

"Any luck finding an apartment?"

She noticed the slight timber of hostility laced in his tone, and she wasn't sure if he was making small talk, or whether there was a point to these questions?

"No luck so far." Nice and vague, without an admission, keeping *her* tone as positive as possible.

"Really?" Todd stopped lining coffee carafes on the folding table and glared directly at her.

A cringe seized her, but she tried her best not to outwardly show it. The suspicion that he knew she lied, that she'd been found out, made her skin crawl. But she held herself in check, hoping he'd end the game of twenty questions.

"I thought more people would be here setting up. Do you need help?" She purposely withdrew her gaze from meeting his and scanned the area. "Where's Evan?"

"Over at the municipal building."

Oh, no. The planning board. "Is everything all right? Are they giving him a hard time?"

"No, they're helping him. You're the only one giving him a hard time."

"Me?" She pressed a hand to her chest, then secured the collar of her jacket tighter around her neck, hoping to distract him from the hot flash of red she felt heating her face.

"I don't know what your game is, but we don't play games here. We take things straight up. Our liquor, our jobs, our friends."

She gripped her collar tighter. "That's one of the things I like about Cedar Ridge."

"Really?" He eyed her like a prosecutor interrogating a witness. "How's your job going?"

Her job? Where was he going with *that* question?

Her insides bounced into a jumble of nerves, but she merely shrugged to convey nonchalance. "It's a job, pays the bills."

"Are you getting settled in the new office building?"

"It's working." These questions caused her stomach to lurch in panic. She took a step back as he moved in closer.

"Good," he said. "I just got a new job, so I know what it's like."

Phew. Just small-talk. She relaxed her hands from her collar as her shoulders loosened. Forcing a smile on her face she said, "Congratulations. Do you like it?"

"Yeah, people are *real* nice." His demeanor seemed to lighten, and he turned his attention back to the task of arranging coffee carafes. "I've met everyone there. I have to. I'm the new daytime maintenance guy. Had to make sure I get to know all the employees and their offices, in case they need something. Been there a month now."

"That's good." Nora exhaled, relieved that the inquisition passed. "I hope it works out."

"So, how about you?" He looked up at her then, aiming an uncomfortable stare at her. "Where did you say you work?"

Darn. She had hoped the conversation would stay on him. "I'm an office assistant."

"In the new office building?"

"Mm-hmm." She pushed her glasses up higher on the bridge of her nose. A mumble wasn't the same as lying. Right?

"Funny thing about that." His cordial demeanor changed back to suspicious. "My new job, it's at the same building."

Nora couldn't stop her eyes from bulging wider, and he noticed. He definitely noticed.

"Yeah, you don't work there. No one, and I mean no one, ever heard of a Nora Langston. So what gives?"

Oh, no. She didn't want to lie even more, but she needed to protect her image in town. Too much rode on her keeping up the façade. Her job—she didn't care about that anymore. But the Cavanaughs—they meant a lot to her. This village meant a lot to her. Evan meant a lot. *You're falling for him.*

She resolved herself to MC's suggestion as it crept through her thoughts at the most inopportune times. "Okay, you got me." She puffed out a large, loud breath as a streak of panic cut through her. "I'll tell you the truth because you're Evan's friend, but please, what I'm about to tell you, please don't tell *him*."

"Why not?"

"Because I don't want him hurt." She also didn't want Julie and Arlene hurt any more than MoonBurst could potentially hurt them.

"If you're not who you say you are, you've already hurt him. He hasn't trusted a woman since his wife ran off on him."

So she *had* left him. Evan hadn't said a word about it. Neither had Arlene. Or anyone for that matter. But why? It was as if the subject had been taboo, no one saying a word about her. Why would a woman leave such a great guy like Evan? And why would she leave their precious daughter?

"My name is Eleanor Langston Bainbridge. My father calls me Nora."

He folded his arms across his chest and glared. "Okay. So why is it so important that we don't know who you really are? Are you on the run?"

"What?" How could he think that she'd be the type wanted by the law? The most she'd ever done wrong was get a parking ticket.

"Any warrants out there with your *real* name on them?"

"Of course, not!" How had things gotten this out of control? Her simple lie of omission had snowballed into a giant iceberg. She needed to come up with an explanation, a plausible explanation that would satisfy Todd and quell his suspicion. There were so many reasons why she was here and why she needed to lie. MoonBurst, her parents, Harrison . . . Harrison!

Nora cleared the tight lump in her throat and swallowed hard. "My parents want me to marry a guy I don't love. I didn't want them to find me, so I gave a different version of my name."

Todd snickered. "You're kidding, right? An arranged marriage? Why didn't you say no?"

"I did. But the family pressure was too much. Coming to Cedar Ridge is kind of a new start for me."

He cocked his head slightly as his eyes narrowed. "And the job?"

"I work in the city for now. Come here on weekends when I can."

It was sort of the truth. She couldn't tell him the entire truth, but this story did sound believable, because it *had* been true—until she had set her father straight on not marrying Harrison. She still needed to confront her mother, but Todd didn't have to know that.

"Look, I don't want to hurt Evan. The last thing I expected to find here was a nice guy. I love Arlene and Julie. I came to help today because Arlene told me about the blind taste test."

His gaze scrutinized her, but this time, she didn't squirm because 99.9 percent of her story was true. She focused directly on his eyes, holding her ground.

Finally, unfolding his arms, he asked, "So, when are you gonna come clean with Evan?"

She thought a minute. "Just after this thing with MoonBurst is settled. He's got enough on his plate to deal with."

"You're right about that." He bent to pick up a case of coffee. "Okay, I won't say anything. For now. But I'm warning you, if you hurt him, I'm gonna tell him everything. And I'm not above letting your family know either."

Wow. The guy acted like a member of the mob. But she couldn't blame him. He was sticking up for his friend, and having a loyal friend like Todd was rare.

She nodded. "You've got a deal."

Grateful to have dodged that bullet, she couldn't help wonder when it would surface again.

~ ~ ~

"Hey, there you are," Evan said as Nora walked through the large, double wooden doors into the municipal building foyer.

"Todd told me you were here." She stepped to the side giving him room as he carried what appeared to be a heavy box. "What's that?"

"Coffee grounds. I spent last night grinding all the beans so it would be easier at all the test locations."

"Todd said you set up different places around the village."

"Yep. This way, we won't miss anyone. George and the guys will be here, Todd's at Grover's Park, Mom's helping Molly at The Cookie Cottage, and Elliot Hansen agreed to man a table outside Ridge Grocery."

"Elliot Hansen?"

"He owns the store."

"Oh, I didn't know that." She shrugged a shoulder. "Looks like you've got it all covered. What about the Bean & Brew?"

"I'll be there in case anyone needs more supplies."

"And how are you getting MoonBurst coffee?"

She hadn't heard anything about the company participating. In fact, they didn't seem to know about it, so more than likely they were going to find out about it on the five o'clock news. Bruce and his "team of three" were going to be angry. Serves them right. She had tried, tried to get them to move their location to a different town, but they refused.

"Adam's in charge of acquiring MoonBurst coffee."

"Acquiring?"

"Yeah, he drove around to all the different MoonBurst stores and bought up as much as he could." He winked as he picked up another box.

How did Adam do that? The closest MoonBurst stores were scattered throughout the next county, nowhere near Cedar Ridge, which was why this location would be perfect for their expansion.

"Evan, we're here!" George announced. "And we're ready to kiss some ass."

"Don't you mean kick some ass?" Walter asked.

"I thought we already got gas," Howard said. "Didn't we, Walter?"

Walter nodded, then Nora saw his sad, puppy-dog frown turn into a smile when he spotted her. "Oh, praise be Jesus. My angel is here!"

She went to him with open arms and gave him a hug that felt wonderful. "How are you, Mr. B.?"

"I'm fine now that you're here."

She backed away slightly, but kept her hands on his upper arms. "I have something for you in my car. I'll be right back."

Nora left the men in the foyer and ran to the parking lot. By the time she returned, her heart pounded as she caught her breath. The high stamina she used to have a few years ago had dwindled from her years of sitting behind a desk crunching numbers every day. Once she got her life settled, she'd have to look into some sort of workout. Maybe take up jogging through the village or around Wilkensen's Pond. And right then, she realized she'd found the place she longed for, to make Cedar Ridge her home. A place where she belonged.

True, genuine happiness filled her, making her giddy. When she stepped in front of Walter Buchannan, she almost burst with enthusiasm. "Here you go!" She presented the box to him, and he just stared at it. "Open it," she said with a giggle.

"What is it?" His gnarled hands gently lifted the lid and surprise lightened his mocha-colored face. A sparkle of joy showed in his eyes, warming Nora's heart. "Cornbread?"

"Not just *any* cornbread. It's from Sylvia's in the city."

"Nice touch, Langston," Evan whispered in her ear as he passed with another box of grounds. "You drove all the way into Harlem?"

She hadn't noticed him standing so close, but as his words laid a warm breath on her earlobe, a tingle quickened under her skin. "Thank you," she whispered back, and for a moment, his gaze clung to hers. "It wasn't a big deal. Walter's worth a little extra trip."

Keeping her mind on Walter did little to dispel her attraction to Evan. Now, the stakes were higher that she not hurt him, especially, since Todd mentioned his wife's abandonment.

The air sizzled with so much sexual tension between them, she worried one of its sparks would set off an explosion by hitting the fluorescent lights above. She didn't want to break the connection, but she knew she had to.

"Where do you want me?" she asked.

Evan's gaze had been fixated on her face, but now it slowly roamed her body from her neck traveling to her hips. She forgot about everyone else in the lobby, her focus solely on Evan. She heard nothing but the beat of her own heart, the one Evan had jumpstarted.

"I can think of a few places—" The sparkle in his eyes danced with mischief, but then he broke the connection and slid the box onto the table. "—but right now, I think you're safer staying here with the guys."

His declaration confirmed he had felt the attraction as much as she. Wanting to see which direction this impractical attraction could lead—and accepting the magical spell this village had on her—she ran with the impulse of wanting to push his buttons. "Safer for whom?"

"You're playing with fire, young lady." He glanced at her with a crooked smile, then began removing zip-type plastic bags from the box. "I think Howard would be upset if he saw you flirting with another man."

Gratefully, his comment broke the mounting tension she had trouble deflecting. It also helped that Howard sent her his trademark wink when she glanced at him. Thank God he hadn't heard Evan's remark, and thank God the three gentlemen were hard of hearing.

"I hope this blind test works." She helped him unload the plastic bags of coffee and waited for him to respond.

After a few seconds, he finally continued the conversation. "I'm with you on that one. I told Adam to make it fair. No fancy stuff. Their regular and decaf, against mine."

Good. A fair contest. It would play better for the media that way, too.

She hoped with all her might that the Bean & Brew won. She admired Evan's determination to save his business, even though she was sure Bruce and company would certainly laugh at his efforts. But she wouldn't. It just made him more likeable, more respected, and as much as she tried to deny it, more desirable.

"Do you think the board will deny MoonBurst's application if you win?" She wondered if he had some insider information that he hadn't shared.

George moved in close to her. "They have to. After my speech at the meeting, they agreed to."

Nora jumped, not realizing the older man had heard some of their conversation. "Your speech?"

He snapped the suspenders lining his chest. "Yes siree. I took command of that meeting and told Whitmore he didn't have a choice."

Nora looked over at Evan for confirmation.

He shook his head and mouthed, "Adam."

Nora held in a snicker and turned her attention back to George. "That's good to hear, George. I'm sure the board will do exactly that."

Evan's decision not to dispel George's account of what really happened proved the level of respect and devotion he had for his elderly friend. Another guy, not as comfortable with himself, would have set the old man straight. But not Evan.

Each time he did something like that, Nora had another reason to care about him.

That definitely was *not* in the plan.

~ ~ ~

Evan invited everyone who helped him work the taste test back to his house for a celebration. While he was grateful to Nora for arranging television coverage, the Bean & Brew had been crawling with people, none of whom were buying coffee. When the test was over, he closed the doors and his crew of volunteers met up at his place. From what the village council and the planning board had said, it appeared votes at each test location favored the Bean & Brew coffee over MoonBurst. But he wouldn't be comfortable until he personally saw the results.

He excused himself from the celebration taking place in his living room, the voting ballots in hand. The quiet of his bedroom provided time to go through the ballots, gaining an exact tally that he could report to his eager supporters.

Sorting through the sheets collected at each location, Evan made a pile for MoonBurst votes and a pile for the Bean & Brew. But when he got to the end of the loose ballots, a packet of papers was left. The ballots from the municipal building were neatly fastened with a paper clip, complete with a handwritten summary sheet attached to the front.

For someone who claimed not to be good with numbers, Nora not only tabulated each of the ballots, she also divided them into gender and approximate age. The only thing missing was an actual spreadsheet of the figures.

His idea that Nora helped the guys with the testing had worked well. Between the three of them, he wasn't sure they understood what Evan needed, but she was there, guiding them, helping them, and she seemed to enjoy them, too. Whenever she was around, the three old men lit up like Christmas trees. And that's just what Walter needed. The man wasn't himself since Dolores died. Evan knew it was hard on anyone married for 56 years, and happily, too, to lose the person they loved.

He stopped tallying, remembering how long it took his mother to get over his father's death. He had thought she'd never survive the deeply entrenched depression of losing him. But slowly, her life became whole again, more so this past year. Losing one parent had been difficult enough at that time, but losing the other to depression took a toll on him and Julie. He was grateful it worked itself out. And if Nora had helped to temporarily ease Walter out of his funk, well, then, Evan was grateful for that, too.

He realized he had been grateful to her for more than a few things. She was great for the guys, great for Julie. His daughter finally got back some of that spunk she lost all those years ago when Miranda left.

His mother liked her, too. He noticed how she'd gotten a kick out of mothering Nora. He didn't think Nora liked it at first, but as the weeks went on, he saw signs of her looking for Arlene's approval. From that comment she made about her father the other day, he suspected she may have come from a dysfunctional family, but he wouldn't jump to any conclusions.

Whatever happened in her past was done. It shaped her to be the kind of person everyone around him truly liked. And, yeah, if he was honest, even he had to admit he enjoyed seeing her, too. Enough that he'd begun to look for her when she wasn't around.

One thing did puzzle him, though. Why was she only around on weekends now?

The first two weeks that he met her, she came to the Bean & Brew during the week, during lunch breaks, and a few days when she took off from work. After that, he'd only seen her on weekends. It was as if she vanished from the planet during the week.

He'd have to ask her about it, but right now he needed to get back to her summary sheet. It saved a whole lot of time and made his job calculating the test results quicker. Evan scribbled the numbers into two columns on a notepad, then totaled them. The results confirmed what his friends and the village council had told him.

Bean & Brew won by a landslide.

Every participant got two identical samples of coffee, and whether they lived in Cedar Ridge, or were tourists just passing through, they overwhelmingly voted for his brew on both coffees, especially his decaf.

Armed with the proof that his coffee was preferred over the coffee giant, he went back to the living room to give his friends and family the final totals.

He hoped it would be enough to convince the village fathers to deny the mega-company's application. If not, he'd have to think of another tactic to slay this dragon.

~ ~ ~

Nora helped Adam's mother, Molly, set out plates and napkins for dessert. The Cookie Cottage's coconut caramel surprise cookies were a nice snack for everyone to nibble on while they waited for Evan's report.

She grabbed a bottle from the case of water Elliot brought with him from Ridge Grocery. The last thing anyone wanted to see or drink was coffee, so the water hit the spot.

While everyone chatted about the day's events, Nora quietly sipped her water taking in the sight while she leaned against the dining room and living room archway. These people, whom she hadn't known a few weeks ago, had welcomed her into their fold. She didn't know if it was because they were naïve or just plain nice.

She preferred nice. Although, each time she thought about it, a huge pang of guilt wedged in her gut. They took her at her word that she was who she said she was. They judged her actions as someone who helped them and showed true concern.

In the cynical, watch-your-butt world she lived and worked in, she had known there was a different way of life waiting somewhere for her. She aspired to find a life that had more meaning, purpose, importance. And it wasn't until today that she realized she'd finally found it.

She felt a warm comfort as Arlene's arm wrapped around her shoulder. "You were a tremendous help today. Thank you."

"I didn't do anything different than the rest of you."

"Oh, yes, you did." She chuckled. "You babysat the geriatric set. That was no small feat."

Nora chuckled then, too. "They were fine. It was more fun than work."

"I'm glad you enjoyed it. But let me tell you, you made those guys feel like they contributed. Like they mattered." Arlene kissed the side of her head. "Thank you for that."

Sincere gratitude was a two-way street. Nora's gratitude grew with each moment she spent with the woman. Arlene had shown her more acceptance and love than her own mother ever had. "It was my pleasure. And thank you."

"What in the world for?"

Nora swallowed the tiny lump tightening her throat and wrapped her arm around Arlene's waist. "For making me feel like I'm one of you."

"Well, you are. Or you will be, once we get you settled into an apartment."

The apartment. Second time today that subject dangled in front of her. While she truly wanted to move to Cedar Ridge, the idea of everyone finding out her secret kept her from totally embracing that idea.

"Mmm, have you tasted these cookies?" Nora released her arm from Arlene, reaching for the tray of Molly's cookies, trying to deflect Arlene's comment. "They *are* delicious."

"Yes, they are. Molly's cookies are the best." She called over Nora's shoulder, "We had so much fun working the taste test together. Didn't we, Mol?"

"It was wonderful!" Molly answered as she scrambled through the crowded room toward them. "That sign Evan posted outside The Cookie Cottage really brought them in. Doubled my sales for the day. We should have a taste test every Saturday!"

"I'm not too sure that would go over well with Evan."

Arlene removed her arm from Nora's shoulder. "What do you think, Nora?"

A weekly taste test? Sure, Evan's coffee was excellent, but did Molly actually think he'd win every weekend? And could Evan financially afford to give away that much free coffee all the time?

Oh, she could just imagine how happy Molly's son, Adam, would be to go every weekend into the next county to purchase multiple bags of MoonBurst coffee at multiple locations.

"I think this one test will do the trick," Nora finally responded.

"I agree. And we have *you* to thank for the media coverage, too. That should carry some weight with the planning board," Arlene said with an affirmative nod.

The media. Nora glanced at the cable box to see the time. "Quick, turn on the TV," she said to Arlene.

"Julie!" Arlene called. "Turn on the TV, sweetheart."

She turned to Nora. "I don't know how to turn those darn things on. I have a different provider."

Julie did as instructed, and the group huddled together as they watched the evening news.

Nora stood between them all, like she belonged. Because she did. For the first time in her life, she didn't feel like the black sheep or the oddball who didn't conform. She was accepted for who she was, not what she had.

When the warmth of another kind followed, she turned to see Evan next to her, his strong hand closed around her shoulder. Everyone allowed him to wiggle into the center of the group as they quietly waited for the television reporter, who had interviewed some of them earlier, to deliver his report.

"Coffee wars. Can a small-town coffee shop take on coffee giant MoonBurst? We'll have a report after the break."

Evan's supporters erupted into rowdy cheers. They hooted and hollered so loud, Nora nearly covered her ears. When she looked over at the men patting Evan on the back, shaking his hand, and the women kissing his cheek, she knew he was their hometown hero. No matter how this challenge turned out, Evan gave it his all, and so did his friends. They were a community bonded by love.

Nora rooted along with them, wishing for Evan's success. Right then, she knew what she had to do. Her loyalties had officially shifted. Yes, she had an inkling when she came to town this morning. But she wasn't fooling herself any longer. Her heart wasn't back in the city. It wasn't with her job or her promotion. Her heart was here with these people, people who cared for one another, people who always looked out for one another.

She wanted to be like them. But in order to do that, she needed to be truthful. To break ties to her old life so she could start fresh. And quitting her job was her first task.

Yes, she knew she'd have to tell everyone who she really was and why she originally came to Cedar Ridge. And she also needed to share what was in her heart. And hopefully, after that, she'd still be welcomed into their lives.

Hopefully, it all wouldn't backfire on her.

Chapter 10

"Daddy, puh-lease."

Evan groaned. He hated when Julie begged.

"Please can I stay over Gramma's?"

Arlene nudged her son. "Come on. The kid hasn't slept over in weeks. It'll save you time in the morning getting her ready to come over to my house for church."

She did have a point. And after all he'd done today, sleeping in tomorrow morning would be a help before he had to crawl out of bed to open the store.

"Okay." He turned to Julie. "But don't talk Grandma's ear off all night. She needs her sleep."

"Are you saying I'm old?" his mother asked as she fake-punched Evan's arm.

"No. I'm trying to keep Julie's storytelling to a minimum so you can get some sleep."

His mother chuckled. "Don't worry about us. We'll be fine. *You're* the one who needs a good night's rest."

"You're not kidding," he said as he helped Nora gather empty water bottles from around the room.

Julie gave him a tight hug along with a sloppy kiss, and his heart melted at how much he loved her. "Bye, Daddy. I love you."

"I love you too, pumpkin."

"Nora, do you need a ride to The Comfy Quilt?" his mother asked as she neared the door.

"No, thanks. I've got my car."

"All righty. Don't you two stay up too late, if you know

what I mean!" Mom said with a wink, and taking Julie by the hand, out the door she went.

"Maaa . . ." Evan groaned and turned to Nora. "I'm sorry about her."

Nora swiped a hand in the air, like it didn't bother her, but he did notice how her cheeks flared bright pink.

She lowered her eyes and pursed her lips, as if she were trying to smother the laugh that she appeared to be hiding. She timidly glanced back at him. "Your mother is adorable. She's such a . . . mother, you know?"

He raised his eyebrows. "A what!?"

"No. No," she rushed to correct her answer and reached out to lay her hand on his arm. "She's a motherly type. You know, caring, loving, even when she's busting you."

"Oh, so you're *not* insulting my mother?" He held back the mischievous impulse of wanting to give her a hard time. "I'll let you slide this time."

"Thank goodness." She let go of his arm and plopped onto the couch like a rag doll, all loose and lazy. "I'd hate it if I had to suffer another task like today's as punishment."

He followed to sit next to her. "So, if I demanded you make it up to me by working another taste test tomorrow, you would?"

She rolled those purple blue eyes at him. "Only if you needed it. Let me repeat myself, I *meant* your mother is motherly, so I don't really think a punishment is in order."

Her lips curled into such an enticing smile, he had to hold himself back from tasting them. He liked when she smiled. It turned her eyes a deeper shade of purple. "Yeah, I guess Mom's a good mom."

"Take my word for it." She teasingly patted his knee. "She's the best."

"What about your mom?"

Nora hesitated, like she didn't want to go there. But the loaded comment she just dropped needed clarification.

He thought a minute, then lowered his voice. "Is your mother still alive?"

"Mother is *not* the cookies-and-milk kind of mom."

"Mother?" *Okay, so she's alive.* "Why so formal?"

"That's the way she wants it. Our relationship is more like a business arrangement. She's the CEO of the family, and I have to do what she wants if I want to keep my *job*."

"Ouch."

"Yeah, so you see, when I say your mother is motherly, it's a sincere compliment." She picked at a few errant pieces of lint from the pillow sitting between them. "You're a lucky guy to have a mother like her."

"I know I am. She's great with Julie—without smothering—and she let me take over the family business even though she owned half of it with my father for almost thirty years."

"Because she trusts you."

"And I trust her. Trust is really important to us, you know?"

Seeing her appreciation of his mother confirmed what he'd been feeling all along. He loved how neatly she fit into his life with his friends. How neatly she fit into his family. Like she was the missing piece needed to complete them.

"Thank you for everything you've done." He couldn't keep from taking hold of her hand. "When that reporter came on TV and said, 'David may just have slain Goliath,' I nearly bounced off the walls." His thumb gently rubbed the back of her hand, and the softness of her skin had him wondering how good the rest of her would feel.

"You've got to be proud of all you did today. A vote of seventy-six percent in favor of your coffee is fantastic." She giggled. "You kicked ass, just like George said you would."

"I guess that's better than kissing ass." He laughed, too, repeating George's words. Nora's lips, though, were another thing entirely. Plum and moist as she scraped her teeth over that lucky bottom lip just tempting him to kiss her. He hadn't felt this kind of attraction in years. Even with her ponytail and those ugly brown-rimmed glasses, he was so attracted to her that some of his body parts were going to rebel if he didn't kiss her.

He leaned sideways, closer. "Would it be okay if I kissed you?"

Her eyes widened in surprise. "You're asking permission?"

He shrugged and a momentary hesitation skidded through him. "I don't want to ruin our friendship by going with the impulse, especially if you don't feel the same way."

"That's very chivalrous of you, sir."

"Yeah, that's me." He couldn't hold back the cocky grin he flashed at her. "A true gentleman."

She lowered her chin, but kept her gaze on his lips. "Do you kiss like a gentleman?"

"There's only one way to find out."

As he leaned his head toward hers, a sweet floral scent spread throughout his senses. Touching the side of her cheek with his fingertips, the softness of her skin had him wanting to explore all of her. But he knew the reaction was much more than physical. For him, the desire went hand in hand with trust. Trust to allow another woman to infiltrate that vulnerability he carefully protected for years, enabling him to let down his guard, so even a simple kiss was symbolic of his protective walls crumbling and allowing someone to matter.

As his lips touched Nora's, a quiver shot through them, then jolted to the pit of his stomach. Dormant urges he'd been holding in check forced their way back to life. It had been so long since he kissed a woman, he felt like a nervous teenager trying to keep from exploding too soon. His tentative pressure on her lips wasn't at all what he wanted. Raw anticipation surged through him, but he controlled it, slowly shifting a fragment away.

"Yes, you are a gentleman," she whispered and her gaze was back on his lips again.

"You say that like it's a bad thing." His control wavered as he went with the urge to run his fingertip over her moist lips.

"Let's just say I thought there'd be a tad more fire behind it."

"So you're disappointed."

"Mmm, a little."

He drew her tighter into his arms, her breasts connecting with his chest as all sorts of thoughts of how he wanted to take it farther rushed through his mind. "I like a woman who knows what she wants."

"Not too aggressive?"

"No. It's a turn-on." He carefully removed her glasses and placed them on the end table next to the couch. As his lips made contact with hers again, he took his time, running his tongue over her top lip then the bottom, tasting, gently sucking her bottom lip until it swelled. He carefully released her hair from that annoying ponytail holder and when her hair fell free, he plunged his hands into it, grasping the nape of her neck, gathering her closer.

With her securely in his arms, he finally crushed his lips to hers, devouring her mouth, exploring and coaxing her to accept him. When her lips slowly parted, their tongues danced with an intense heat that had his body revving and his mind charging ahead with thoughts of taking it to the next level. He pictured her naked in his bed, and he knew he'd gone too far—a pubescent teenager on a mission to get laid. He reminded himself that he was a father. A father who needed to protect his daughter from heartache. And he was also a lonely man who needed to protect *himself* from heartache. If he jumped too quickly, it would satisfy the burning urge, but what would it do to his life? He was just beginning to trust, so he needed to take it slow, needed to be sure that his trust wouldn't be destroyed again.

~ ~ ~

Kissing Evan meant trouble. And Nora didn't know how to get out of it.

She clutched the back of his shoulder blades as his lips pressed against hers. His hands explored her hair, her neck, caressed her shoulders and arms, pressed her tightly against him so that she felt the evidence of his excitement.

She wanted to give herself to him. But how could she do so when he didn't even know her real name? She hadn't been honest with him. Couldn't.

But the honesty in his kisses nearly plunged her into tears because of Todd's warning earlier this morning. She didn't want to hurt him like his wife had. She had no intention of walking away from him either, not when he made her feel whole and wanted. His desire for her wasn't formulated because of a business deal—a means at gaining a position with her father, as Harrison's were.

Evan wanted her for *her*, or for who he thought she was. She couldn't go on deceiving him like this. She had to confess who she really was before this went too far.

But how?

The truth would devastate him.

While he struggled to pay bills and defend his business against her company, she led a completely comfortable life. Her social standing in the tony Upper West Side neighborhood only reinforced the depth of the Bainbridge pot of gold.

How could she tell him she was sent here to put him out of business?

She didn't deserve an upstanding guy like him. She was a fraud. A liar.

Nora slowly withdrew her lips from Evan's. She caught her breath as she felt the smoldering breaths that escaped from his swollen lips.

God, he was hot.

But she had to stay focused.

"Easy there, cowboy. Okay, you win. You are *not* a gentleman in the kissing department."

"Too much?"

"No. Just right." She placed her hands on his shoulders to ease a fraction away, but no wanting to lose contact. "I think we need to slow down a bit. After all, we've only known each other a few weeks."

He lowered his head and leaned it against hers. "It seems like a lifetime."

To her, too. Oh, this man knew how to touch that emotional place she had buried deep inside that longed to have someone unearth. But she needed to be strong. Needed to tell him who she really was. It was only fair.

"I need to be honest with you."

He lifted his forehead from hers and his questioning eyes seemed to bore through her. "Is this going to be an 'I like you as a friend' speech?"

"No." She shook her head wanting to be sure he knew how she really felt. "I'm totally attracted to you. But we don't know that much about each other. Or rather, you don't know much about me." Letting her hands slide from his shoulders, she clutched them together to rest in her lap.

He nodded. "True."

She had to be careful. If she told him the complete truth, he might call his friends to remove her to the village border. Todd would probably have her banned from all of Sussex County.

"I'm thirty-one years old."

"Really?" His eyebrows rose in surprise. "I thought you were younger. I'm thirty-two."

"Thanks for the compliment." Her mother would attribute her ageless complexion to good breeding. "I have two brothers. One older, one younger."

Evan seemed to relax as he angled his right ankle on his left knee and laid one arm across the back of the sofa, barely touching her. "Do you have a favorite?"

"Maybe not a favorite, but I get along better with the younger one. He's a little more laid back than the older one. Older one's a little too intense for me. How about you? I've never heard you talk about siblings."

"Only child. Mom wanted more, but it wasn't meant to be. I wish I had two brothers to horse around with."

"I guess I can understand that. Dalton and Hunter used to drive Mother crazy chasing each other around the house." And then Mother had the nanny handle them. Did you grow up here?"

"Yep. In the same house Mom lives in. How 'bout you?"

"Upper East Side. Then I moved out on my own." Careful, don't give out too much, too soon. "Before I came here, I lived in the city."

"New York?"

She nodded. "I still have an apartment there until I can find one here."

"Where abouts?"

She hesitated, sure he didn't know the neighborhood. "99th and Amsterdam."

"There's a great restaurant on Broadway. Carmine's."

"I love that place. Hey, wait. How do you know that?"

"I used to eat there a lot."

"When?" She eyed him warily. He no more frequented that Italian restaurant than she loved country music.

"When I lived on 85th Street."

She took hold of the pillow between them and tapped his arm with it. "You lived on the Upper West Side?"

A hint of a smirk rimmed his lips. "I'm not the country bumpkin you think I am."

It seemed she wasn't the only one keeping secrets. But at least his secret wasn't trying to take her job away.

"Okay, I need details," she said, truly interested, bending one leg under her on the sofa cushion, she rested the pillow in her lap and turned her body toward him.

"After I graduated—"

"You went to college?" She knew the question was inappropriate, but it just blurted out.

His hand went to his chest. "Do I seem that uneducated?"

"No! Since you work in a coffee shop, I thought you've been working there since high school."

"I *own* the coffee shop," he said with a single nod, then smiled and tweaked her nose with his fingertip. "Something you also didn't think me capable of when we first met."

She lowered her head and peered up at him with a grimace. "Sorry about that."

He chuckled then his fingers began playing with the strands of her hair that had fallen on her shoulder. "Yeah, it was fun listening to you threaten to have me fired that first day."

"There goes that assumption thing again."

"Exactly. So back to my story. When I graduated from NYU, I got a job working at New York Life as an actuary."

"Really!?" Now she really felt like a snob. Not only was he educated, but he had a high-salaried job right out of college. So much for thinking he lacked ambition by working for minimum wage. "How long did you work there?"

"Up until four years ago." His prone body seemed to stiffen with his words. "When Dad died."

She laid a hand on his knee. "I'm sorry."

"Thanks. I still keep thinking one of these days I gonna go in to open the store and he'll be behind the counter waiting for me, busting me about coming in late." A sad smile wavered across his lips. "Every day I wish for it, and every day I'm disappointed."

"Sounds like you were very close."

"We had been, when I lived here. I worked in the store on weekends, you know, summers and after school. Once I went to college—and then lived in the city—it was hard to be as close." He aimed his eyes away from her and focused on the strand of her hair he was playing with, twirling it around his finger. "We talked on the phone all the time, but it was never the same." He turned his gaze back on her. "How about you? Are you and your father close?"

Her father. Oh, boy. "Yes, and no."

"Care to explain?"

"We're close when it comes to business. I try my best, he encourages me, but I'm not sure he understands my strengths."

"The idea, assistant thing." He nodded, agreeing with the lie she'd told him.

She stopped breathing for a second, then exhaled. She had to be as honest as possible now, because she couldn't bear the constant lying. "He knows I'm capable, but doesn't think I'll amount to anything unless I work for his company."

"Does he have a large company?"

She couldn't tell him her father was Colin Bainbridge, president of Bainbridge Enterprises. He'd know she was lying about who she really was because she wasn't using the Bainbridge name.

Think. Think!

How can I tell him the truth without telling him the truth?

"He dabbles in several enterprises." Which was true. Bainbridge Enterprises encompassed a few key businesses. It wasn't the largest company in the country, but it wasn't the smallest, either. "It's medium sized, does all right."

"I take it you don't want to work for him."

"Definitely not. It's hard enough keeping our personal relationship intact. Working with him would be a juggling act. Besides, I want to make it on my own. Gain that sense of accomplishment."

"I know what you mean. Dad wanted me to partner with him in the store when I graduated high school. The day he moved me into the dorm at NYU, he told me it wasn't too late to come back home. He used to joke that we could be coffee moguls."

"That's great that you were able to joke around. Joking was viewed as a waste of time with my family. Although, there were times when Dad would try to lighten things around the house, but Mother immediately put an end to it."

"So you got along better with him than your mother?"

"Definitely," she said with a firm nod. "We've come to an understanding, sort of an alliance, so we can survive living with Mother."

"Mother." Evan smirked and shook his head. "Do you call him Father?"

She giggled. "No, silly. Dad or Daddy, depending on the mood or the situation."

"Well, that's good. I couldn't imagine calling my mom, Mother. Usually, it's Ma."

"If you met my mother, you'd understand." But enough about her. She thought she knew a lot about him, but evidently, he had a completely different life before the Bean & Brew. "Okay, you lived in the city until four years ago. Was Julie born there?"

He nodded. "Almost didn't make it to the hospital on time. I thought she was going to be born in a cab."

"Oh, I couldn't imagine that!"

"Yeah, well, when a baby wants to be born, you don't have much choice."

"So you were . . ." She counted back in her head. "You were twenty-six when she was born?"

"Yep."

"That's young." She clutched the pillow in her lap close to her chest. At twenty-six, she was busy carving out her career at MoonBurst. Back then, having a baby wasn't even on her radar.

"Sure was. Seems I've got a knack for doing things before everyone else. Got a job before my friends, got married before them, first one to have a baby, and the first one to get dumped. See, there's a big problem when you do everything before everyone. You learn by your mistakes. And I learned big time."

There it was. Finally.

Nora didn't have an appropriate response. But she knew she had to acknowledge it.

"How long were you married?"

"Three and a half years." He shook his head and frowned. "Things hadn't been going well. She resented the baby cutting into her social life. She left me babysitting almost every night that last year we were together."

"How could any mother resent a tiny baby?" Although, she practically lived it by the way her mother had treated her. Mother doted on her two brothers. They were *men*, the "be all and end all" of her mother's existence.

"Beats me. Julie was a good baby, too. She slept all night, woke up happy. Miranda just didn't want to be tied down."

Not sure if she should ask, Nora decided to anyway. "Was Julie an accident?"

"Hell no. Miranda wanted to be the first to have a baby. Since we were married almost two years, I agreed it was time. I made enough money, and I wanted a bunch of kids. I figured, if we started young, by the time the kids were in college, we'd be in our fifties and able to enjoy a long retirement."

"Sounds like a practical plan."

"It was. But after she got pregnant, she started saying she wanted a baby because it would be cute to dress up like a doll. And when she started to gain weight, she complained because the baby was making her fat." His sullen expression had Nora's heart aching for him. "That's the first clue that we made a mistake."

"How could she not realize she was going to gain weight? Didn't she ever see a pregnant woman?"

"That's Miranda. In her head, *she* was going to be different. Maybe gain ten pounds and shed it right after the birth."

Nora dropped the pillow on the floor by her feet and took hold of his hands. "That's so sad, for you, and for Julie." The understanding in his eyes showed her that he appreciated her concern.

With his free hand, he took hold of one of hers and rubbed his thumb across the back of it. "Yeah, but we're better off this way. We're happy. We would have been miserable if Miranda came with us."

"So, Miranda never came with you to Cedar Ridge?"

"Nope. When Dad died, I told her I wanted to quit my job and run the store. She went ballistic."

"Didn't she see you were trying to help your family?"

"Nooo . . ." He shook his head resolutely. "She hated it out here. Too quiet, no social scene."

"But that's part of the charm of Cedar Ridge."

"Not in her eyes. She wanted the city night life."

"So you and she wanted different things?"

"Oh yeah. We dated in college and got along great. Wanted the same things in life. Once we graduated, she became obsessed with the social scene, going to clubs so she could be seen, shopping at all the designer boutiques, eating at the best restaurants. I was in love with the girl I met in college and was busy working my butt off to make a good living that I didn't pay attention to how she had changed. She kept demanding. I kept giving. Before I knew it, I was married at twenty-four and working seventy hours a week."

"Wow. My life sounds so boring compared to yours."

"Believe me, there's nothing exciting about it. The day after I told Miranda I wanted all of us to come to Cedar Ridge, she left me and Julie."

"I'm so sorry." Nora clasped his hands tighter.

"Poor kid cried for weeks. She was so little, she didn't understand her mother was a selfish—"

He cut himself off, and Nora was glad he did. She wouldn't have been able to stop herself from adding to the litany of comments on what kind of horrible woman could leave her precious two-year-old. Especially a child as lovable as Julie.

Nora gently slid one hand free from his grasp and cupped the side of his cheek. "I know it was difficult, but you and Julie belong here. You're home. Like you said, you're both happy here."

"We are. And it's Miranda's loss that she'll never know her daughter."

"And it's my good fortune that I got to know you and Julie." She couldn't stop herself. This man stirred all kinds of feelings in her. Empathy, sympathy, loyalty, respect and, yes, even desire.

She leaned toward him and placed a gentle kiss on his cheek.

His arms wrapped around her in a protective embrace where she never wanted to leave. The pressure of his warm, inviting lips had her holding onto him, savoring the emotions he poured into the kiss, the rawness of baring his story to her, trusting she'd understand.

Slowly, she felt her mind falling deeply for this man she didn't even know she wanted. Falling for the life she found here with him. And as he slowly lowered her to the sofa cushion, her body melded with his as it pressed the length of her. Not only did she let her body give into that temptation, she allowed her mind to go to that emotional place she kept from any man she'd been with. She'd shared her body with only a few select men, but her mind—her emotions—those were hers and hers alone, not to be shared with anyone. Emotions brought heartbreak. But now, she allowed Evan to unlock that emotional vault. A dangerous concept for someone who initially had no intention of allowing a man into her life.

And with Evan, her mind couldn't control what her heart dictated. Her heart overrode any logic her brain emitted. The gliding of his tongue, the softness of his lips and the nibbles of his teeth, had her mind responding along with her heart.

Yes, she hadn't been totally honest with him. But this was a start. She only hoped that when she finally did tell him the entire truth, his heart would be too invested to walk away.

Chapter 11

Evan knew he was in trouble.

When he saw that Miranda's abandonment of Julie had truly upset Nora, he knew his vow not to have a woman in his life had to be broken.

Nora needed to know he came as a package deal: him *and* Julie. There was no separating the two. And Nora understood that. Accepted that.

She and his daughter had already formed a bond, and now that he realized the reason for Julie's admiration, the attraction he felt for this woman surged loud and strong.

As his body feasted on the softness of hers, he suppressed the urge to take it further. It had been many years since he'd made love to a woman. There had been two hook-ups over the past four years, but they were sex, plain and simple. Since Miranda walked, he pledged he'd never let himself be vulnerable to a woman again. Because an honest woman didn't exist.

But she did exist. An honest, loving, thoughtful woman who magically appeared in his life right when he needed her. She filled that lonely void that surrounded him, satisfied the anticipation of having someone special to talk to every day, and now filled the physical intimacy he hadn't realized he craved.

As she welcomed him to ravish her mouth, he accepted the challenge. She'd been there for him with his daughter. Been there helping him fight that damn coffee company threatening his business. And now he hoped she'd help him with the burning need to unburden the sexual frustration the past few weeks had brewed.

The heat in her responses signaled a green light. All systems go. He could have her right here and within a few minutes, his body would finally get the release it desperately needed.

Wait. *What?*

What the hell am I doing?

He wasn't sure if what he felt for Nora was the real thing, but if there was one lesson he learned from his past, it was to take his time and think things through. If he needed a release, he could take care of that himself. Making love was a different matter.

If and when he made love to Nora, it wouldn't be a wham-bam kind of thing. He'd take his time, show her how much she meant to him. Give, not take.

He slowly removed his lips from her neck and that sweet, warm spot that he wanted to explore further. Lifting his head, he looked into the cloudiness of her violet-blue eyes. Seductive eyes.

"I'm really sorry for getting carried away." He went to rise from her, but she yanked him back.

"Don't apologize for something we both want."

A groan slipped from his throat. "You're not going to make this easy on me, are you?"

"If you mean you've got me all excited and now you're walking away, yeah, I am."

"You were right earlier." He pushed several strands of hair away from her eye with his fingertip then ran his finger down the softness of her cheek, aching to continue its journey lower. "We just got to know each other. I don't want to mess this up."

"You're doing just fine," she purred.

"Thanks. But I mean if this thing between us is going to work, I'd like to take it slow. I've got Julie to think of."

"Julie!" Nora pushed him off of her and bolted up with him nearly falling on the floor. "Oh, my God! Julie and your mother sit on this sofa!"

"What's that got to do with it?" He steadied himself on the couch cushion.

"I agree with you. This is *not* the place." Nora glanced around the room. "Nor the time."

She looked so cute, all worried about doing it in the living room. "All right, relax." He gathered her into a hug, keeping it friendly enough so he wouldn't jumpstart his groin again. "When we do it for real, I'll make sure we're not on any communal furniture. Deal?"

She nodded. "Deal!"

~ ~ ~

Just after midnight, by the time she snuggled into the fluffy mattress of The Comfy Quilt, Nora's body still hummed from the way Evan's mouth had devoured hers. If that was an indication of what the man could do with his mouth, she couldn't wait for the surprises he had in store for her. Her skin still tingled and her nether regions ached just thinking about it.

As she rolled over, pulling the blankets tightly around her neck, the annoying vibration of her phone skidding along the wood top of the night stand kept her from relaxing.

"Darn," she moaned, not wanting to reach for it. It didn't matter. All the important people were here in Cedar Ridge.

She stared at the phone, willing it to stop, but realized she hadn't received a call in over twelve hours, so she grudgingly picked it up. Bruce's name and number appeared on the screen.

"Hello, Bruce."

"You don't know how lucky you are that you finally answered. I've left you three messages over the past two hours."

She figured that. Thus, the main reason she had kept the phone off, but in the back of her mind, she knew he'd call after the media coverage aired the taste test. "It's Saturday night, almost midnight. And my day off."

"I don't care if it's Christmas. Did you see the evening news?"

Oh, yes she did. And if he knew she had arranged it, she'd be fired on the spot. Maybe that wasn't a bad thing. But she didn't want something like that following her, and she certainly didn't want to burn any bridges. "No. I haven't. I've been enjoying my weekend." Helping the Bean & Brew's efforts had given her a great sense of accomplishment, of purpose. Much more than any other project she'd done for Bruce in the past.

"That damn town will be my undoing," Bruce barked in her ear. "Your report was late, so our vote had to be postponed. Now that Bean & Brew guy held a taste test. Who the hell is he? I thought Thomas and Arlene owned that store?"

Nora rolled her eyes then closed them tightly rubbing her right temple. He had a way of ruining a perfectly perfect day. "Didn't you read my report? You were a little sloppy in your initial discovery." Her eyes slowly crept open. "Thomas is dead."

"So who's this guy?"

Her cheeks puffed out as her breath slowly released from her mouth. "His son." *A very caring, loyal son who's ten times the man you are.*

"Great. So instead of dealing with a middle-aged couple on the verge of retirement, we're dealing with a hot shot who likes to give television interviews." Silence lasted only a moment and then, "All right. He wants a fight, he's going to get a fight. Starting bright and early tomorrow morning, your weekend is over. I want you back in Cedar Ridge to find out how they got hold of copious amounts of *our* coffee. Then I want you to make sure everything is in place for our meeting with that one-horse village planning board. Our lawyers are formulating the proposal, and I don't want anything to go wrong."

Back in Cedar Ridge bright and early. Done, she thought with a touch of humor. "Bruce, I'm not an investigator. I gather data. I don't have any idea how to find out how they got hold of our coffee." She smiled as she pictured Adam Carlson's handsome face. "And I'm not the negotiator who schedules your meetings with the board."

"I want that info on my desk by Monday morning."

"Bruce, it's Sunday. Locals don't mill around he— in Cedar Ridge on Sunday. It's the fall tourist season." She'd almost given it away that she was snug in the tiny village already. "I'll try, but I can't promise."

"What's with you, Bainbridge? You've never had a problem delivering on other projects. Why has this one slowed you down?"

Slowed down? That's exactly what she needed and why Cedar Ridge fit her so well. The people slowed their pace, enjoying life. Even with all the tourism, they transferred that same laid-back lifestyle to those who visited their village. A step back in time when people mattered, not money.

"I'll report back to you when I have the information," she said. "I'll keep in touch,"

"Yeah, like I believe that one." *Click.*

Nora put the phone on the nightstand and plopped her head on the down-filled pillow. The light from the full moon splayed through the window blinds adding peacefulness to the room. Putting Bruce out of her mind, she drank it all in. Tomorrow she'd come up with some sort of plan on how not to give Bruce what he wanted. But once she was able to settle things back home, there would be one thing she'd be sure to give him.

Yes, and that would be her Independence Day. The day she handed in her resignation.

~ ~ ~

Coming early to the Bean & Brew was the perfect start to an autumn Sunday morning, and Nora couldn't wait to see Evan again. But when the line of customers began at the door, she knew it would be a while before she'd have him all to herself. She skirted the line and scooted behind the counter.

"Thank God the cavalry is here!" George greeted when he noticed her. "Here, you take over. I'm too old for all this work." He lifted the white apron over his head and handed it to her.

"Me?" she asked as she held the apron out in front of her, not sure if she should don it or not.

"Somebody's gotta. Arlene is at church and that line isn't getting any shorter."

Nora glanced back at the row of people, then her eyes landed on Evan who bounced from the grinder to the doughnut rack to the milk station with the speed of an Indy driver. She couldn't remember the last time she helped in one of her company's stores. In fact, now that she thought about it, she'd never done counter work before. But Evan clearly needed help, so there had to be something she could do.

She tied the apron at the back of her waist and asked, "Where do you want me?"

Evan stopped for a second, got a devilishly sexy gleam in his eye, then it cleared. "How about you check people out after I give them their orders?"

"Okay. Where do I find the prices?"

He stopped again. "Uh, coffee is a dollar, doughnuts and danish are two dollars, and newspapers are each marked with their prices."

"Got it." She nodded and took her place behind the cash register, taking a few seconds to familiarize herself with the buttons. "Okay, who's next in line?"

It took a while for her to get the hang of it, but by the time she glanced at the clock and realized two hours had past, she finally felt comfortable doing the job he gave her. As things slowed down, she was able to talk to a few customers. That Cedar Ridge magic worked overtime today, and oddly enough, she actually enjoyed herself as she connected with some of the residents she hadn't had a chance to speak to until now. More importantly, a sense of pride filled her at helping Evan. He needed her, and she was able to come through.

When Julie bounded into the store, she squealed when she saw Nora behind the counter. "Are you working here now?" she asked, giving Nora a hug.

"No," Nora said, wrapping her arms around the six-year old's shoulders. "I'm helping your father this morning because it was really busy."

"Daddy, can I help, too?"

Evan ruffled the top of his daughter's mop of curly brown hair. "Did Grandma drop you off?"

"Uh-huh. She had to go to the Ladies' Aux, Aux . . ."

"The Ladies Auxiliary."

"Yeah, that's it. She said I need to stay here for a little while, then she'll come get me. Can I please help?"

"Okay, but only until it gets busy again. If the line gets long, you need to go sit with the guys until the line goes down."

"Yipee!" She jumped up and down. "I need a apron."

"In the back closet, on the bottom shelf." As his daughter ran to get it, he turned to Nora. "I hope you don't mind having her around?"

"Why should I mind? She's a great kid. Besides, it is your store and she's your daughter. She belongs here."

"Yeah, I guess you're right. But a lot of adults don't like being around kids."

"I'm not a lot of adults." Once again, the magical pull had surfaced. She had been one of those kinds of adults a few weeks ago, and just like magic, "I loved being around Julie."

"I can see that." When he winked at her, her heart melted. "Thanks for all your help this morning."

The sincerity in his eyes had her wanting to tell him how important he and Julie were. Especially after they'd almost made love last night. She slid closer to him, knowing her heart was on her sleeve. "It was my pleasure. I really enjoyed it."

"Okay, I'm ready!" Julie had the apron loop around her neck, but it hung past her knees to her feet and dragged on the floor.

"Come here, sweetie, let me fix this." Nora pulled the apron high up on Julie's chest, and with a fold, raised it off the floor to tie at her waist. "Okay, you're all ready to work."

"Hey, Nora, could you give me a hand with these boxes?" Evan held open the basement door.

She rushed to grab a box and held the door with her hip so he could scoop up another box from the stairway. They deposited the large boxes on the floor near the grinder. With a box cutter, Evan sliced open the first box and withdrew a sleeve of disposable cups and handed it to Nora who tore the plastic wrapping to reveal a stack of cups. She then squatted to refill the lower shelves. "I don't know," she heard Julie's panicked voice from behind her.

"Norrraaaa!"

Nora pivoted on her heals and found Julie running to her. She grabbed the stainless frame of the shelves with one hand to keep from falling over as Julie flung herself into Nora's arms.

"What's the matter, sweetie?" Nora balanced her weight and wrapped Julie into a hug, then rose with her in her arms. Julie tightly tucked her face into the crook of Nora's neck.

"That scary lady wants a vanilla tea somethin'," she mumbled.

"What scary lady?"

Julie pointed without looking to the other side of the counter. "That one."

Nora's stomach flip-flopped and she gulped hard, not sure what she should do. A strange protective surge bolted through Nora's heart and she held Julie extra tight.

Nora heard Evan's footsteps coming from the basement stairs and when he was in the kitchen, she heard him asked, "What's going on?"

"Sweetie." Nora slowly lowered the child to stand on her own and guided her attention from the woman to Julie. "Why don't you stay here and help Daddy. I'll take care of the lady."

She eyed Evan who was coming closer and ushered Julie toward him, then she squared her shoulders, and felt the tightening of her jaw as she faced the woman on the opposite side of the counter.

"Mother . . ."

In true Joan Langston Bainbridge form, the matriarch of the Bainbridge clan stood with an arrogant air of superiority cloaking her. Her perfect clothes, perfect hair, and perfected scowl caused permanent frown lines to bracket her mouth.

"Mother, what are you doing here?"

"When your father told me you were in this dreadful place, I didn't think you were going all Jane Goodall. Look at you, for God's sake. You don't look like yourself."

Nora pushed an errant strand of hair out of her face that fell from her ponytail and pushed her glasses higher on the bridge of her nose. "Nice to see you, too, Mother."

"You need to clean up right now, put your face on, get rid of those hideous glasses and end this foolishness. You're coming home."

Nora stroked her ponytail for extra measure. "No, I need to take this conversation elsewhere. In case you haven't noticed, this is a business, not a conference room."

"Are you actually working here, with these—these people?" Her mother huffed out a deep breath and crossed her arms over her chest. When they actually didn't make it all the way because of the bulk of her designer coat, Nora suppressed a smile.

But that smile quickly turned sour when her mother's words hit a nerve. Nora scooted around the counter into the table area and, taking her mother by the arm, ushered her near the back table where Julie normally did her homework.

"How dare you come in here and insult my friends."

"Friends? Have you lost your mind?" She waved in Evan's direction. "Look at these people. They're certainly not *our* kind."

Oh, how Nora hated that attitude. Yes, she had been guilty of it on more occasions than she cared to admit, but once she realized people were no different no matter what they did for a living, she tried her best to take them as they were. Thankfully, Cedar Ridge had opened her small mind, and she was grateful she finally saw the light.

"You cannot come in here and insult good people. People I care about."

"Care about? Please . . ." Mother averted her eyes and stuck her nose higher, keeping her posture rigid. Then she aimed her eyes back onto Nora. "I've always had to direct you because you've tended to stray away from what's right. You need to stop this madness and come to your senses. Harrison and a job are waiting for you at B.E. Honestly, you never did know what was good for you."

Nora momentarily ignored her mother and glanced at Evan and Julie. Watched him place a dollop of whipped cream on Julie's nose. Seeing the delight on the child's face caused Nora's heart to sing with joy. But that joy quickly turned to boldness as her thoughts and her tone transformed into strength. She looked her mother directly in the eyes. "*Everything's* changed, Mother. I know exactly what's good for me. I'm happy here."

Joan uttered a sophisticated groan and rolled her eyes. "After all the years I've spent giving you the best of everything, this is what you settle for?"

"Those were things *you* wanted, Mother. I wanted love. And acceptance. And I'll be damned if I'll settle for the same type of relationship you and Dad have. I told you a long time ago, I'm not marrying Harrison."

Nora thought about her job and the promotion she intended to give up. She no longer felt the need to prove to her mother that she could make it on her own. It wasn't worth her time or energy. The importance of her life couldn't be measured by wealth or ambition. And she certainly had no intention of settling for a marriage that wasn't based on love.

She glanced at Evan and Julie again. The life Nora had lived in the city with her family wasn't real, there were no emotions involved in any of it, no love. Her new life from this point was going to be based on the life she discovered here in Cedar Ridge, by the people who meant the most to her. The people who loved her.

"I'm sorry, Mother, we don't serve your kind of coffee in this store. You won't find what you want here. But I have."

~ ~ ~

When Julie opened the front door of Arlene's cozy, ranch-style house, the aroma of homemade pot roast enticed Nora's taste buds. After receiving the Sunday dinner invitation, she took a leisurely two-block walk from The Comfy Quilt to Arlene's. The thought of a family dinner thrilled her like never before.

Initially, breeding pushed her to "dress" for the occasion, but Arlene insisted it was just a casual family dinner, nothing special. But to Nora, it was more than special. It was a chance to see how a real family interacted, how they shared an evening meal.

Taking Arlene's advice, Nora dressed comfortably in a neat pair of cords and a tank under a ribbed sweater. Normally, she would have brought a bottle of wine as a token of appreciation, but she wasn't sure if that was appropriate. So she opted for something they all could enjoy, even Julie, and had stopped off at Ridge Grocery for a nice bottle of sparkling cider.

"You're here!" Julie wrapped two little arms around Nora's waist.

"Yes, I am, and so are you!" She kissed the top of Julie's head.

"Come here." Julie dragged her by the hand. "I have to show you . . ."

Nora followed her through the comfortable living room into the kitchen.

"You made it!" Arlene stirred a large pot with steam rising from it, warming the tiny, but efficient kitchen.

"Hello!" Nora said as she held Julie back from yanking on her arm. She placed the bottle of cider on the counter next to the stove.

"That wasn't necessary." Arlene rotated the long-neck bottle to read it. "Oh, but this is such a nice treat. Thank you." She leaned over to kiss Nora on the cheek.

"Come on." Julie urged by pulling her arm. "You gotta see it." Out the back door they flew with Julie pointing to the redwood picnic table that rested in the middle of the deck. "See!"

Nora spotted it—not knowing why this was so important—but she knew she'd better act like it was. "Wow. That's a really big pumpkin! What are you going to do with it?"

"Carve it!" Julie giggled while she jumped up and down. "Daddy said we can all do it after dinner."

Carving a pumpkin. The whole family together. Not Julie and the nanny. But Julie, her father and grandmother. What a wonderful family tradition!

Nora knelt in front of the little girl. "You're going to have so much fun!"

"Correction—"

Nora's heart skipped as she recognized that deep voice that already had her blood simmering.

"—*we're* going to have fun carving it."

Evan's broad smile welcomed her like a warm hug. "You can't come for dinner and then leave. It's not good Mischief Night manners, right, Jules?"

"Right!" She giggled behind her hand and her eyes sparkled as she gazed adoringly at her father. "You gonna stay, Nora?"

Nora's heart gushed at the idea of being included in their family tradition. She was so entrenched in this family she didn't know whether to cry with joy or cry in panic. They were so open and giving and trusting.

"Well, what do you say?" Evan's eyes teased and his smile arched to the left.

Oh, but he was hot. And loving, and caring to his family.

Guilt began a tug of war with her heart.

This family showered all their trust upon her, and she repaid them by hiding her identity.

Seeing the unquestionable plea in both their expressions, she pushed aside the guilt and went with her heart.

"I'd be honored to carve your pumpkin with you. But I have to warn you, it's been years since I've done it."

"Don't worry. I'll show you how to do it," Julie reassured as she hopped down from her father's arms.

"Yeah, don't worry," Evan said with a twinkle in his eye as he winked. "It's like riding a bike, and other things. Once you do it, it all comes back to you."

Nora looked him squarely in the eyes, lowered her chin, and tried to summon her most sultry voice. "What makes you think I forgot how to carve and . . . other things?" She turned away and left him on the deck as Julie yanked her back into the house.

"Come on," the little girl said. "You gotta see my doll collection."

She followed Julie into the first bedroom of the one-level home. Bruce had instructed her to get info on the Cavanaughs business, and if he saw her now, she'd surely lose her job. She hadn't yet figured how she was going to quit on good terms, but right now, she needed to place her undivided attention on Julie's mission to introduce her to her dolls.

A tall, wooden and glass Curio cabinet held a beautifully delicate doll collection. "Are these your grandmothers?"

"Nooo." Julie shook her head and her ponytail swung wildly. "They're mine."

"Why aren't they at your house?"

"Gramma keeps 'em here so I won't ruin 'em. They're not for playing."

Nora marveled at the beauty of each one. "I can see that. They're gorgeous. That's a lot of dolls."

"Gramma gets me one for all my birthdays."

Nora counted and turning her gaze from the dolls back to Julie. "I thought you were six?"

"I am."

"But there are seven."

"She got one the day I was born."

"Oh, right." The day she almost made her entrance in the cab. Nora would be surprised if Julie knew that story. "Which one is that?"

Julie pointed to the one on the top shelf on the left. "That's Jessica."

Nora felt her eyebrows shoot upwards. "Jessica?"

"I named them."

"Why Jessica?"

"Because I like that name."

"Is this the doll you got for your first birthday?" She pointed to the one next to Jessica.

"Uh-huh. She's Samantha. And that's Kayla, that's Fiona, Brianna, Alexa, and that's—" The pint-sized princess looked at the doorway as if checking they were alone, then whispered, "—that's Isabella."

Okay, Nora would play along. It had been decades since she played a kids' game, and she couldn't help notice all the names ended in 'a.' "That's a nice name. I like it."

"Me, too." She continued, whispering, "I named her for my mother." She glanced back at the doorway. "If I had a mother, she would be pretty, so I gave her a pretty name."

Nora's mouth quivered and she dropped to her knees, wrapping the child in her arms, stroking her hair. The poor kid didn't even know Miranda's name. Nora hugged her a little tighter and whispered in her ear, "Isabella is a beautiful name, sweetie. Don't worry, I'll keep your secret."

She wiped at her eyes, trying not to let Julie see the emotions that overcame her. She realized right then that by cutting herself off all these years, she didn't allow herself to feel, to get involved enough in life to ride the tide that came along with living, truly living.

She didn't like these feelings gripping her now, but she knew that the sadness and heartache she felt for this child also brought an awakening.

She loved Julie.

Pure, unconditional love for a child that garnered both joy and sorrow.

That's what had been missing from her life. Her sterile existence forbade her from enjoying life, from opening herself to the vulnerability of caring about another person, no strings attached, and having that person care about her.

Now she knew the secret to Cedar Ridge. It wasn't the village that was magical. It was the people. And her journey led her here so she could find the missing pieces to make her life complete.

God knew she was upset with Bruce right now. But she was also grateful to him. If he hadn't sent her to Cedar Ridge—to these people—she never would have experienced true love.

Looking at the love in Julie's eyes, Nora knew she would never be the same again.

Chapter 12

"Daddy, can we keep the store?"

"I don't know, but we're gonna try."

Evan aimed an unspoken warning toward Nora and his mother as he passed the platter of pot roast. "I'm going to meet with the board tomorrow in a closed meeting. See if the taste test and the TV coverage changed their minds."

Nora took hold of the platter, trying to steady her hands as the question of the Bean & Brew thrust another stab of guilt at her. She turned the platter toward Arlene, who picked off two slices of meat, then Nora took her own, hoping the apprehension she felt didn't show on her face.

"You know what?" Arlene said. "I don't want to talk about the store for the rest of the night." "Let's enjoy our meal, and talk about it tomorrow." She tweaked Julie's nose. "Do you have everything you need for your costume?"

"Uh-huh." Julie nodded before a forkful of mashed potatoes made it to her mouth.

"What are you dressing up as?" Nora asked.

"A fairy princess." Her eyes sparkled like the bedazzled head pieces on her collectable dolls.

Of course she was, Nora thought with a chuckle, thankful for the change in subject. "Oh, you're going to make a beautiful fairy princess."

"Thanks!"

In her Manhattan neighborhood, Nora had seen kids trick-or-treating in her building, but for the past few years they no longer went door to door. She remembered hearing something about kids gathering in the pool room for treats, but she never contributed.

Come to think of it, she was kind of a Scrooge when it came to holidays. Too busy working, no time for celebrating—or even decorating, for that matter. Went along with her empty lifestyle.

"Nora, can you come trick or treating with us?"

It seemed Julie wanted her to do everything with the family. While it was unusual because Nora's own family rarely did anything together, Julie's invitation seemed a perfect opportunity for her to get back into the spirit of the holiday and experience a *real* family tradition. "I don't have a costume. Do I have to get dressed up?"

"Good Lord, no," Arlene interrupted. "Just bring yourself."

"I'd love that. It's been years since I went house to house."

"Huh?" Julie asked.

"They don't go house to house anymore," Evan said between chewing bits of pot roast. "The kids meet in the school parking lot, and the parents hand out candy from their cars. Called Trunk-or-Treat."

"Yes, it's safer that way," Arlene said with a wave of her hand. "With all the crazy people in the world, you've got to be careful what they hand out."

She hadn't thought that would be a problem, especially in Cedar Ridge. Everyone appeared so nice, but she guessed all types of people lived where you'd least expected.

"Yeah, it's a little weird, but it is safer," Evan added. "The kids also go around to the stores." He turned his attention to his daughter. "I've got a bucket full of chocolate all ready for them."

"Reese's Pieces?" Julie asked as she bounced her fanny around in her chair.

"Yep. A bunch of other stuff, too."

"Goody!"

"Okay, finish your dinner. We've got a pumpkin to carve," Arlene said to Julie. Turning to Nora with a broad smile, she laughed. "You, too, young lady."

~ ~ ~

"That was so much fun," Nora said as she and Evan strolled down Primrose Lane to The Comfy Quilt.

"You liked it?" he asked.

"Absolutely. You've got the *best* family."

"We're all right." He glanced at her then, noticing the glow from the streetlamp causing the ends of her black hair to shimmer. He was surprised when she arrived at his mother's house with her hair down, like it had been the first time he met her. Right now, it was all he could do not to take her into his arms and plunge his hands into its silkiness, so he kept his mind on keeping her conversation going. "I guess you haven't done too many family things in a while."

"Try in a lifetime. Mother never wanted us or the house to get messy. Daddy was always away on business."

"What kind of fun was that?" he asked, trying to keep the conversation light while he fought the urge to put his arm around her.

"It wasn't. That's why I loved tonight."

What he loved was the way her eyes lit up like a Jack-O-Lantern right now. The spring in her step—more like a hop—showed her excitement. It was kind of cute; she was kind of cute with that knit hat covering her head, looking all relaxed and happy.

Trying to slow her pace, he took hold of her hand, feeling the chill of her soft, tender skin, so he tightened his grip.

Leaves blew around their feet as they ambled the two blocks. As the waning harvest moon cast a healthy glow to the neighborhood, Evan watched Nora's eyes sparkle with delight when a few kids ran past, rolls of toilet paper in hand.

"At least mischief night is still the same," she said.

"Yeah, not too bad. Elliot keeps all the eggs in the back refrigerator unit at Ridge Grocery for a few days, away from the kids, so they don't egg the neighborhoods. When customers need eggs, they ask him to get what they need."

"That takes all the fun out of it for the kids."

"Sure does. But it's okay. Once you get your car egged, you don't want it happening again."

"Is it really that hard to get off?"

"Oh, yeah." Enough of this egg talk. He wanted to find out when she'd be living in town so he could see her more. "So, how's the apartment hunting going?"

"I haven't started looking yet. But soon. If you know of any place, can you let me know?"

"Sure." Keeping her here would now become a priority. After he saved his store.

"I'm getting things settled. Probably go back into the city on Tuesday, give notice on my lease, tie up a few loose ends."

"That's great. I'm sure Sarah will be disappointed. She likes having you around."

"Did she say that?" Nora asked, as if she was surprised that the owner of The Comfy Quilt thought of her that way.

"Sure did. Everyone likes having you around." He stopped walking, then gently drew her close. "Especially me." Giving into the urge, he finally kissed her lightly on the lips. "Thanks for coming to dinner. It meant a lot to us."

"It meant a lot to me," she said, her voice heavy like caramel syrup, just like the first day he met her. Although, this time, her lips stayed close to his, and the warmth of her breath mingled with his. The idea of protecting her from the cold guided him to wrap his arms around her, cloaking her body in warmth.

"I have an idea," she whispered.

His body jumped to attention. "I'm listening."

"Why don't you come up to my room? It's kind of chilly, and I could use someone to keep me warm."

She read my mind.

The thought of the two of them keeping each other warm had his body ready, willing, and able to do his part.

"Lead the way, my lady," he said, sweeping his arm for her to lead. "You can use me *all* you want."

~ ~ ~

Nora's insides trembled as she closed the door to her room at the inn. It had been a long time since she'd been with a man. Something she didn't do often.

The few men she had been with were more of a convenience. Always neat and practical. No drama. No guilt. She'd made sure to let them know from the onset that she wasn't interested in a relationship. Just a sexual attraction, no emotional attachment. And they'd been all right with that.

But this time, she didn't have the need to give her neat and practical speech. She wanted to be close to Evan. To capitalize on the feeling of acceptance she felt this evening with him and his family. To wallow in the acceptance he showered on her for just being herself.

"In all the years I've lived in this town, I've never been in one of these rooms," Evan said as he surveyed the sitting area of Room 6.

"I like it. It's cozy, sort of a snuggly place to hide from the cold."

He enfolded her in his arms. "Still haven't gotten used to the temperature around here?"

She looked up at him with a flirty gaze. "I'd say right now the temperature is heating up nicely."

As he lowered his mouth toward her, she sighed, sensing his eyes trained on her lips. "Glad my services are working," he whispered. His lips gently grazed hers, then lightly dragged across her cheek to her ear and whispered, "Like I said, use me all you want."

Shivers prickled Nora's neck as his hands reached to unbutton her jacket. As she did the same, and their outerwear fell to the floor, she realized her mind began to cut off her emotions in that routine that always played out whenever she was with a man. Instead of just enjoying herself this time with a man she trusted and cared about, and giving in to a wave of emotional satisfaction, she continued to guard herself, as she'd done all her life. She needed to put aside the "logic" she always brought to intimacy and concentrate on how wonderfully Evan made her heart feel. But the difficulty of letting go kept interfering and she struggled to push past that annoying practice, needing to be honest with herself and focusing on how she truly felt about Evan.

Plain and simple, she had strong feelings for him. But not just him. He came with a wonderful, loving set of baggage that she whole-heartedly embraced. She loved Julie and thought the world of Arlene.

But Evan. Oh, Evan. There were so many reasons to fall for a guy like him. His devotion to his family. The tender way he handled his daughter; his consideration for his mother, and the determination to keep his father's legacy alive. Nora admired how his honesty fostered loyalty from everyone in Cedar Ridge.

But most of all, Nora reveled in the way he made her feel, like she mattered, that his life was complete whenever they were together.

And as his hand roamed the curves and plains of her body, as heat rose deep within her, she sensed that destiny had a hand in bringing them together. Even though she knew Cedar Ridge wasn't the magical place she thought it to be, fate had drawn her to him. If she truly wanted to enjoy her time with him right now, she needed to put herself out there and open her heart. While that thought frightened her, somehow, she knew with Evan, it would be worth the risk.

~ ~ ~

There had been times when Evan knew sex was a bad idea. This wasn't one of them.

Trust meant everything to him. Too much to lose, too much heartache allowing another person that kind of control over him again. And while his body screamed for release, he knew being with Nora was more than just physical. She enabled him to open his heart by proving her devotion and concern for Julie. She had woven herself into his life, his family, and even his business. He couldn't believe she had gone the extra mile with television coverage for the taste test. His ex had never done anything like that for him. Nora was by his side in every aspect of his life. She was honest and real, completely opposite from his initial impression, and he counted his lucky stars that she'd found her way to him.

As he kissed that tender spot just at the hollow of her neck then ran his tongue across her collar bone, he knew this wouldn't be a one-night mistake like the two others he had since Miranda walked. Unlike those two situations, being with Nora put his trust and vulnerability on the line—the well-protected trust that she had slowly earned. He trusted her with his daughter which, in turn, meant he could trust her with his affections.

When their bodies molded to each other, he felt the walls sheltering his heart break down, allowing her in.

This was it. The real thing. He stopped a minute, needing proof that her heart was in it as much as his. He surveyed her face, searched her eyes, then carefully removed her thick brown frames that blocked what he needed to see, gently tossing them on the nightstand. When he stared deeply into her trusting eyes, reassurance met his gaze, confirming they were both ready to plunge into something neither of them had anticipated a few weeks ago. Yes, this was definitely right for both of them. He felt the yearning in her heart radiating from her soul, certain that if he was going to fall, he wasn't falling alone.

~ ~ ~

The next morning, Evan was glad to see Nora walk into the store. If he ever needed a partner, it was now. Both emotionally and physically. But the physical would have to wait another grueling ten hours if she'd be willing.

Last night, she was loving and attentive and made him feel whole again. It wasn't just the sex. The emotional sharing of their bodies had hit him hard.

Her showing up right now was the icing on the cake. When their eyes connected, that deep communication that only lovers share shown through in her secretive smile, totally brightening his shitty morning.

"How are you today?" she asked as she stood on the opposite side of the counter and gave him that look that said, *I can't wait until tonight.*

"Better, much better." He took hold of her hand and his insides came alive. "Now that you're here. Give me a minute. I'll meet you at a table."

He made her usual mocha decaf, brought it the table, and took a seat across from her. Man, that vanilla scent from her shampoo smelled all sensual and inviting, but he needed to keep his thoughts on something more important than jumping back into her bed again. At least for now.

"I need to apologize," he began.

Surprise jumped to her eyes and her shoulders hitched. "Why?" she said slowly.

"For leaving you so soon last night."

"Oh." Her shoulders seemed to relax. "I thought you were going to say we made a mistake."

"Mistake?" He shook his head and reached for her hands again. "No way. Last night was one of the best nights of my life."

She lowered her chin and fixed a flirtatious gaze at him. "Mine, too."

"I didn't want to leave."

"As much as I wanted you stay the night, I understand that you couldn't because of Julie."

"Actually, Mom figured I'd be late, so she let Julie have another sleep-over."

Along with that lingering gaze, he definitely noticed that lover's smile settle back on her lips. "Why didn't you come back?"

"I thought about it." Staring at her moist lips, he rubbed his thumbs over the back of her hands. They were warm from being wrapped around her coffee mug, but not as hot as her body had been last night. "If I came back, I never would have made it into work on time this morning, along with missing the meeting."

She giggled softly. "You *definitely* would have been late."

"So you're not mad?"

"How could I be? You're the most loving man I've ever met."

That went a long way to bolster his ego. Having Nora in his life was like winning the lottery. Only better.

She gently released one hand from his and sipped her coffee. "How did it go this morning with the planning board?"

Ah damn, she broke that steamy spell she had floating around him. Okay, back to reality. "It didn't. Looks like they're leaning to a yes vote."

Her coffee mug landed on the table with a thud. "What about the blind taste test and the TV coverage?"

Evan let go of her hand and sat back against his chair. The excitement of being with Nora suddenly evaporated when the reality that all his hard work trying to save his business didn't make a difference. "They didn't care about all that," he said with a shrug. "Said the media coverage worked well because the village home-page hits rose by thirty percent."

"That's good for tourism, but what does that have to do with approving MoonBurst?"

"It doesn't. What they like is that MoonBurst promised to hire only Cedar Ridge residents for their new store." Yeah, it sounded great, but that didn't help his cause one bit. "The council pushed the planning board in hopes that'll help everyone who doesn't have a job."

"Wait a sec." Nora cocked her head, her eyes and mouth braided together into a giant question. "They're under the impression MoonBurst will only hire Cedar Ridge residents?"

"Yep. And with the way the economy tanked a few years ago, we've got a lot of people collecting unemployment. That's why the village decided to go tourist, bring in customers for all the sagging businesses."

Nora didn't answer for a second as her questioned expression told him her mind was working, then she finally asked, "I don't understand? Did MoonBurst actually say they were only hiring residents?"

Why did she have the need to process that fact? Why did it matter so much? "That's what Mayor Farley said. Why, what's up?"

Nora hesitated, her mind quickly searching her memory bank. She'd seen the proposed contracts and nothing like that had been stated. In fact, she had skimmed a small clause that mentioned hiring, but she couldn't recall it stating anything about only hiring resident employees.

Bruce wanted her final report today, and she initially intended to leave tonight, but after spending a few hours last night with Evan, she wanted to extend her stay one more night. And with this new information, going back to the city to tie up the loose ends became more urgent. First thing tomorrow morning, she'd head back to take care of things and also do a little digging to find validity to MoonBurst's hiring plans.

Something wasn't right, and she needed to get to the bottom of it.

Bruce would have to wait. Again.

~ ~ ~

As soon as Arlene arrived later that evening, Evan was out the door. He couldn't have his daughter permanently sleeping at his mother's, so he asked her to sit for him at his house while he went to Nora's.

This time, he didn't mind the enthusiasm in his mother's eyes at the mention of Nora. She liked Nora. A lot. Which made the situation convenient without a lot of explanation.

When he arrived at the inn, the anticipation of seeing her intensified during his four-block trip from his house. He'd taken his truck in order to get there quicker, but locating a parking space took longer than if he had walked.

At the antique reception counter, Sarah smiled at him when he asked her to call Nora's room. And when Nora had given the okay for him to go up to the second floor, Sarah raised an eyebrow, but also gave him and approving smile.

Yeah, that was the problem living in a small town. Everyone knew everyone's business.

He took the creaky, brittle wooden stairs two at a time, took note of the busy, flowered wallpaper on the stairway walls he hadn't noticed last night when Nora guided him to her room. More flowers adorned lighted sconces lining the hallway walls. Too many flowers for his taste.

Just as he raised a hand to knock on Room #6, it opened. A silhouette of soft light behind Nora highlighted her beautiful face. No makeup, her silky black hair rested gracefully around her shoulders. She was his own true angel sent from Heaven to save his lonely heart.

As he entered, the candlelight around the room silhouetted a peek through the light fabric of her nightgown. Yeah, he'd prefer a short little scrap of soft material, maybe in hot red, to cover just a few of her scrumptious curves, but he had to admit, the soft yellow, almost see-through knee-length thing she wore made his body throb.

"I thought we could talk a little, if that's okay?" She pointed to the loveseat and small oval coffee table. Two wineglasses and an unopened bottle of white sat waiting.

"Talking is good." Although, he'd love to explore what lie beneath that thin nightgown, he could handle taking a few minutes to talk, knowing the wait would be worth it.

After pouring the wine, they each took hold of a simple stemmed glass and she *clinked* hers to his. "To new beginnings."

Not too much of a wine guy, he gulped it instead of a sip. "Hmm. Pretty good." He took hold of the bottle. "Verde, huh? Never heard of it."

"Neither have I. It came highly recommended."

"Elliot?"

She nodded.

When he noticed her lick her bottom lip, he took another swig to tamp down the urge to skip the cordial conversation and get right down to business. "I prefer a good brew, but this will do."

"Sorry. I didn't think beer would be as romantic."

He leaned in closer and whispered, "Sometimes, beer's got nothing on wine." He dipped his index finger in his glass, then rubbed it along her bottom lip. "Just depends on what you do with it." When her tongue peeked out again to lick it, he adjusted his butt against the couch cushion, easing the pressure in his jeans. "If you want to talk, you better make your tongue behave."

"Only if you control where you put your finger."

Oh, he could think of a few places, considering he knew almost every inch of her body after last night.

Phew. He needed to cool off. "So, what's on your mind?"

"Julie."

That quickly turned down the temperature in his pants. "What's wrong with her?"

"She told me something, in confidence, but I think you need to know about it."

"She failing math?"

"No. It's not about school. It's about her mother."

What the hell?

Now any chance of the two of them exploring each other's bodies was gone. The mention of Miranda turned him off quicker than a light switch. His neck and shoulders instantly tensed at the mention of her, so he blew out a huffed breath, trying to remain calm.

"What about her?"

"Does Julie know her name?"

Evan didn't understand where *that* came from. "She doesn't need to know her name. The woman doesn't exist."

He knew a look of disapproval when he saw it. His mother had been giving him that same look regarding the same subject.

"She didn't die," Nora gently said.

"No. She evaporated. Walked out one day and never came back."

"Has she tried to see Julie?"

He shook his head. It killed him every day that that witch might show up out of nowhere and demand custody of his daughter. She didn't care about his little girl.

Whenever mothers went to school functions, Julie's mother was absent. Sure, his mother stepped in, but it wasn't the same. Every Mother's Day, he made sure to plan something special so Julie wouldn't feel the pain of not having a mother. He knew it was a lot for a kid her age to handle. She *did* have a mother somewhere, but the woman didn't want anything to do with her.

"No. Like I said, she walked out and never looked back. She said she didn't want to be a mother or a wife anymore." He felt his heart splitting into two, felt himself kicking into protective mode to ward off the pain. He didn't want to go where this conversation was headed. "Is there a reason for all these questions?"

Ouch. That came out harsher than he wanted. Unfortunately, Miranda brought out that side of him.

"The doll collection," Nora said softly. "Julie explained it to me when I was at your mother's."

"I don't get it. Mom started that collection for her. I never understood the fascination. Just more frou-frou stuff to clean. What's your point?"

"Did you know Julie named the dolls?"

"Yeah, what's the connection?"

"The doll she got for her last birthday, the one named Isabella. Do you remember it?"

Vaguely. Tall doll, brown hair, frilly dress, just like all the rest. "What about it?"

"Julie told me she named her for her mother. She said, 'If I had a mother, she would be pretty, so I gave her a pretty name.'"

"Damn," he whispered as his heart slammed into his ribs. "I thought I was protecting her."

The warm touch Nora placed on his shoulder gave him some comfort, but nothing could make him feel better about messing with his little girl's world.

"It makes sense that she'd wonder about her mother. Do you mind my asking what you *have* told her?"

He inhaled deeply, held it a second, then slowly let it go. "I said some kids don't have a mother or father. She just had me and Grandma. She seemed to buy it, so I went with it."

"Was that when she was younger?"

Nodding, he remembered the first time the question came up. She was three and she believed everything he said. A few times after that, she asked, and he kept up the lie. That was that. Eventually, she never asked again, and he never offered further explanation.

"Why is it coming up again?" He knew he was whining, but raising a kid on his own was hard. Without a hand book, he sometimes felt like he was floundering in a pond of quick sand.

"She's really bright, and she is getting older. She probably sees other mothers. Some pregnant ones, too. She's old enough to realize she had to have a mother in order to be born."

He thought a minute and then said, "Ah, damn. Adam's wife is pregnant." He scrubbed a hand across the back of his neck. "She asked all kinds of questions when Laurel started showing. I answered them truthfully, but I never . . ."

"She's a perceptive kid. I'm sure she realized it before she even asked you." She placed a reassuring hand on his arm. "Don't beat yourself up."

"I screwed up big time."

"You're doing the best you can. It must be difficult keeping the truth from her. No child wants to know they're not wanted."

The empathy in her eyes told him she cared about Julie enough to sideline her own desires to help him through this. They could have been naked, making love right now, but she chose to put it off in favor of helping his daughter. His trust in her just increased a truckload.

"Would you like me to help you sort out what to tell her about Miranda?"

"You'd do that?"

"If it would help? I'm not an expert on family issues. God knows, my family is a mess. But I do know what it's like not to feel like you're enough. That your mother doesn't want you. After all these years, I still feel the pain. But I also don't want to interfere."

He turned to her and placed his hands on her upper arms. "It would help. A lot."

"Whatever I can do, let me know. I love that little girl of yours."

Right then, Evan knew he no longer needed to protect his heart from Nora. She wanted to help his daughter for one simple reason: she loved her.

Perfect. Because he knew Julie loved Nora, too.

And so did he.

~ ~ ~

As despair covered Evan's face, Nora knew his heart was tearing into tiny pieces. When he reached for her, she willingly fell into his arms.

He's spent four years protecting his daughter, but now it was time for him to be truthful. And she'd be there to help him. To help Julie.

For the past few weeks, her own evasion of the truth had twisted her stomach into a knotted web. And right now, it twisted again with the possibility that a lie could drive a wedge between Evan and his daughter. She'd seen it over and over in her own family. After observing the Cavanaughs, and everyone else in Cedar Ridge, she'd learned relationships flourished when there was honesty between loved ones.

And that's what she wanted with Evan.

A relationship.

To be a part of his life.

She loved his devotion to his family, his number one priority, even if protecting them caused further problems. At least his intentions were sincere, and because of that, she knew he and Julie would get through this.

She loved his unwavering loyalty to his friends. His generous nature aided them without question, and they never hesitated to repay his kindness. He lived the 'treat others as you'd want to be treated' lesson, a lesson she now intended to follow.

She loved his passion for his business, his commitment to his customers, his determination to fight MoonBurst to keep his business alive.

In short, she loved him, but love couldn't thrive without honesty, so she would be unable to tell him until she was ready to share the truth of who she really was.

Because of him, she opened her heart and rode an emotional journey she had programmed her heart from feeling. He drew her into his world and gave her a purpose— not just a bottom-line type of purpose of supporting her empty lifestyle—but a true purpose where humanity comes first while all else pales.

The connection they just shared about Julie had her rejoicing that she finally let go and allowed him to break down the barriers she carefully crafted. As their hands found their way to the vulnerability of each other's bodies, she knew their shared love and concern for Julie had bonded them forever, bringing them emotionally closer.

And just before they crested over that threshold of lovemaking, Evan held back, cupping her face in his hands.

"I love you," he said as his mouth came down on hers, smothering her response.

Her heart and body surged right along with him, but she couldn't utter those same words back to him. She hadn't been totally honest with him, so her heart wasn't free to be given. Not yet.

~ ~ ~

As another hour passed, Evan rolled toward Nora and crooked one arm under her head wrapping the other around the softness of her belly just skimming the edges of her breasts.

He had been right about her the first day she walked into his store. She looked like an angel promising eternal life. After two nights together, she'd brought him to his own piece of Heaven. And he loved this fresh, unpretentious version of her much better than that hot-looking polished corporate raider. This version was real, and warm, with a great sense of loyalty. But more importantly, she was honest. In a million years, he never thought he could trust again.

"Hey, it's late," he murmured against her hair. "I'm going to have to go."

Her hand gripped him tightly. "Do you have to?"

He nodded, kissing the side of her head even though his body and heart wanted to stay. "Julie."

"You're right." She released her hands, then gently nudged him from her bed. "Go. She needs you to be home."

"Hey, you don't have to be so pushy about it. I thought you like having me here?"

"I *love* having you in my bed. But I also love your daughter. You need to go."

Not only was Julie his priority, she was also Nora's. Another reason to love her. "One more kiss?"

Her violet eyes teased as she smiled up at him. "You can't resist just one kiss."

"Sure can."

As his mouth captured hers, the fluid dance of their tongues enticed his body to wake up, which wasn't a good thing if he intended to leave. Man, he wanted to stay.

"Mmm," he moaned when his cell phone rang and he grudgingly released her. "Who's bothering me at an important time like this?" Leaning over the side of the bed, he grabbed his jeans that were strewn on the carpet and retrieved his cell from the pocket. He squinted at the number on the display then put the phone to his ear.

"Hey, Ma, I was just leaving."

He moved the phone away from his ear when her voice sounded loud enough to fill the room, but he couldn't make out what she was saying because she was talking a mile a minute.

"Wait. Wait. Slow down. What happened?"

As he processed her words, he felt the blood drain from his face and his heart beat loudly in his ears. Life suddenly ran in slow motion, and he heard himself respond to his mother, but wasn't coherent of the words that fell from his mouth. He hit the end button, then jumped from the bed.

"What's wrong?" Nora asked. "Is it Julie?"

Pushing one leg into his jeans, he stumbled, rushing his second leg into the denim. "No, it's the store!"

"What happened?"

"It's gone!"

Chapter 13

As Nora sped her car behind Evan's truck toward the Bean & Brew, her initial reason for coming to Cedar Ridge churned in her head. When she envisioned putting the Bean & Brew out of business, she never imagined this.

Traffic swelled when she reached Elm Street. She crept slowly, inching her car around police barricades when an officer waved her on. Even though all the fire trucks blocked the view of the building, Nora saw plumes of gray smoke billowing high above them.

At last week's meeting of the Sussex County Expansion Project, she had tried to stop, or at least postpone, the demise of the Bean & Brew. Now, that demise seemed inevitable. Wiping tears from her eyes, she parked her car next to Evan's truck and ran to join him, holding onto his arm with one hand and rubbing his back in support.

"Thanks." His eyes welled with a flood of tears, and she held on as he began to move.

They hurried together toward the sidewalk, only to be stopped three stores away from Evan's shop by Todd decked out in his fire fighter gear.

"No way, man. I can't let you any closer."

"Come on. It's my store." The anguish in Evan's voice felt like a stab to Nora's heart.

"I know." Todd lifted the face shield from his firefighter helmet. "You won't do anyone any good if you get hurt." He grabbed his friend by the shoulders and turned him away from the building. "Nora?"

"I'll take care of him." She took hold of Evan's arm with both her hands, but glanced at Todd. "Please. Try to save the store."

"We're doing our best."

"I know." Thank goodness Evan's friend was one of the volunteer fire fighters. She gently guided Evan across the street, where a small crowd of people stood behind the police barricade. As they reached the area, Adam rushed to them.

"You okay?" he asked Evan.

Evan just shook his head, the tears he'd been holding back now poured down his cheeks.

Adam turned his attention to her. "Is he all right? Was he in the store?"

"No, he was with me, but I think he's in shock."

Adam gave one affirmative nod. "It'll be okay, buddy." He put his arm around Evan's shoulder. "We'll all help you rebuild."

Evan stared blindly without a word.

Nora couldn't begin to know how he felt right now. She'd never had everything she worked so hard for, destroyed. How can someone come back from something so devastating?

The problems he faced earlier about Julie paled in comparison to this. She knew it would be difficult to address Julie's issues at the same time as dealing with his options for his business.

But, with MoonBurst threatening to open, would he just take his losses and move on? Or would he be determined to rebuild?

Just then, Arlene and Julie showed up—Julie in her pajamas under her coat. As they neared Evan, Nora sensed it was her turn to back away. As much as they had welcomed her into their lives, she was not a Cavanaugh. As the three of them held onto each other and sobbed, Nora saw the horror on their faces and heard the grief in their cries; she knew their love would be the catalyst to get them through this tragedy.

With Evan's determination, his sense of responsibility and loyalty to his father's memory, Nora would bet an entire year's salary he'd rebuild the Bean & Brew.

He was that kind of man.

~ ~ ~

After a sleepless night pacing the floors between his bedroom and living room, Evan needed to go to the store. Todd said the inspectors still needed time to investigate and deem it safe before anyone, including *him*, could go in. But he needed to see for himself that it wasn't all gone, that the Bean & Brew would be waiting for him just like always.

At four a.m., he jumped in his truck and drove onto Elm Street. Barricades blocked the sidewalk of his storefront.

It wasn't a dream.

Icicles dripped from the utility wires connected to the building. With all the commotion earlier last night, he didn't realize the temperature dropped enough to freeze. As he drove to the parking lot behind the building, puddles of ice dotted the asphalt ground, black soot licked across the cement façade from the outline of the windows and door. More barricades and caution tape cordoned the area.

He sat a minute, wondering how it all went wrong. The business had finally moved forward the way he had envisioned. After four long years of loneliness, Nora now brought joy back into his life. Last night, he felt like a man who had everything. A great family, a rewarding business, and a woman who loved him.

To literally be ripped out of Nora's warm, loving bed to watch his business burn was the worst nightmare he'd ever had. Worse than when Miranda had left. He tried to deny it happened all night long, but the evidence that lay silently in front of him proved him wrong.

He stepped out of the car, and the noxious smell of burned wood and wires hung in the early morning air. He walked around the frozen puddles, staring at the back of the building. The door was gone and a light peeked through the back of the store, radiating from the streetlamp through the large, plate-glass window in the storefront.

Climbing over the barricade, he shuffled toward the caution-taped doorway and covered his nose with his hand. The stench nearly cut off his breath as he stuck his head in the doorway.

His equipment stood covered in charred fragments of wood and molded waves buckled the laminate countertop. Anything that had been plastic melted downward like dripping taffy. Mugs lay broken, covered in soot.

All the hours he put into the place, all the ideas and promise for success were now out of reach. No business, no customers, no purpose. It was all gone.

Every day for the past four years, he came to the store, hoping his father would be there. And now that hope was gone. The irrational chance to see his father one more time wouldn't happen. The opportunity to keep his promise to take care of his mother and the coffee shop was now obliterated by the flames. Everything his family had worked for was destroyed.

Evan dropped to his knees, ignoring the cold water seeping into the denim from the puddle he knelt in. His gut wrenched in emptiness, the lingering odor of smoke aided his tears, choking him.

His father and the business were gone.

And they were never coming back.

~ ~ ~

It was time.

After two days of ignoring Bruce's messages, Nora finally returned his calls. The disgust she felt at Bruce's pleasure over the fire at the Bean & Brew turned her stomach making her more determined to resign and move permanently to Cedar Ridge.

During the recovery from the fire, her priorities were Evan, Julie, and Arlene, spending as much time as possible with them, running errands, taking Julie to and from school, and even bringing Julie to the park yesterday afternoon for her park day. It was the least Nora could do since Arlene had been so distraught over the fire and could barely function. Besides, she loved spending time with Julie.

Today, the fire marshal said Evan would be able to go into the store to view the damage, and from what Todd had told them, luckily, there wasn't much, just the back kitchen area.

Arlene didn't want to see it, said there were too many memories of what she and Tom had built together. So Nora decided to be there for Evan for emotional support.

She used to view emotional support as a waste of energy, that a person needed to "man up" as her father always said, not letting emotions rule them. But that thinking was wrong. She understood that now. Evan's emotions were raw and justified. The man nearly lost everything he had worked for, and she wanted to make sure she was there for him.

On her way to see the damage, she took a detour to Ridge Liquors, thinking a little liquid courage might be in order.

As she entered the Bean & Brew's front door, other than the heavy smell of smoke, she almost wouldn't have noticed anything different had she not looked toward the back of the store. The coffee shop was in better shape than Evan had described. The putrid stench overpowered the small shop, but for the most part, the back of the shop had sustained most of the damage. She found Evan standing in the middle of the table area with a large object dangling from one hand.

"What do you have there?"

When he turned his watery gaze at her, he took hold of the item in both hands to show her. "I failed him." The shiny, varnish finish of his father's wooden mug holder was lost to streaked soot.

She placed a gentle hand on his shoulder, giving a comforting rub. "No, you didn't. You did everything you could to keep this place going. What did the fire marshal say?"

He bowed his head, letting out a deep breath. "Electrical short. In the grinder. That's why most of the fire is in the back. Water sprinklers in the ceiling kept it contained until they got here."

"I see the water damage," Nora said as she looked around the store. "The insurance should cover that, right?"

He shrugged one shoulder without a word.

Nora put the six-pack she held on a table, gathered two long-neck, brown bottles, twisted off the caps and handed one to him.

He stared at it like he'd never seen a bottle of beer before. "Isn't that your brand?"

He nodded, but made no move to drink.

"Good." She took a short sip, allowing the bitter beverage to tingle her tongue. Not bad considering she hadn't had a beer since college. "So, what's the plan?"

"Plan?" He finally looked at her as if seeing her for the first time, his eyes swollen and red.

"Yes. Your plan of action to rebuild."

Evan shook his head and shrugged again, carefully placing the mug holder on the table next to the six-pack. "I dunno. Maybe, collect the insurance, clean this place out and move on."

"Move on?" She stepped to face him, staring him square in the eye. "As in not own the Bean & Brew anymore?"

"Yeah. What's the use?" he said in a long sigh, and he looked away from her. "MoonBurst is coming. Why rebuild? I'm going to be put out of business."

"Excuse me?" She grabbed him by the forearm, forcing him to make eye contact. "I mistook you for someone I know. I thought you were Evan Cavanaugh, from the Cedar Ridge Cavanaughs."

His gaze broke from hers, and he lowered it to the floor. "What's your point?"

"I know you're hurting right now, but Cavanaughs don't give up. We need to rebuild this coffee shop, maybe put in a few new touches and make it even better."

He finally looked up at her then. "We?"

"Yes, I'm ready to roll up my sleeves, but I need our fearless leader to tell me what to do."

She noticed a tiny smirk at the corner of his lips. "Do you now?"

"Yes, sir." She playfully punched his bicep. "Are you with me?"

The smirk grew into a slow smile as it inched from the left corner of his mouth.

She moved to stand next to him, surveying the rubble in the store, then bumped her shoulder to his arm. "We got this." She *clinked* her bottle to his. "We've totally got this."

~ ~ ~

"Damn. This is a lot of paperwork."

Evan knew repairing the Bean & Brew would be tough, but the repairs were a piece of cake compared to the mountain of paperwork and phone calls he had with the insurance company the past two weeks.

Nora had been right. He was a Cavanaugh. And Cavanaughs didn't give up.

It also didn't hurt that he had a real go-getter like her by his side to help kick him in the ass and snap him out of the depression he had allowed to swallow him. She was a gift to him and his family, and he didn't know how he would ever repay her.

And, she was also right that he hadn't let his father down. The fire hadn't been his fault even though he initially convinced himself it was. They'd been having problems with the grinder for several months, and even though he recently had it repaired, once the aging unit shorted again, it was too much for the equally aging electrical system of the building to handle. The short hadn't tripped the electric breaker, so now the owner of the building had to upgrade the entire electric supply for not only his store, but the three other stores in the building.

Once he realized he wasn't at fault, his focus on rebuilding became clear. There was no way he'd let his father's legacy die. Evan had finally come to terms that his father was gone, but that wouldn't stop him from making his father proud. And if MoonBurst wanted to come into his territory, he was ready for them.

Somehow, some way, he'd find a way to slay that dragon. With Nora by his side, and the love of his father in his heart, he was ready for the fight.

~ ~ ~

An emptiness filled Nora's heart as she headed back to New York. She didn't want to leave Evan and his family. But she still needed time to officially hand in her resignation and move forward. The quicker she got those tasks done, the quicker she could go back to the people who had given her a happy heart.

With the renovations finally under way, Nora left Cedar Ridge and the Bean & Brew in the capable hands of Evan and his friends.

Evan had a lucky bank of friends to count on. Todd and Adam helped on their days off, while Walter, Howard and George came each day to greet customers and residents, giving everyone updates on the store's progress. Molly,

Adam's mother, sent urns of coffee and trays of cookies from the Cookie Cottage, and Nick sent over sandwiches from the Acropolis Diner.

As much as she hated to leave, Nora knew Evan would be all right.

Even Arlene had eventually shown up a few hours each day to "supervise." It gave Nora great comfort that Arlene loved her suggestion of full-wall bookshelves that could be stacked with old classics, a few just-released paperbacks, and a generous set of magazines for patrons to enjoy with their coffee. But, what the woman especially loved were the four overstuffed chairs that were Nora's grand-opening gift. She knew the guys would appreciate them, since the chairs were positioned in a small nook in a cozy corner, giving them a little privacy. Arlene even went to a yard sale and purchased inexpensive end tables for that corner.

Things were magically progressing nicely back in Cedar Ridge. Now Nora needed some of that same magic here at home. She put her bags down on the white living room carpet, placed her mail on the glass console table near the door, and hit the *Contacts* button in her cell. When she pressed *Send*, butterflies danced in her stomach with all the vigor of a freight train.

"Hi, Dad. Am I interrupting something important?"

"Nora! I always have time for my best girl."

Since when?

"Dad, I'm your only girl."

His patented, faux laugh, the one he used on clients when he didn't give a damn about them, rang through the phone. "True. What can I do for you?"

"I'm going to hand in my resignation today."

"It's about time. Does that mean Harrison's finally going to be on my team?"

Why did her family always do that?

"No, Dad." Nora pinched the bridge of her nose and closed her eyes. "This is about *me*, not him."

"Well, yes, of course. I'm sure you two have come to an agreement, so I'll expedite his arrival."

Blowing out a frustrated breath, she rolled her eyes. "We haven't come to anything. I haven't seen or spoken to him in weeks. I'm quitting my job for *me*."

"What about that promotion you were in line for?" His tone softened. "Did you not get it?"

"The promotion is irrelevant." Picking up a letter from her mail, she glanced at it, but really didn't read it. "It's not what I really want."

"Ah, then. That means you're coming to work for me."

Noting the satisfaction in his tone, she slapped the letter back onto the table top and repeated, "No, Dad. I won't. I'm moving. Out of the city."

"So, you'll commute. The island isn't a bad commute. Neither is Connecticut."

"Not the island, and not Connecticut. It's New Jersey." She waited, already predicting his reaction. A few dead seconds clicked by.

"This is a big step," he said quietly. "What company wooed you?"

She chuckled at that, and then cringed as she awaited his reaction. "No company. I don't have a job yet."

The sound of him clearing his throat rumbled through the phone. "Let me understand this. You're moving out of state, to New Jersey of all places, without a job?"

When he put it that way, it did sound irresponsible, but somehow she knew it was the right move.

"There's nothing wrong with New Jersey. Cedar Ridge is a great town with wonderful people. I know I'll be happy there."

"Cedar Ridge? I told your mother you were there, but I thought it was a phase, that you'd leave whenever you got that Aunt Bea, Andy Griffith crap out of your system. I can't believe you want to stay there. It's not even in Bergen County, for God's sake. Have you thought this through?"

She felt the butterflies flitter away as a renewed confidence pushed them aside. "Yes, I have." Quickly she strode to the floor-to-ceiling window overlooking the city, disappointed it wasn't the tree-lined streets of Cedar Ridge. "I'm not asking your permission. I wanted you to hear it from me instead of someone else." Mainly, Harrison. Let's see how that jerk was going to find another way up her father's butt.

"Have you told Harrison yet?"

"No. As I said before, I haven't spoken to him in weeks." She needed to break this connection between her and Harrison once and for all. "Harrison has a vested interest in the Bainbridge fortune, not me. He's played you in hopes of gaining a position by marrying me."

"I know what Harrison's capable of, but your mother assured me that you cared for him. That he's a good fit for you."

There was only one man who was a good fit for her.

Evan.

Because he loved her.

Evan, who knew nothing of the Bainbridge fortune. Who liked that she was independent and could take care of herself. Who was more than willing to share his family with her.

How could Harrison be a good fit? She didn't even know his family. "Look, Dad, Mother and I don't agree on this. I'm going to pick a guy who's trustworthy, loyal, responsible, and who cares about everyone around him. Someone who truly loves me."

"Nora, that kind of guy doesn't exist." The exasperation in his voice came in loud and clear, but then he controlled it. "Well, if you can find one who loves you, grab him. Being loved is very rare."

"I know, Dad." Boy, did she know. Her parents barely spoke to one another over the years. Dad tolerated all the rules and societal etiquette her mother imposed on him and the family. Forced to kowtow to Mother's rules because it was *she* who brought money to their union, who had funded the beginnings of Bainbridge Enterprises with part of the Langston fortune.

"Believe me, Dad. I will hold out for love. Thanks."

When the call ended, she mentally checked that task off her list. Glad that difficult encounter was over, it was now time for the sole reason for her return. Picking up her handbag, she headed for the office.

After the brief, fifteen-minute commute, she was behind her desk, keying in her password on her computer so she could back up all her files onto a flash drive. Before she spoke with Bruce about her resignation, she needed to do some investigating into who had leaked the Expansion Project to the media a few weeks ago. Someone had made her job extremely difficult, and even though she had her suspicions, she wanted to know for sure. A call into *The Star-Ledger* newspaper was in order.

"Hi, Tracey. This is Nor— Eleanor Bainbridge from MoonBurst. I'm calling to double-check the last article we sent you."

"You mean the one about opening the new locations?"

"Yes. I wanted to make sure Lindsay Wilson gave you all the information needed."

"Let me check." After a moment of silence, Tracey said, "Ah, here it is. Harrison sent it. Looks like we have everything, so no follow up is needed."

Yeah, that's what she thought. When Nora heard the name, it confirmed her suspicions. She'd make it a point to let her father know in case if Harrison tried to weasel his way into her father's good graces.

Nora ended the call, took the file folder containing a hard copy of her resignation letter and made her way to the 23rd floor.

Bruce was about to get a shocking surprise.

~ ~ ~

Nora helped as much as she could to rebuild the store. While she had no experience with construction, she cleaned debris, washed and painted walls, and mopped more floors than she ever did in her lifetime. Her mother would be appalled!

With a final sweep of the dining area, she noticed a woman standing in the doorway, curiously looking in the direction of the new reading nook. The grand opening wasn't for another week or two, but the store had been open to the regulars. This woman didn't look familiar.

"Can I help you?" she asked.

"Not really," the woman said, and after a few seconds, she asked, "Is that little girl the owner's daughter?"

Nora glanced at Julie sitting on one of the new upholstered chairs doing her homework. The poor thing was home sick from school again, this time with an ear infection and a horrible cough.

"Yes, she is," Nora said with a touch of concern.

"Is there something wrong with her?" the woman asked in an odd way.

Nora didn't know who this woman was, and with that question, she didn't care to. Why was she concerned about Julie? And what was wrong with the way Julie looked?

"She's fine," Nora finally answered. "She's not feeling well. She's home sick today."

When another ferocious cough barked out from Julie, the woman stepped back with a grimace.

"Don't worry," Nora said. "She's not contagious. Just another one of her ear infections. The cough's a new development, but if you stay on this side of the store, you'll be safe."

"Ugh!" The woman kept staring at Julie. "Does she get sick often?"

"She's a kid. They usually do." *What is her problem?* "Is there something I can help you with?"

The woman crinkled her nose, then pulled her gaze from Julie's direction as if it was painful. "Is her hair always like that?"

Julie's hair looked fine. The usual ponytail was cute with the curly-Q ribbons hanging from it.

Clearly, there was something wrong with this woman, and Nora didn't like the fact that she kept commenting negatively about Julie. Her protective side swelled and she responded from her heart, "She's a great kid. We're very proud of her."

"We?" the woman asked, clearly surprised.

Nora didn't like the tone of that question. "Julie's a special little girl. We all love her."

"And you are . . .?"

What was with this woman? "I'm, ah, a friend of the family."

"The family, as in Evan?"

All right, this was turning awkward. Time to put an end to it. "Yes, Evan and Arlene and Walter, Howard, George, you know. The Bean & Brew family."

The woman eyed her. Somehow Nora thought the woman read more into that statement. Yes, she loved Julie. How could she not? She and the child shared a joint hero worship. But the accusatory questions made the hairs on the back of Nora's neck stand erect. Were her feelings for Evan that apparent that a stranger picked up on them? And was this woman really a stranger?

Nora hesitated, then gave serious attention to the woman. Noticed a familiarity to her face.

Just then, Evan came in the front door after getting lag bolts at Donaldson's Hardware. He stood facing the two women, his eyes narrowed, then his hands started shaking. Nora immediately noticed the skin from his neck up to his forehead turn a purplish red. He looked like he was going to explode. And then . . .

"What the hell are you doing here?"

Chapter 14

"Nice to see you, too, darling."

"You need to leave. Now." Evan reined in the impulse to rattle a few choice words at her. It took all his willpower not to throw his ex's designer ass and Tiffany-coated neck out of his store.

"I'm a customer," Miranda said. "I'm not leaving until I get what I came for."

"We don't serve what you want."

"Well, what I want isn't on the menu." He noticed her eyes trained on his daughter. "Don't go there, Miranda. You walked four years ago. Don't come in here and undo everything I fixed. You didn't want her then, you don't want her now."

"You don't know what I want."

"I know what you don't want, and that's not to be tied down with a family, especially a child. Leave her alone. You've done enough damage."

"Things are different now." She held up her left hand and the blinding sparkle of what seemed like a hundred diamonds glared in his eyes.

"You finally hooked a sugar daddy. Good for you. Now go back to whatever penthouse you flew out of and leave me and *my* daughter alone."

"She looks like me, doesn't she?"

Just then, Julie started a coughing fit and Miranda bristled.

"No. She's a beautiful kid inside and out. She's nothing like you."

Julie's cough became harsher, and Evan was grateful to Nora for rushing to her side with a glass of water and a tissue.

"Oh, now, darling. Don't be bitter. We just wanted different things. There's no reason we can't find some common ground on this."

He moved to within a few inches of her. Her expensive perfume almost choked him. "I'll fight you with everything I've got. Stay away from my daughter."

"Dear, dear, Evan. You won't win this one." She flashed that obnoxious ring at him again in mockery.

"Get out," he said between gritted teeth.

A snarky smile spanned her face and she turned to leave. Over her shoulder, she simply said, "You'll be hearing from my lawyer." Then out the door she went.

Evan's entire body shook. He couldn't even speak when Nora came to his side. His lips trembled uncontrollably and he couldn't see clearly through the tears that flooded his eyes. His worst nightmare had come true. He tried to put it out of his mind for four years, but he knew, in his heart and in his head, that Miranda would come riding in on her broom one day and swoop his daughter out of his arms.

He slowly lowered his body onto the chair that Nora slid close to him. "She's going to take my little girl from me. I've got to get a lawyer," he said in a slow mumble.

"She's not going to take Julie from you. Julie doesn't even know her."

"*You* don't know Miranda. When she wants something, she gets it. That rock on her finger proves it. Bet he's bank rolling the best attorney in New York."

"Don't you have an attorney?" Nora asked.

He shook his head. "Not anymore. Mendelson, the guy who handled everything when she left, died a few months ago. I guess I can call his partner."

Nora walked to the counter, retrieved a pen, and ripped

a blank guest check from its pad. Flipping it over, she wrote a name and number.

"Here." She handed the paper to Evan. "Call this guy. He's one of the best family law attorneys in the city. Call him and you'll never have to worry about losing Julie ever again."

"How? How can you be so sure?"

"Trust me. This guy will make sure you keep your little girl."

~ ~ ~

Two weeks later, Nora sat across from Walter at a table in the Bean & Brew, helping him with his crossword puzzle. Evan walked toward her and handed her a crumbled piece of paper.

"What's this?" she asked, noticing a phone number scrawled in pencil on the sheet that looked like it had been torn from a guest check notepad.

"Amanda Russell has an apartment for rent. It's about five houses away from the inn on Primrose Lane."

"Primrose Lane would be perfect." Two blocks shy of the village center, but still residential. A great location to ease her into small-town living. And with living so close to the inn, maybe she'd be able to foster a friendship with Sarah. "I still have three months left on my lease, but my landlord said if I get someone to take it, I can leave before that. When's it available?"

"End of the month. Right after Thanksgiving. And speaking of being thankful, I need to thank you for giving me that attorney's name. He seems to think my chances of winning are really good. Pretty impressive, too. Hunter Bainbridge? How'd you get a connection like him?"

Uh-oh. Yes, she knew she'd taken a chance referring Evan to her brother, but Hunter was the best and Evan and Julie deserved the best. She was grateful her brother agreed to keep her identity a secret. But he'd made her promise to level with Evan which she had every intension of doing soon.

And Thanksgiving? She hadn't realized the holidays were coming so soon.

"Nora, are you going to have Thanksgiving with us?" Julie asked as she sat on the other side of Nora, coloring a fraction worksheet.

"We always have room for one more," Evan said, wagging his eyebrows. "Fight you for the drumstick."

"You can have the drumstick. I'm a breast girl when it comes to turkey."

He leaned close and whispered in her ear, "I'm a breast guy, too."

She smirked and playfully smacked him on the arm. "I know you are."

Thanksgiving.

Time to give thanks. Thanks to the Cavanaughs for including her. Thanks to the people of Cedar Ridge for embracing her. Thanks that Bruce didn't have a coronary when she handed him her resignation.

Coronary, no. Payback, yes.

The man had her do every last bit of work possible before she left. Her last two weeks at MoonBurst not only fried her brain, it also kept her from coming back to Cedar Ridge, until now. When she had finally arrived this morning, the Bean & Brew gang practically rolled out the red carpet, treating her like royalty. Her own family never behaved that way on the rare occasions that they saw her.

Her family.

Thanksgiving.

Spending a home-town Thanksgiving with Evan and Julie would be a dream come true, sharing a loving family holiday.

But she *did* have a family, even though the five of them seldom acted like one. The thought of their typical stuffy

Thanksgiving gave her pause. Mother meticulously dressed, Daddy grumbling that he needed to make a business call to Europe. Hunter still trying to convince them he was gay, her parents still refusing to believe him, and, if they were lucky, Dalton would be there. No, that was unlikely since he made it perfectly clear he wanted no part of the "family charade."

Nora inwardly cringed at the thought that she'd be forced to forego her laid-back, friendly "Nora" identity for uptight *Eleanor.* The five of them, all dressed in their holiday finery, taking their assigned seats at the elaborate table set for twenty in their lavishly appointed dining room, befitting the perfect photo cover for *Better Homes & Gardens.*

Her family would politely eat the perfectly prepared meal that Mother's cook toiled over, and her mother would gush like she had created it herself. Stilted conversation with everyone acutely aware of the land mines that lurked below the surface.

Thanksgiving in the Bainbridge household. Truly nothing to be thankful for.

She'd choose a casual, homespun dinner cooked by Arlene any day, especially since Nora truly enjoyed Sunday dinner with them a few weeks ago. She could practically smell the bird roasting in the oven, Arlene fussing over the rest of the meal dressed in her comfortable elastic-waist pants and turkey-embellished sweatshirt. Julie would be excitedly watching the Macy's Thanksgiving Day Parade in her pajamas, while Evan patiently waited for the plethora of football games to begin as soon as Santa made his end-of-the-parade appearance. Just the thought of Evan sitting casually on the sofa with his hair tousled, his T-shirt and jeans tightly molding his body, his bare feet resting on the coffee table. Oh, it made her heart yearn to be with him.

It would be just what she always wanted: a loving family living in a real home.

Her mind drifted to how she Nora, not Eleanor, could arrange to spend the day with Evan instead of her family. Snuggling with him on the sofa after the holiday meal, maybe have him come back to the inn. Waking up in his arms the next morning, the official start of the Christmas season, would be such a cherished gift. But, of course, she knew that couldn't happen. He needed to be home with Julie. *But a girl can dream, can't she?*

"What do you say?" Evan asked, a smoldering gaze colored his eyes with just a hint of mischief in them.

"Puh-lease?" Julie sing-songed.

"Let me see what's happening with my family, and I'll let you know. Deal?"

Julie bounced her head in a sharp nod. "Deal!" She slid from her seat next to Nora and hopped to one of the comfy chairs in the nook with George and Howard.

Evan took advantage of the empty seat then moved his arm around her shoulders and kissed her temple. He'd been doing that sort of thing all day since she returned, and it gladdened her heart that he had no problem letting others know they were together. Not like Harrison. He'd proposed numerous times, yet never showed any signs of affection. *That's because Harrison was a business deal. Evan is the real deal.*

"I really like the changes you suggested for the store," Evan said. "The guys like them, too."

She glanced at Walter across from her who nodded and grinned, then at George and Howard seated in the grouping of upholstered chairs. They seemed to enjoy the comfy nook that Evan, Adam, and Todd built in the far side of the table area.

"I see they claimed their own spots. It's nice of them to allow Julie the extra seat." She leaned in close. "Who do they let sit there when Julie's at school?"

"No one. It's reserved for Ma so she can get off her feet and relax when the store's quiet."

"Well, the store doesn't look like it's ever going to be quiet again. You haven't even had your grand re-opening and business is already brisk."

"Yep, sure is. Speaking of which, I better go help Ma." Before he rose, he quickly kissed her on the mouth.

The bubble of joy that filled her had her giggling like a sixteen-year-old. Her life had completely turned around. Right now, her time would be consumed with looking for a new job, finding a new place to live, and starting a new life with a man who truly loved her. The only thing she had to do was come clean and tell him who she *really* was and why she *really* came to Cedar Ridge. In fact, tonight seemed the best time to do it.

She quickly grabbed his arm to halt him. "Is it possible for you to come by the inn tonight?"

He wagged his eyebrows at her again. "I thought you'd never ask."

"Well, that, too. But we need to talk about something first."

His eyebrows knit together and he frowned. "Sounds serious."

"Yes, and no." Oh, yeah. It was serious, but with all the love between them, she couldn't help but be optimistic. "I don't think it's anything we can't resolve."

"Okay. Tonight it is."

"Thanks."

When he turned to go back to work, she took a cleansing breath. The sooner she told him why she'd come to the village, the sooner they'd be able to get past the dishonesty that threatened their relationship.

Evan deserved to know the truth, especially since her alliance was with him now, not MoonBurst.

She just hoped he'd understand she never intended to hurt him or his family. Her initial mission was to put him out of business, but falling in love with him changed all that. That's why she helped him rebuild his business after the fire. That's why she quit her job. Now all she had to do was help him fight MoonBurst, and then they'd be able to live happily ever after.

Yes, it could all work out, just as long as he was receptive when she finally told him the truth.

~ ~ ~

Yesiree, life was back on track, and this time, Evan had Nora to share it with. Just thinking about tonight had his insides jumping around like the beans in his new grinder.

She'd seen him at his lowest after the fire when he was all moody and depressed, yet she stuck around anyway. He'd be eternally grateful for the help she gave not only him during that time, but to his mother and Jules, too.

And during the rebuilding, her suggestions to add a few special sandwiches, a full line of teas, and a few frou-frou coffees perked up the menu that went along with the new perked up décor. After next week's grand re-opening, hopefully nothing would stop him. And for that nagging 300-pound gorilla in the room—MoonBurst—he'd handle that when the time came.

For now, his thoughts and energies had to be on increasing his customer traffic, which swelled solidly each time the door opened. A quick glance at the line of tourists in town for the weekend Harvest Festival, and Evan said a silent prayer that this constant flow would continue. Even a few suits from the new office building decided to venture over. Nora probably told everyone who worked with her there to check out his new store. It filled him with pride that she'd always be there for him, looking out for his best interests.

"I see everyone is enjoying themselves," one of the suits said as he approached the counter.

"We aim to please," Evan responded, happy at the upturn of his business. "What can I get you gentlemen?"

"Large black regular," the heavyset guy answered.

"Here or to go?"

The man looked around the table area and shrugged. "Why not? Let's have it here."

The men with him nodded their approval.

"Black straight up it is." Evan reached for a Bean & Brew mug, and just as he placed the cup under the grinder spout, the man called over to him to stop.

"Wait, change that. Nutmeg Pumpkin, light and sweet with a milk foam," the guy said in a rush, then let out a boisterous laugh as he joked with his friends, all of them seeming to laugh at Evan.

"Got it." *Yeah, I got it all right.* The guy would have to try harder if he planned to give Evan a hard time. He quickly made the Nutmeg Pumpkin coffee order and presented it to the customer. "Here ya go. One Nutmeg Pumpkin Latte."

"Did I say latte?" The guy raised an eyebrow and turned his attention to his friends who all shook their heads like the good minions they were. "I'm sure I didn't say latte."

"You're right, you didn't. But coffee light and sweet with a milk foam is a latte. I'm sure you're aware of that."

"Humph." The guy reached into the pocket of his suit jacket for his wallet.

Evan hadn't seen a wallet retrieval from a suit jacket since he worked in the city. He eyed the guy. Custom suit, manicure. Wasn't from around here. Doubted he even worked in the village office building.

The orders from the guy's friends went quickly, a few laughs projected again toward Evan, but he let them roll off his back. They'd be on their way soon enough.

The men laughed in loud conversation as they stood near the counter waiting for an available table. When they finally sat, their conversation noticeably turned to whispers and stares.

What the hell is that all about? Evan thought.

One of the guys motioned his chin toward the nook area as another aimed his finger in the same direction. George, Nora, and crew were unaware they were the topic of discussion, especially since Nora had her back to them. Evan doubted she even knew they were in the store. But why the attention on his friends?

He kept pace with the line of waiting customers, his mother struggling to fill pastry and bagel orders. Adding a limited number of sandwich choices to the menu had helped increase sales. Yeah, the workload also increased, which made keeping up with the demand of a long line somewhat difficult, but the profits were well worth it.

The line grew longer as the minutes clicked by, and he hadn't time to give those suits a second glance. Nora slipped behind the counter. "How about we break up the system? You're the coffee master," she said to him. "You do coffee, I'll do sandwiches. Is that okay?"

"You don't mind?" he asked.

"I can't sit and socialize while you two are going crazy. It's the least I can do."

"Okay. Great." He turned and yelled to Arlene, "Ma, you stay on pastries and bagels."

"Got it," his mother responded as if she were relieved to have some of the pressure lessened.

As the three of them danced into a rhythm churning out orders, Evan loved the team work. So unlike Miranda, Nora got right in and worked her butt off. Not only was she the creative idea person she claimed to be, she was also a hard worker.

"Grilled chicken with roasted peppers and basil," Evan called to Nora.

"Do you want that plain or spicy?" she asked.

He abandoned the peppermint coffee order he was preparing and leaned in next to her. "The customer wants it plain, but I'm partial to spicy."

"Not in front of your mother," she whispered.

"Hey, Ma's cool with it." And he thanked his lucky stars she was. He laughed and went back to his order.

"I haven't seen you this happy in years," Arlene said, placing a plated, tissue-wrapped bear claw on the prep counter to complete his coffee order.

He glanced over his shoulder at Nora, who was talking with a customer. "She's everything I've ever wanted."

"I'm so glad to hear that. We love her, you know."

"And—" He leaned to kiss his mother's cheek. "—I love her, too. Plan on another place setting for Thanksgiving."

"She's coming?" Arlene asked in surprise. "What about her family?"

"Not sure." Wow, the mist of the strong mint aroma hit his nostrils as the coffee rushed into the cup from the spout. "Jules invited her and she didn't say no." He quickly placed a top on the disposable cup.

"Well, it would be nice," his mother said. "But I'd still like to know why she wouldn't spend the holiday with her parents."

Pulling a brown bag from the shelf above the prep station, he placed the coffee and pastry into the bag. "I'll ask her later, okay? Then I'll report back."

"I don't want a report, I'm just curious."

Evan raised both his eyebrows at his mother, thinking, *Yeah, sure.*

"Stop that." She glared at him. "I care about her."

"And I appreciate that. Don't worry, everything will be fine."

"Hey!" Evan jumped as Nora backed into him, her body trembling as if it was hot-wired. "What's going on?"

"I'm n-not sure. I-I'm not feeling well."

"Hold on." He dropped the bag on the counter and retrieved a stool from the side wall. "Sit down."

She did so, but all color drained from her face. He wasn't sure if she was going to puke or pass out.

Evan ignored the line of customers and drew a glass of water for her, but she refused it.

"Take some deep breaths," Arlene said, also turning her attention to Nora.

Within a few minutes, Evan heard grumbling from the line of customers.

"I'll be right with you, folks," he yelled, knowing he couldn't let them down, but his concern for Nora was his main focus at the moment. Her hands trembled and her coloring hadn't returned yet.

"Excuse me, everyone," someone from the table area called out. "I understand your disappointment in not getting service."

Evan looked past the line of customers to see the heavy-set suit standing as if he were going to give a speech. "Let me reassure you that you won't have to go through this inconvenience in the future. MoonBurst Coffee will be opening just down the street in two short months. You'll never have to wait for service again. That's my promise to you and the MoonBurst brand."

The crowd briefly remained silent, then Evan saw a few go to the guy to ask questions while others shook their heads in disbelief. The guy's proclamation sucker-punched Evan, momentarily leaving him dumbfounded.

"Evan, is that true?" a lady in the line asked.

"N-No. MoonBurst hasn't been approved yet," he said in a rush. In his mind, he tried to deny it, tried to remain optimistic, but his last visit with the planning board hadn't gone well. MoonBurst all but had it in the bag.

What was wrong with him? Yeah, he wasn't on his game because of the pressure of possibly losing Julie, but his new lawyer assured him it would all work out.

Damn. How many catastrophes could one guy handle at a time? His business was under attack and he stood rooted in his spot, letting that corporate asshole all but close him down. Snapping out of the nightmare that now became his life, Evan needed to take control of the buzzing confusion in his store, take back control of his business.

He stepped close to the counter and raised his arms to gain everyone's attention. "Folks, there may have been rumors about MoonBurst, but nothing's firm yet."

"Uh-huh. I beg to differ," the guy said with a mocking laugh. "The plan has been in the works for months. And thanks to Eleanor, it's a done deal."

"Eleanor?" Evan asked. "Who's Eleanor?"

The guy pointed his finger in the direction behind Evan. "Your new employee."

"What new . . .?" He glanced at Nora sitting on the stool. Her skittish expression and pasty pallor silently screamed something was terribly wrong.

She slowly rose, clutching her stomach, and crept near him behind the counter.

"That's what I wanted to talk to you about tonight," she whispered.

He turned to her. "You're Nora. Nora Langston. What the hell is he talking about?"

"Nora?" The blowhard came closer without Evan realizing. "She's Eleanor Bainbridge. An employee of MoonBurst."

"*Former* employee," she corrected, but she didn't look Evan in the eye.

Gradually, confusion turned to anger, slowly churning to a boil in his gut. Had everything she told him about herself been a lie? Was it all a scam?

"Maybe so, but you did your job well." The suited asshole turned to address the customers. "Now let me reassure everyone, MoonBurst will take care of all your beverage needs just after the new year. Be sure to look for our grand opening with our new menu."

The inside of Evan's body erupted into an uncontrollable rage. He'd known better not to trust another woman, but he so badly wanted someone to love, he allowed himself to be led into the biggest betrayal of his life. What Miranda did to him was nothing compared to what Nora, or Eleanor, or whatever the hell her name was, had done.

"Evan, let me explain," Nora pleaded.

When she went to place her hand on his arm, he snapped it away, almost stumbling.

"Is that why you suddenly felt sick?" he asked in disgust. "You knew he was going to make that announcement."

"No. No. I didn't. When I saw him, I had no idea why he was here. He was upset when I handed in my resignation two weeks ago. Remember I told you that?" She stepped toward him and the sorrow in her eyes did nothing to convince him her act wasn't part of the master plan.

"Don't." He raised his hands to block her from coming nearer, then lowered them both and said through gritted teeth, "Get out. Get out of my store."

"Evan, no," she pleaded. "You don't mean that."

He couldn't look at her. It hurt too much, and the anger erupting inside him made it hard to remember he was a gentleman.

"Get out," he whispered. "And don't ever come back again."

Chapter 15

Nora's entire world crumbled when she saw the hurt flaring on Evan's face.

She'd wanted to be the one to tell him who she really was and why she ended up in Cedar Ridge. But Bruce had a different plan for her. One that apparently included revenge.

Why?

Why had he come to the village? How did he know to find her here? Why would he purposely hurt Evan by publicly announcing he intended to put him out of business?

It was unethical and cruel.

But at least it was straightforward and honest.

Unethical and cruel belonged to her. She'd been the one who lied. The one who'd snuck around in plain sight collecting information to supply to the company. The one who'd known how vehemently Evan distrusted women, yet she'd continued the lie, earning his trust, taking advantage of him in order to delay the truth.

None of that had been her intention, nor had it been her intention to fall in love with him and his family. But it had happened, and now all of them would have to live with the scars from her deception.

Nora haphazardly scanned the store for Arlene, finally settling her dazed stare on the woman. The hurt displayed on her face plunged into Nora's heart as she focused on the sadness in Arlene's eyes. She knew that look all too well. Had received it hundreds of times from her father.

Disappointment.

Not only had she deceived Evan, she had deceived his mother, the woman who'd opened her heart and accepted Nora for who she was, with no expectations other than just being herself. The woman had showered her with an unconditional acceptance that she'd never had from her own family.

Nora tried to peer through the thick saltiness of heavy tears. Scanned the crowded store for the little person who unexpectedly changed her life.

Julie.

They had shared so much. One of the happiest days of Nora's life was when Julie shared her doll collection and her special secret. Nora's heart had ached for the void Julie obviously felt, but that same heart had rejoiced because Julie had trusted her.

Now, because of her, that precious child would never trust her again.

Nora continued to search the sea of faces that glared at her now, searching for one more glimpse of the little girl. Before coming to Cedar Ridge, she never imagined herself having children, but Julie changed it all. Now, not having the chance to be a mother to Julie, not having Evan in her life, caused a stabbing pain to slice through her.

Finally, through the cloud of tears, she found her. Exactly where Julie was supposed to be—in the arms of her father. Evan knelt next to his daughter, his arms around her tiny neck, his lips moving. As he had done in the past, Nora knew he was reassuring his daughter in that soothing tone he used to comfort Julie, telling her everything was going to be all right.

But it wouldn't be all right.

Nora ached to run to them, to tell them how sorry she was and how wrong she had been in the beginning and how she loved them both so much that she planned to give up her life in the city to settle in Cedar Ridge with them.

But that was all a dream now.

A fairy tale without a happy ending.

The sobs she tried to force down revolted, causing her chest to heave. She clutched her stomach at the pain radiating across her middle and choked as her breath grew heavy and labored. Tears blurred her vision and she hopelessly turned toward the door, knowing she had to leave, but not being able to take the first step away from everyone and everything she truly cared about.

The weight of everyone's judgmental eyes cloaked her with awkwardness and ridicule. Never had she been so ashamed of her actions. Regret pounded her head and heart. If she had only fessed up sooner, then maybe, maybe she wouldn't have been shunned by Evan, and maybe, being honest wouldn't have had the impact of Bruce's grand stand for revenge.

But maybes didn't cut it in the real world.

Gathering her dignity, she dragged herself to the door. As her trembling hand reached for the bar across the glass door, Nora turned her head back one more time, for one more look at the family she had lost. One more look at the man who was nothing at all what she had initially wanted, but everything she now loved. His glare told her loud and clear that he wanted nothing more to do with her. Arlene's bewildered gaze confirmed the distrust that most likely formed in the woman's heart; and Julie, the sight of the downcast expression on her quivering lips and sad eyes shattered Nora's heart into a million pieces. She had hurt that darling little girl.

Nora squeezed her eyes tight as she turned away and took that final step out of the Bean & Brew, away from everything dear to her. Once on the sidewalk into the cold, overcast fall day, she cried out the pain of her broken heart. She didn't give a damn about her public show of emotion. This pain, this emotion, was totally appropriate.

If there was one thing she'd learned from Cedar Ridge, emotional involvement meant you were truly alive. But without Evan and the Cavanaughs in her life, she felt as if she had nothing left.

~ ~ ~

"Son of a b—"

A few hours later, Evan glanced at the blood on his hand, the one he just slammed into the wall.

It had taken all his strength to keep his reaction concealed, not to scare his daughter and explode in front of her. And especially to keep his cool in front of a store filled with unsuspecting customers. None of them understood the fury that boiled below his skin. He had waited until closing, and with each minute that clicked by, the boil's intensity increased.

Yeah, they all heard that asshole's announcement that MoonBurst would be riding into town like a hero to save the day. And everyone thought the possibility of losing his business was what sent his mood south and his temper short.

His gaze glanced toward the nook.

"I can see an L-shaped bookshelf right here."

It had been a mere three weeks since Nora shared her idea of the nook, her eyes brimming with excitement.

"And a few comfy chairs right here."

Her enthusiasm had guided him to make her vision a reality. She and his mother had been so proud when they found the perfect chairs on a joint shopping spree. *"I just love them,"* Nora had said.

And all he could think of at the time was how much he loved her. How happy and complete she made him. How she had helped him get a lawyer who would keep him and Julie together. How good it felt to be able to open his heart and trust again. Love again.

Now that thought sent his anger raging through his body

as he stormed toward the nook. Books flew off the shelves, the chairs landed sideways, toppled in a fit of rage.

He found himself surging toward the blackboard, smearing the new sandwich choices from the black slate with the sleeve of his flannel shirt.

Zeroing in on the back of the store, he headed straight for the sandwich prep station he custom built to *her* specifications. Packages of artisan breads flung through the air, condiment bottles tumbled to the floor like struck bowling pins. If he could, he would have hurled the brand-new sandwich/salad refrigerator Nora insisted he buy across the kitchen, but that wasn't a good life choice since the damn thing was at least three hundred pounds of stainless steel.

He foolishly thought he had a future with Nora. Thought he had found a true partner. Thought he'd be able to give a loving mother to his little girl. He was so wrong.

He looked around at his empty store, void of customers, and realized the symbolism of all the new items discarded and strewn around.

"Empty, just like it will be when MoonBurst opens. And a mess, just like my life."

He slumped against the metal cabinet across from the new grinder and slowly slid down until his butt hit the floor. He stared up at the wooden mug holder he had painstakingly restored after the fire. His eyes bounced to the holder and the picture of his father secured to the wall. His vision clouded and he wiped his eyes with the back of his hand.

"I'm sorry, Dad. I tried. I wanted to make you proud. I wanted to find what you and Mom had." Hot tears streamed down his cheeks, their saltiness seeping into his mouth. "I guess I was naïve to believe I found it. I'm sorry."

He heard the creak of the new back door. Lowering his head, his hands went over his ears. Whoever it was, he wanted them gone. "Go away!"

"Oh my now. Would you look at this mess."

Evan released the tight cupping of his ears, but kept his eyes closed. "Walter, this isn't a good time."

"Oh, I'd say it's the perfect time," the elderly man said in his usual gentle tone. "I figured you needed this."

Evan felt the soft kicking of Walter's shoe against his own to gain his attention. He didn't want to be disrespectful, but he didn't feel like socializing right now. "It felt good when I trashed it, but it's gonna be a bitch to clean up."

"That's not what I'm talking about."

Evan finally opened his eyes, realizing puddles of mustard, chipotle mayo, and some other strange messes were at his feet. He glanced up at Walter standing nearby. Light bounced off the six-pack of brown glass bottles his friend held out to him.

"When a man grieves, he does it alone so no one sees," Walter began. "The way I figure, you've got two issues going on. Nora and the store."

"No. I have one. The store."

Walter popped the twist top off a bottle and offered it to him.

Evan pulled his body from the crap on the floor, ignoring the mass of sticky gunk on the butt of his pants, and took the beer. "Thanks."

Walter nodded. "You know, son, we're all hurting in one way or another. Your mom's hurting because she misses your dad. I'm hurting because I miss my Dolores."

"It's not the same."

"Maybe. Maybe not. But the difference is that *we* give into the grief instead of fighting it."

Evan took a swig of beer, resisting all of Walter's logic. "I'm going to lose my store. How does giving into grief stop that?"

"It might not. But by fighting the grief, and not acknowledging it, you also can't open your head and heart to find a solution."

"I tried." He took another swig and glanced at the shambles that was his business. All the beer in the world wouldn't make the pain go away.

"You did." Walter patted him on the shoulder. "And your father would have been proud. But you're not finished."

Evan glanced at Walter then. "How so?" Every time he thought he was making progress with the business, something came along to set him back. After this blow from Nor— Eleanor and MoonBurst, he knew he had lost the battle.

"You're letting this thing with Nora cloud your judgment."

"Her *name* is *Eleanor*. And I'm not letting her cloud my judgment." He rotated the bottle in his hands, trying to stave off his nervous energy. "She's not real. She's a manipulator in the destruction of my business."

"Well, it might look like that now, but think back. She did help you."

"Helped with what?" He frowned at his friend, knowing Walter was wrong on this one. "Building my hopes so she can watch them crumble? What kind of person does that?"

Walter's dark-brown eyes turned an expectant gaze at him. "Did you let her explain?"

"There's nothing to explain." Evan placed the bottle on the counter and ran both hands through his hair, then cupped the back of his neck. "She set me up."

Walter shook his head. "Things aren't always so clear cut. There's always an angle we don't see."

"You mean the one where she pretended to care about this place?"

Walter shook his head again. "I don't think she pretended. She wouldn't have stood by you through all the rebuilding if she was pretending. And she wouldn't have helped out Arlene and Julie the way she had if she didn't care."

Walter did have a point. Maybe she did care about his mother and Jules. But there was no way he'd be convinced she cared about the Bean & Brew. That was all a ruse to have him believe they could work side by side, that she . . .

Damn. She had lied. She led him to believe she loved him.

His frustration returned again, but he needed to rein it in. The store couldn't afford more damage than he already inflicted, and Walter didn't deserve to witness another shit fit from him. "I was played, Walter. Plain and simple." And it hurt like hell.

"I wouldn't be so quick to judge," the older man said with a pointed finger. "I think she was honest in her feelings for this place, and for you and Julie."

Were Walter's former cop instincts kicking in, or . . .? "I think you've got a soft spot for her because she brought you cornbread."

"Could be," Walter said with a smile. "But I'm a pretty good judge of character. There's a genuineness about her. She tries hard not to let her emotions get the better of her, but they do."

"I think you're looking for something that isn't there."

"Maybe. But she did bring you out of your self-imposed exile. That has to count for something. And she did get that fancy city lawyer to help you with Julie."

Evan thought about that for a minute. Nora taught him to trust again, only to be crushed. Again. She taught him to be open to change, but that change wasn't going to do any good because she made sure her company would put him out of business. And now, she had him second-guessing if his lawyer was on the up and up, or just another scam.

What a fool.

Walter could make all the excuses he wanted when it came to Nora. As far as he was concerned, she was a fraud and no longer existed.

~ ~ ~

She cried herself to sleep, but after what seemed only a few minutes, Nora was awake again, reliving Evan's last words.

"Get out. And don't ever come back again."

Each time she recited those harsh words in her head, the pain sliced through her heart again and again. The one and only man she ever truly loved now hated her.

Her tireless effort to control her feelings now collapsed in a heap of sorrow and disappointment. She had royally screwed up her life.

No one was to blame but herself. She'd come to Cedar Ridge with the intent of putting Evan out of business, just like she'd done several other times in several other towns. Each time, she purposely blocked out how it affected each shop owner. It was neater that way. She didn't have to deal with the guilt associated with her actions. Her career goals had been at the financial and emotional expense of someone's hard work.

But it backfired terribly this time.

This time, she'd broken all the rules her father had taught her. No emotions, no second thoughts, no involvement. Go in, get out, and collect your reward.

Except this time, she reaped the unexpected reward of falling in love which was so much more valuable than money.

The love of a good, decent guy was far more priceless than a promotion to the 23rd floor. For once, she felt loved, truly loved. For once, she felt she belonged, was accepted for who she was. And finally, after all these years, she had the courage to tell her mother to back off and let her live her own life.

With Thanksgiving right around the corner, this was the season of thanks. But suddenly Nora had nothing to be thankful for.

Everything good in her life was all gone. The family she admired, respected, and loved wanted nothing to do with her. The hatred on Evan's face cut through her heart, dissecting it into a million pieces, never to be healed again.

Evan had been in love with Nora. Right now, she wasn't sure which person she truly was. Eleanor lived life as others expected. Nora lived with an open heart and open mind, free to live as *she* chose. And Nora wouldn't roll over and accept that there was nothing she could do.

"How am I ever going to get him back?" She hugged her pillow and rolled over on her side. "I can't live without him, without Julie."

Her eyes searched for the answer in Room #6 for one last night. She couldn't give up. She had excelled at everything in her life. Loving Evan was the most important of all, and she couldn't let him go without a fight. She longed to be with him, to grow old with him, raise Julie, and give her a few siblings. To be mothered by Arlene, maybe capture some of that Cavanaugh strength that kept them close and able to take on the world.

So why wait? If she wanted to be a Cavanaugh, she had to think like a Cavanaugh. She needed to think like the fighters the three of them were. How they turned each bad situation around that was thrown at them.

Evan's determination to take on MoonBurst was the same kind of resilience she needed to get him back.

If she loved him, she had to fight for him. And the only way she could prove to him that she truly did love him was to help him fight for his business.

For several hours, possibilities ping-ponged through her brain as her heart ached. And as dawn finally broke and peeked through the blinds of the room's windows, she was almost sure she knew how to do it.

Nora, not Eleanor, intended to win back the man she loved.

~ ~ ~

At 6:15 a.m., Evan already felt as if he'd put in a full day at the Bean & Brew. Last night, after Walter left him in the rubble of his store, he spent hours cleaning the mess, then finished it off by coming back in at 4:00 a.m. It was his mess. He needed to clean it alone. Besides, the hard work took his mind off the possibility of losing his daughter. With everything coming at him at once, it was a miracle he hadn't lost his mind.

Hours later, when his mother walked into work, she obviously noticed a few spots on the new upholstered chairs, but she'd been kind enough not to bring it up.

As customers, friends, and family came into the store, they had tiptoed around yesterday's events, and Evan was just about ready to punch something over the frustration of again having to hold it all together, pretending everything that went down yesterday never happened.

"How you doin', buddy?" Todd joined him behind the counter and gave him a concerned-brother type pat on the shoulder.

"I've been better." Even when Miranda had walked out on him and Jules, it didn't feel like this. Oh, it had hurt, hurt like hell, but it hadn't surprised him because his marriage had been having problems for a few years as he and Miranda had slowly grown apart.

But this . . . He hadn't been ready for this. Being blindsided and lied to by Nora had his heart aching and his ego obliterated. How could he have been so stupid to trust another woman and let his daughter be so vulnerable to be hurt again?

"Hey, you got a minute?" Todd asked. "I need to talk to you about something."

Evan recognized that look. It was the same somber expression that was on Todd's face the night of the Bean & Brew's fire. Evan nodded, jutting his chin toward the table reserved for Julie's homework. "We can go over there."

He purposely settled himself on the chair with his back to the store. He'd had enough sympathetic eyes on him during the morning rush and wasn't in the mood to see any more pouty glances, hoping they wouldn't ask questions, questions he had no answers for.

He stared at the new faux marble tabletop, the one Nora had insisted would make the new store décor pop. She was right, but he tried to shake it off. Every inch of the store was a giant reminder of her, so he pulled his attention to Todd who sat across from him. "What's up?"

Todd let out an exasperated whoosh of breath. "The, uh, day of the blind taste test." The uncomfortable silence was only a few seconds, but to Evan, it felt like a lifetime. *Come on, man, get on with it.* "Nora told me something that I promised not to tell you."

Evan squinted at his friend. "What are you talking about?"

Todd's clasped hands fidgeted on the tabletop, then his gaze roamed out over the store. After a minute, he looked directly back at Evan. "I called her out on not working at the Medical Arts Building."

"I don't understand," Evan said, because he didn't. Where was Todd going with this?

Todd explained how he had to get to know everyone in the building and how it seemed Nora wasn't employed there. "So I told her I wanted the truth, because no one plays games with my friend."

"I appreciate that," Evan said, still confused. "What did she say when you told her that?"

"I don't know." Todd drummed his fingers on the table top. "Something about starting over here, hiding from her family, so she didn't tell us her real name. There was also something about them wanting her to marry some guy she didn't love. She promised me she was going to tell you after everything calmed down with this MoonBurst bull shit." Todd raked a hand through his hair. "I should have told you about it that day. I'm sorry, man. I really screwed up this one."

Evan hadn't seen Todd so upset and frustrated since his wife had been diagnosed with cancer. He'd been a loyal friend, and Evan knew how convincing Nora could be when she wanted to. "Don't sweat it. We were all taken in by her."

"But if I had told you sooner, you could have stopped her from putting you out of business. And maybe you wouldn't have fallen in love with her."

His friend did have a point. But he also knew in his heart that seeing the way Nora had treated Julie seemed genuine. If he wasn't so damn mad at her, he might be willing to try to look at this entire situation objectively. But she'd broken his heart, and had broken his spirit. "It wasn't love, it was need. There's a difference."

"No, you loved her." Todd shook his head. "And I'm pretty sure she wasn't lying about loving you."

"How can you say that?" Evan snapped. "She didn't even tell me her real name, and that lie about working at the office building . . . She kept that one going for a long time, too."

"I know. But if her story was true about hiding from her parents, that could be why she gave her nickname. Didn't you say she had problems with her family?"

The day her mother had come to the Bean & Brew popped into his brain. The woman carried a Cruella de Vil attitude, minus the spotted getup. A few heated words had been shared between Nora and her mother, ending with Nora sending her packing. He remembered it had taken a good long while for Nora to calm down after her mother had left.

Was that altercation about a guy? An arranged marriage? "How did she sound when you talked to her about this guy she was supposed to marry?" he asked.

"She seemed really frustrated with her parents. And she pleaded with me not to tell you. I'm pretty sure she was being honest then. She even came clean when I called her out on not working for Medical Arts."

Todd was putting doubt in Evan's mind, and Evan didn't like it. The last thing he needed was hope that maybe all that went down between Nora and him could be resolved. She had taken advantage of him and made a fool of him. He loved her and that played into her scheme to run him out of business. He could deal with what Nora had done to him, but he couldn't handle what her betrayal did to his daughter. Julie finally had a potential mother figure in her life, someone to love her, but it was all a lie. For that, Evan would *never* forgive Nora.

~ ~ ~

Evan had to get out of the store. Business was at a crawl and his frustrated temper from the night before ignited again.

After Todd left and the morning rush settled, Evan left his mother in charge and headed to Wilkensen's Pond, thinking that maybe he could let off some steam with a brisk jog around the water's edge. As he drove past the village municipal building, he slowed his truck, rolled down his window, then stopped. "What's going on?"

Winston Farley's face swelled to an exasperated red as his eyes bulged. "They're protesting! You've got to make them stop!"

"Me? You're the mayor, you stop them." He watched the group slowly walk in a large, single-file circle in front of the municipal building steps. "If I remember my history classes, aren't citizens allowed to protest? What are they—"

That's when Evan noticed the words on one of the posters. Only two were actual poster-size, handwritten in markers. A few people held 8 ½" x 11" sheets of paper that simply read, NO MOONBURST.

"Ah, Winston, I had nothing to do with this." But, it felt damn good though, even if the outcome was doubtful. Evan had lost hope at the meeting, and then again yesterday when that MoonBurst asshole had said it was a done deal.

He scanned the protesters, happy to see a few of his customers. Maybe the situation wasn't as bleak as he thought. With all the community support behind him, maybe now there was a chance.

"You might not have initiated it," Winston continued, "but it's because of you that they're here."

A bright tuft of white hair appeared through the crowd. One by one, people slowly walked and then he saw them. The guys. Howard's white hair in stark contrast to colorful knit hats and dark jackets. His unmistakable, limping gait accompanied by his sturdy, black cane was followed by George raising a sheet of newsprint, then Walter who waved and directed his friends' attention with a point toward Evan.

They hobbled their way to the truck, presenting Evan with grunts and groans as they caught their breath when they finally reached him.

"Gentlemen." Evan nodded. "What's going on?"

"We're protesting!" George said, holding up his newsprint with the words STOP MOONBURST written in wide black marker. He directed it to the mayor. "Exercising our constitutional right to peacefully demonstrate." Walter and Howard nodded, looking like a pair of geriatric bobble-head dolls.

"Did you guys organize this?" Evan asked.

"Nope," they said in unison.

He examined the crowd again. People of all ages participated in the march, but none stood out as someone passionate enough to organize such a thing. Then he looked back at the guys. Their expressions reminded him of the three monkeys: hear no evil, see no evil, speak no evil.

"Okay, I give. Who's in charge of this fiasco?"

The three simply smiled and shrugged.

"Guys?"

"Remember our conversation last night?" Walter finally asked.

"Yeaaah," Evan said slowly, not sure which part of the conversation he was referring to.

"Things aren't always as they seem," Walter said.

Evan's gaze snapped back to the crowd. No. It couldn't be. Nora couldn't have organized this protest. And if she did . . . Why?

"Is she here?"

All three of them shook their heads, disappointment clearly marking their faces. "No," George said, "she left after we got things going."

"Did she say—"

"All she said was that she needed to leave town," George interrupted. "She didn't want to upset you anymore than she already has."

This wasn't the act of someone who intended to put him out of business. Neither were all the improvements she suggested for the store after the fire. Maybe he had been wrong in not letting her explain. But his heart ached so much he just couldn't see past the rage and hurt. Hopefully, that jog around the pond would help him see things clearly.

"You need to think long and hard about all this, Evan," Howard said. "We're here for you."

"I know, guys, and I appreciate it. Thanks for the protest." He shot a glance at Winston Farley. "I hope it works."

Chapter 16

Nora jumped at a knock on her apartment door. The front desk always called her when guests arrived, so it probably was one of the maintenance guys or delivery people. She slowed her breath to calm her nerves and sprinted to the door. A peek in the peephole had her groaning out loud when that 100-watt smile appeared along with an obnoxious wave.

"Eleanor, I know you're home. Now won't you be a good girl and let me in? We have a few things to discuss."

"Oooo . . ." she ground out between her teeth. She needed to deal with this nightmare once and for all. Opening the door, she demanded, "How did you bribe the front desk to let you come up?"

"I told them I have a surprise for you, which I do." Harrison entered her apartment, one arm suspiciously behind his back. "*Voila!*" With a flourish, he presented a small bouquet of Calla Lillies to her.

"Flowers? They let you up here because of flowers?" She refused to take them, then closed the door. Nora knew she shouldn't let him stay, but she needed to finish this chapter of her life once and for all. Channeling her inner Nora, she charged further into the living room, then turned to face him and crossed her arms over her chest. "The only reason I let you in is because we need to end this charade."

"It's not a charade. I never wanted anything more than I want this." Harrison took several large steps toward her, then got down on bended knee. "I know I haven't—"

"What in the world do you think you're doing?" She stepped backward, almost falling over the glass coffee table.

He slid a teal-colored box from his suit jacket pocket and opened it. The gleam of an enormous diamond encircled by an array of equally stunning miniature diamonds caused her to gasp. "Marry me. Make me the happiest man on earth."

A sputter of laughter escaped her mouth. She needed a distraction to take her mind off of Evan, but a marriage proposal wasn't what she had in mind. And certainly not from Harrison! It was Evan she had hoped would propose to her, only Evan. "Happiest man on earth?" she snickered. "I'll bet. You think there's a hefty inheritance attached to me, but do you think I'd actually marry you so you can get your hands on the Bainbridge fortune?"

Harrison rose then and came toward her, but stopped short when she raised her hand to him.

"Not one step closer," she warned.

"Look, I know we've had a few *miscommunications*, but we can work them out," he said in a placating tone. "Now that you're no longer working for the company, I can take care of you, provide for you. We're a perfect match. We *get* each other."

"We *get* each other?" With a head tilt, her eyes squinted and her mind raced to find logic in that statement. But there was none. She shook her head slowly, attempting a final shot to end this fiasco. "You're only half right. I totally get *you*. What you don't get is that I'm not interested. The last thing I need is a man to take care of me. If you truly *got* me, you'd already know that." *I don't need a man, but I do want one, one who doesn't want me.* Nora sighed with a heavy heart.

"What I do know is that your parents have given me their blessing."

Nora peered at him with a sideways glance. "I'm sure my mother was pleased. She was always a sucker for a good-looking guy. But my father . . ." Nora turned and walked to the floor-to-ceiling windows, overlooking the roof-top terrace of the apartment building across the street. The trees reminded her of Cedar Ridge and all the wonderful people who took her in as one of them. Her heart yearned for everyone she left behind. Especially for Evan. Before she knew it, Harrison was at her side, open box in hand, the extravagant engagement ring sparkling in the glow of the city lights.

"Eleanor, this has nothing to do with the Bainbridge money. And I'm sure your father knows that, that's why he's given us his blessing."

She narrowed her gaze at him. "What exactly were my father's words?"

"He's always wanted me to help him run the business. You know he's been after both of us to work for him."

"Oh, you're always well versed in evading important questions, aren't you? I suspect that you're not after the Bainbridge fortune because you know that it's not worth nearly as much as the Langston money, so you came up with this engagement idea and pitched it to Mother, knowing she'd take the bait." She paused a moment and glared at him. "Smart move. But not smart enough. You see, Mother and I aren't seeing eye to eye on things lately. *She* may have loved your plan, but it won't work."

"Your mother assured me that you will be agreeable to our marriage. The woman has always been honest with me, so I'm banking on that honesty now."

"Honesty? What do you know about honesty? You were the one who leaked the merger to The *Star-Ledger,* almost jeopardized my field study. And now you're talking marriage? Did you ever think that maybe love should be part of the equation?"

She took hold of his arm and maneuvered him through the living room to the apartment door. "When I get married, it will be for love, not money. So give that ostentatious piece of jewelry to another heiress. *This* heiress is off the market." She showed him through the open door.

"This isn't over," Harrison said as he walked out of the apartment.

She slammed it behind him.

Glaring at the inside of the closed apartment door, she said, "Oh, yes it is."

~ ~ ~

Thanksgiving.

Was there anything to be thankful for?

When Nora entered her childhood home, that old familiar reflex of tightening her shoulders and stiffening her back kicked in as if it was still a daily routine. The last thing she needed right now was to be a part of this farce Mother called a Thanksgiving family dinner. Didn't matter how elaborate the meal, or how engaging her parents pretended to be, Nora knew she'd still be alone in her heart without Evan in her life. Suffering through another Bainbridge holiday would merely compound her loneliness and depression.

The aroma of a perfectly cooked feast seeped into her nostrils, but she noted it wasn't the typical smells of a traditional Thanksgiving dinner. Every detail of the meal would be flawless from the vichyssoise to the expertly crusted crème brulee.

Ordinary people ate turkey in celebration of the American holiday, but not the Bainbridges. Impeccably roasted pheasant would grace the table, making a statement that the Bainbridges weren't ordinary by any means. For them, Thanksgiving meant four of the five family members struggled to get through yet another holiday unscathed. Her brother Dalton would be a no show, as usual. He had the good sense to stay away and not subject himself to the games mother always played. There would be no love, no laughter, no playing games or watching the Macy's Thanksgiving Day Parade.

Oh, how wonderful it would have been to share Thanksgiving with the Cavanaughs. But Nora had burned that bridge into a pile of ash the minute she lied about who she was. It was naïve to think Evan wouldn't eventually find out the truth. She couldn't blame him for his anger. She deserved it. But that didn't stop her heart from breaking each time she thought of him, each time she remembered being wrapped in his arms, being loved by him. Somehow, some way, she had to get him back. Her heart depended on it.

Inhaling deeply, she made her way beneath the crystal chandelier and tiptoed on the marble-floored foyer toward the kitchen, not wanting her mother to realize she had arrived just yet.

Nora braced herself for the endless lectures on her lack of punctuality and boring stories of Mother's social one-upmanships. And if the subject of Harrison became Mother's obsession again, she'd just get up and leave. There was only so much she could endure in one day.

"Oh, Miss Eleanor," the house mistress greeted her as she came through the swinging kitchen door. "It's so nice to see you!"

"Thank you, Viola." Nora took the woman's two hands in hers and said, "It's so good to see you, too." She leaned in to kiss the older woman on the cheek and noticed she was in her work uniform. "Are you getting any time off today?"

The surprised expression on Viola's face and then the lowering of her eyes revealed how uncomfortable the woman was with the question. "Oh, no, miss," she replied politely. "It's Thanksgiving. Too much to do on such a special day."

Special? Oh, yes, special for Mother. Another chance to wield her power over the household staff. To impress *whom* was the question.

Nora dropped one of Viola's hands and placed her own arm across the woman's shoulders. "Correct me if I'm wrong, but don't you have a few grandchildren?"

The woman's brown eyes beamed with pride. "Yes, I do. Five older and three little ones."

Nora slid her arm from the woman and took hold of her hands again. "So why aren't you spending this family holiday with your family?"

A puzzled frown appeared on Viola's wrinkled face. "Oh, I couldn't do that. Mrs. Bainbridge is depending on me today." She tried to put a smile on her face, but Nora saw that it was forced. "We're celebrating the holiday on my day off next week. Like we always do."

"Next week?" Nora shouted, then lowered her voice again so she wouldn't alert her mother. Although, she heard footsteps moving about in the dining room, which meant her late arrival more than likely caused her mother to be in a snit.

Viola's eyes clouded a little. "Yes. On Monday."

"Monday?" Nora moved a few feet from her, straining her neck to see if anyone was coming from the dining room. "Will your entire family be there?"

No answer.

She came back to face the woman. "Viola?"

"No." She shook her head slowly. "I'm going to my daughter's for lunch, to see the little ones who aren't in school. Everyone else will be back at work."

Ohhh, this wasn't right!

Nothing that had occurred under this roof for the last forty years had been right. Nora suddenly realized that all these years she had taken for granted how Viola and Louise, the family's cook, had put together all of the Bainbridge holidays. How could she have been so blind to see that these women were deprived of spending holidays with their own families? The shame of her own inconsideration overcame her like a tsunami. She had to make this right or she'd be no better than her mother.

"Viola? Is your family celebrating the holiday today?"

The older woman's eyes glistened with tears. She gave one simple nod.

"When was the last time you celebrated a holiday with your family?"

Again, the woman was silent.

Nora swallowed hard, then put her hand on the woman's arm. "It's been a long time, hasn't it?"

With the flood of tears finally breaking through, streaming down her cheeks, Viola raised her gaze to Nora. "Christmas, 1975."

Heaviness plummeted to Nora's heart as she realized how wrong this was. "You started working for my family in '76."

As Viola nodded, Nora took her by the arm and guided her into the dining room where her mother, her brother Hunter, and father were already seated.

"It's about time you've arrived," her mother said. "You're late."

Without a greeting, Nora said, "You need to give Viola and Louise the rest of the day off so they can spend the holiday with their families."

"Don't be ridiculous," Mother tsked. "They're perfectly happy spending the holiday with us." She waved a dismissive, jewel-laden hand at them. "Viola, please tell Louise we're ready for the first course."

"Yes, Mrs. Bainbridge."

Viola nodded and turned to leave, but Nora held her back and glared at her mother. "*Mother* . . ."

After a few heavy seconds, her father interrupted. "Viola, please go into the kitchen and tell Louise to leave the meal. Both of you have the rest of the day off. With pay." He eyed a warning at his wife, then smiled at Viola. "Happy Thanksgiving."

"Thank you, sir. Happy Thanksgiving to you, too."

Viola turned and looked into Nora's eyes with such gratitude, Nora felt as if she'd given the woman a true gift. "Enjoy those grandbabies, today." She hugged the older woman, who then rushed to the kitchen.

"Grandbabies? She's a grandmother?" her mother asked.

"Yes, Mother. She has eight." Nora tightly wrapped her fingers around the back of one of the ornately carved dining room chairs. "How can you employ someone for over forty years and not know that?"

Joan sat straighter, as if stiffening her already rigid back into concrete, and Nora knew she was in for it now. "How can you come into *my* house and give the help the day off?"

"How can you not?" Nora's determination deepened, knowing she was doing the right thing. "It's a holiday. A *family* holiday."

"I agree with Nora," her father said. "Very perceptive of you, princess. Can't believe I never realized it before now."

Nora instantly felt that Cedar Ridge magic working on her again. So many lessons were wrought from her time there. Care and compassion for people, regardless of their social standing, was the greatest lesson of all. Evan taught her that no matter what type of job or how old someone was, everyone needed to be treated with dignity and respect.

Her experience with Arlene, Julie, and especially the guys had taught her the personal satisfaction of being able to help someone like Viola who had been taken advantage of by people like Nora and her family. Correction: people like her mother. Nora no longer wished to be included in the same category as Joan Miller Langston Bainbridge. She wanted to be just plain Nora Bainbridge.

"Have you lost your mind? I don't know what has gotten into you, Eleanor," her mother scolded. "First Harrison, now this?"

The joy Nora felt vanished. "Harrison? What about Harrison?"

"Only that you turned down his proposal and threw him out of your apartment."

"Oh, so he *did* report back to you," Nora said, confirming her suspicions. "He's been buttering you up to get me to marry him."

"So you finally turned him down?" Hunter asked. Her brother knew she had been bucking her parents on this subject for a long time and he had been on her side through the entire ordeal.

"Hold on here," her father said. "Princess, did Harrison ask you to marry him?"

Again, her suspicions were confirmed that Harrison had not spoken to her father about it. Nora stood ramrod straight and summoned all her resolve, ready to do battle with her mother.

She aimed her attention to her father. "Yes, he did. And I did turn him down. He's after the family's money." She turned to her mother. "I don't appreciate you giving him *your* blessing. I've told you, I will *never* marry him."

"I can't believe you gave him your blessing," her father said to her mother. "After all the discussions we had about this over the past few weeks, you still want our daughter to marry that spineless weasel?"

"How dare you yell at me like that." Joan glared at him. "This family has suddenly gone mad." She turned her eyes back on Nora and pointed a finger at her. "Ever since you came back from that horrible little town, you've turned this family upside down."

"No, I haven't." Nora gripped the back of the chair tighter. "I can take care of myself. I refuse to marry someone I don't love. This family is in flux and you won't accept that. It's time we make some major changes."

"I agree," her father said. "And the first thing we're doing is banning Harrison from this family." He peered at his wife from across the table. "Any man who uses our daughter as a pawn and then tattles on her to her mother, is no man I want around my family or my business."

"Thanks, Daddy." With her father solidly on her side, Nora felt the weight from her shoulders lessen.

"Okay, Harrison is gone, and we've given the help the day off," her father confirmed. With his hand outstretched on the table, he smiled. "Sounds like the beginning of a good Thanksgiving."

"*Who* is going to serve dinner?" Mother asked in a huff as she folded her arms across her designer suit, her antique broach gleaming under the chandelier's glow.

"I will." Although Nora was sure Louise had the entire dinner completed and warming by now, she knew she could muddle through it.

"I'll help, too," Hunter said as he got up from his seat. "I do all the cooking at home."

"Really? What chores does Greg do?" Nora asked, opening the door to a conversation she knew would upset her mother, but one that Hunter had been struggling with because Mother refused to engage in such topics.

Hunter winked at her and his smile broadened. "He washes the floors, mows the lawn, and picks up after the dogs. We share laundry duty, though."

The shocked expression on Joan's face satisfied Nora in ways she couldn't explain. Her intention wasn't to upset her mother, but if doing the right thing for Viola and Hunter upset her, so be it.

Exuberant laughter came from the far end of the table easing the tension in the room. "Well played, princess," her father said, joy dancing in his eyes. "Well played."

Nora couldn't help but feel all warm inside. She'd made two truly good people happy today. Of course, her mother would never forgive her, but it was worth it. If she couldn't be with Evan for Thanksgiving, at least being with her father and brother on her own terms might ease the pain a bit. She turned on her heels in search of the first course.

"Hey, if we keep this up," Hunter said, following her into the kitchen, "maybe we can actually have a good Thanksgiving."

"Thanks to you, I know the Cavanaugh's are having a good Thanksgiving." She leaned to give him a hug, grateful for the text he sent her a few days ago with the results. "I owe you big time for that one. Helping Evan keep Julie was monumental." Hunter's determination to keep families together made him tops in family law. All that Bainbridge dis-function fueled his passion to do right by those who were hurting.

"My pleasure. It was the easiest case I've had in a while."

"How so?"

"When I contacted Evan's ex, she said she wasn't interested in custody any longer. Seemed she made up her mind once she saw Julie, but threatened Evan just so she could 'play with his head' as she put it."

"I don't understand. If she wasn't interested in Julie, why did she show up?"

"She has this warped vision to go all 'Kris Jenner' and turn her fiancé's two daughters and Julie into a Kardashian-type dynasty. Her original intent was custody, but once she saw Julie, she said, and I quote, 'All the plastic surgery in the world wouldn't help that kid.'"

Nora felt a stab to her heart on that one. Julie was a truly beautiful child, inside and out. Miranda didn't deserve to be a mother to such a wonderful child.

"So she wants nothing to do with her?"

Hunter shook his head. "Nope. Said 'The kid didn't fit into her grand plan,' especially since her fiancé's middle school-aged daughters are 'the most beautiful creatures on the planet.' She kept thinking Julie was a cute two-year-old she could dress up like a doll."

Nora thought a minute. "That's what Evan said about why Miranda wanted a baby," she murmured to herself. What kind of mother has those thoughts?

Nora remembered when Miranda came to the Bean & Brew. She was grateful Julie had that horrible cough that day to dissuade her mother from pursing custody. Julie was a typical child whose adorable personality made her physically cute. Her wonderful insides made everyone love her. Thank goodness Miranda was too shallow to see that. And thank goodness for that cough. "Does she want to see her again?" she asked her brother.

"No way," he said emphatically. "She's legally liable for child support since Julie's living with Evan. And since she doesn't want any part of the child, I drew up an agreement that waived her child support responsibility as long as she stays away from Julie. It should hold her off for a few years until she gets another hair-brained idea."

"And they don't have to go back into court?"

"As of now, no. If she pursues it, unfortunately, yes. As the biological mother, she's got rights." He studied Nora for a few seconds. "I get the feeling Evan and Julie are much more than just your friends. Are you involved?"

Two weeks ago, that question would have flushed Nora a perfect shade of red and a giddy "yes" would have spurted from her mouth. Today, that same question had her heart plummeting to her feet. "No. Not involved. They're just a wonderful family who deserves a break."

"I know a broken heart when I see one. Want to talk about it?"

Nora shook her head and turned toward the array of food-filled platters on the counter. "We've got a job to do here," she said without looking at him. She couldn't utter a word without a flood of tears letting go.

That's when her sensitive, incredibly perceptive brother took the hint and said, "How about we break tradition and right after the main course, we have dessert in the study and, maybe, turn on the game?"

The game.

The picture of Evan flashed before her eyes. Him holding the remote, his feet up on the coffee table, a beer in his hand. Julie playing with her dolls on the floor under the archway between the living room and dining room, one of her construction paper turkeys from school hanging on the dining room wall. Arlene calling out for an update on the game as she bastes the turkey. The house all warm and steamy from the turkey roasting since breakfast. Oh, how she missed them, but most of all Evan. She could almost feel his arm around her as she cuddled with him on the sofa. It could have been the best Thanksgiving of her life.

"Hey, Ell, you okay?" Hunter asked.

It had been a long time since someone in her family was concerned about her. It felt good, like a Cedar Ridge good.

"I'm fine." She placed her hand on his shoulder and forced her gaze on him. "Let's try to see if we can make the best of this Thanksgiving. And I like your idea of watching the game. Mother will be in a total snit!"

~ ~ ~

A few days later, Nora squeezed the bridge of her nose with two fingers, then massaged both eyes. She devoted a good portion of the morning on her couch typing and clicking her laptop in an unsuccessful quest. The hours spent scouring the internet for job postings in the Cedar Ridge section of New Jersey yielded only three positions with her qualifications. Her decision to give up her life in the city to move to Cedar Ridge with Evan wasn't going as well as she had hoped. She expanded her job search further into the county and even two adjacent counties, but the few she had found were on the ends of both counties. Unfamiliar with those rural parts of the state, she was uneasy with an hour commute each way. Also the twenty-minute Manhattan subway commute to the MoonBurst corporate offices had spoiled her all these years.

But she wasn't giving up. Hope had her organizing the protest last week before she left Cedar Ridge. And hope had her probing her files for anything she could send Evan that would help him fight her former employer. If he didn't want to give her a chance to explain, she was determined to give him something to listen to.

Yes, she had been wrong to deceive him; but that was part of her job. Although, she had gone rogue by getting involved with him, she was pretty sure that was *not* in the MoonBurst Coffee Employee Handbook under her job description.

She placed her laptop on her coffee table and headed for her triple-door, stainless-steel fridge. Opening the bottom freezer drawer, she reached for a carton of BEN & JERRY'S Chocolate Therapy, retrieved a spoon from the white cabinet drawer, and leaned against the gray granite countertop as she plunged the spoon into the frozen treat.

The silky creaminess of ice cream eased her frustrations. The chocolate cookies and chocolate pudding woke up her senses, helping her to think clearer. Some of her best ideas were born at this very spot, with this exact chocolate ice cream. After a few spoonfuls, her cell phone sounded from the living room, vibrating on the coffee table. She scurried into the room and when she recognized the name on the screen, she dropped the spoon and cold container on the table, ignoring the chocolate that ricocheted off the spoon and landed in a happy pile on her white carpet.

"Arlene!?" she answered as her heartbeat kicked into overdrive.

"Hi, Nora," a meek voice greeted. "I mean, Eleanor."

It was Julie!

"It's okay, sweetie. You can call me Nora. My dad calls me that all the time." Her heart rate raced as it thumped in her chest.

"He does?" Surprise rose in Julie's voice. "It's your real name?"

"It's a nickname, like when your daddy calls you Jules." Nora glanced to her bookshelves across the room. So many times this past week she had picked up the stainless root beer mug from that shelf, the one she got at the pumpkin festival with Julie. With each touch, it had caused her to cry.

"Oh, okay," Julie said. "Are you mad I called?"

"No. You can call me anytime," she said then added, "As long as your father knows. I don't want you doing something he doesn't want."

"It's okay. Gramma said I could call. I'm on her cell phone."

"How is your grandma?"

"She's good. She said I need to talk to you, coz I miss you so much."

Nora's heart sank even though she was grateful to hear from her little friend. Friend. Oh, how she had hoped Julie could have been more. Every maternal instinct she didn't know she had kicked into gear whenever she'd been with Julie. "I miss you, too, sweetheart. Did you have a good Thanksgiving?"

"No. It was boring. Daddy and me were sad. Gramma said she needed to cook a lot so she wouldn't be sad." The child fell silent for what seemed a lifetime, but it only lasted a few seconds. "It was no fun without you."

That did it. Nora's tears let loose as her heart broke all over again. Her own Thanksgiving had been better than normal, but it had also been miserable because she wasn't with Evan and Julie. Wiping her cheeks with her fingers, she needed to put her sadness aside and be upbeat for Julie.

"You know what? Mine wasn't fun without you, too. How about the next time you feel sad, you call me? But, only if Daddy lets you. Does that sound good?"

"Yes," she said in a timid tone. "But that means I'll call you all the time."

Oh, boy. While it comforted her to hear that Julie and Evan missed her, Nora needed to bring Julie's normal excitement back. She doubted Evan would let her visit his daughter, but somehow, she needed to do something. *Her* little girl was hurting and not only was she responsible, her heart told her she needed to fix it.

"Julie, I don't know how I'm going to do it, but I promise I'll come up with something to cheer you up."

"O-kay." But the pint-sized munchkin didn't sound convinced. "Nora, can I ask you something?"

"Anything, sweetie."

"Did you lie to Daddy?"

Oh, boy. How could she be honest in a way that Julie could understand? Nora tightly squeezed her eyes and pounded her forehead a few times with her fist.

"Yes, I did," she said in a guilty breath and slowly opened her eyes. "I lied by not telling him who I worked for. You know how I told everyone my name was Nora Langston?"

"Uh-huh."

"Well, my full name is Eleanor Langston Bainbridge. I didn't tell anyone my last name because I didn't want them to find out where I worked. I didn't lie, but I didn't tell the whole truth. Can you understand that?"

"Uh-huh. It's kina like telling Gramma I like her peach pie, even though I like pumpkin better."

Okay, not the same, but heading in the right direction. "Exactly. You didn't tell Grandma because you didn't want to hurt her feelings."

"I never want to do that. She'll cry."

"Good girl. I didn't tell everyone who I was, because I didn't want to hurt them. My job was to see if MoonBurst would work in Cedar Ridge, not to hurt anyone." Yeah, it was a stretch, but sugar-coating it seemed all Julie could handle at her age.

"Okay, good. Coz, I love you, and Daddy loves you, too. Oh, so does Gramma. Can you come home now?"

Home.

That word sounded like heaven, especially coming from the little peanut Nora wanted to mother so badly. No promotion, no pay increase would ever compare to the sound of the child wanting her to come *home*.

Nora swallowed hard and closed her eyes. "I will whenever things get settled." She counted on hope to guide her to tell Julie the right thing. "Until then, you can call me, or even e-mail me. Do you know how to do that?"

"No."

"Okay. Grandma has my e-mail address. Ask her to help you. But remember, only when you have Daddy's permission."

"'kay."

"All right, sweetheart, I'll talk to you soon."

"Bye, Nora. I love you."

"I love you, too."

Nora's hand shook as she pushed the end button and clutched the phone to her chest. Why did love have to hurt so much? She finally found everything that made her happy and she couldn't have it.

Evan had missed her. And he must love her if his six-year-old daughter saw it, too. Hope sprang back into her heart again. There had to be a way she could go "home" to spend the rest of her life with Evan and Julie. A few phone calls and e-mails wouldn't be enough.

Wait.

E-mails.

Nora plopped onto the sofa and clicked through several windows on her laptop screen. She knew that e-mail was here somewhere. When had she received it? Maybe around Halloween? She scrolled down her e-mail inbox. And finally, there it was. The answer she'd been searching for.

Chapter 17

Evan lay on the sofa watching his mother navigate the living room floor, picking up a few beer cans and pushing a pizza box out of her way as she sidestepped the minefield of crap scattered on the carpet.

"Are you going to stew in here all day, or are you going to clean this place up so you can put up a Christmas tree for your daughter?"

He didn't want to hear it right now, so he slung his arm across his eyes. It had been a few weeks since all the shit went down with *Eleanor Langston Bainbridge*. The apparent heir to the Bainbridge Enterprises' Empire must have had a good ol' laugh at his tiny business, tiny house and tiny life.

For several days after she left, he fought the urge to Google her name, but finally gave in when his ego—and yeah, his heart—had him wondering who the hell she really was. He would have been better off not doing the search. With her family's fortune, he wondered why she worked for MoonBurst when she could just sit back and count all her money.

And when he realized she was a Bainbridge, the connection to his lawyer clicked as he realized Hunter Bainbridge, the guy who held Miranda off from snatching Julie from him, was Nora's brother. Evan's involvement with her was so tangled up, his insides felt strangled.

"Julie talked to her, you know," his mother said, yanking the newspaper out from under his feet on the couch.

"What?" He quickly withdrew his shielding arm away from his eyes. "When? Where?"

"On the phone. I gave her permission."

"Ohhh, no." He sprang to sit at the edge of the cushion. "You can't do that. She's my daughter."

"And she's hurting, too," his mother said. "You're both hurting. But you aren't considering her, are you? You're wallowing in self-pity and it's not right." She waded through more crap and turned the wand on the window blinds. Evan squinted and blocked his eyes with one hand as light poured into the room.

She had a point. He couldn't remember the last time he and Jules did something fun since Nora left.

"How's Jules takin' it? The call, I mean?"

"She's fine. I probably should have let her do it sooner because it made her feel better. It would have saved the poor kid a couple of weeks' worth of heartache and confusion."

"Confusion?"

His mother nodded. "All she heard you say was that Nora was a liar. That confused her because she trusted Nora."

"Didn't we all?" he mumbled, and then said, "Well, Julie heard the truth. Maybe it was better that way. Now she won't get her hopes up that Eleanor would be—"

A potential mother figure, but he wouldn't dare say that out loud. The last thing he needed was Julie thinking she could keep up a relationship with Eleanor.

"Phone calls are banned." He pointed at his mother. "You got that?"

The Nora he knew no longer existed. He thought the weeks that passed would have cleared his head, but all it did was infuriate him more, and he dove straight into a tiring depression. He knew he was acting like a bear, but he couldn't help it. The woman broke his heart and ruined his business. *But she did help you keep your daughter.*

"You're being unreasonable," Arlene said.

As if reason even belonged in this conversation. Damn. The conversations in his head were making him nuts.

"And no e-mails, either." His anger and adrenaline kick-started and he picked up his phone from the floor, only to realize zero battery life. He groaned and left the couch to sit at his desk-top desk. "I'll take care of this."

He logged into his e-mail, glanced over the incoming mail, and sat a minute. "Damn."

"What's wrong?"

"I don't have her e-mail address."

"How about that?" Arlene placed the empty beer cans on the coffee table and rocked back and forth on her heels with a smile. "Guess you can't send her a nasty e-mail now, can you?"

"Ma, no disrespect, but you're pissing me off right now."

She crossed her arms in front of her chest with that 'Mom, knowing' look. "That may be, but how about we reach a compromise?"

Compromise? What was going on in *her* head? This wasn't a game, it was his life. As far back as he remembered, his mother seemed to have a built-in BS detector. Always did, and always would, point out when he was acting like an ass. Given the situation, he wished she'd cut him some slack right now.

With a heavy sigh, he finally asked, "What kind of compromise?"

"You allow Julie to contact Nora whenever she wants, and I'll give you her e-mail address."

"You have it?"

She cocked an eyebrow at him. "Would I offer a deal if I didn't?"

He swiveled the desk chair to turn away from her, staring at the computer screen. "That's blackmail."

"No, it's taking care of three people I love."

"Two people," he mumbled.

"Don't correct me." She stayed silent long enough to give him time to digest the offer, but then, "*And* make sure you send her a cordial e-mail saying it's okay. She was worried about Julie contacting her without your permission."

"Oh, come on." He swiveled the chair around to face her with a questioning eye. "You expect me to give her permission to contact *my* daughter? Are you kidding?"

"You owe her that." When his mother planted her hands on her hips and glared that 'Don't mess with me' scowl, he knew she was right.

Sorting through the mess on the desk, he finally scooped up an unused napkin then found a pen on the floor next to his desk. "Okay, what's her address?"

"You're going to make it a nice e-mail, right?"

He bit his lower lip then turned his lips up into a fake smile. "So nice it will give her a sugar rush."

"Smart aleck." She swatted the back of his head. "It's ELB@Bainbridge.com."

"Of course it is." Just as he wrote the second 'B,' he stopped. "Wait a . . ."

He looked back at his e-mail In Box. "Holy shit."

"What's wrong?"

He shot his gaze at his mother. "You're never gonna believe this."

~ ~ ~

It was so good to be "home."

The minute Nora drove into Cedar Ridge, her spirits lifted. She didn't know if it was the clean, fall air or the spell the village wove over her each time she visited. Although, the village looked especially magical now with Christmas decorations adorning the businesses and streetlamps, just like a Norman Rockwell painting. The only detail missing was snow which was predicted to fall tomorrow with a Nor'easter. Good thing she planned to be here before the storm and she couldn't wait to experience her first Cedar Ridge snowfall.

But today wasn't merely a visit. Hopefully, it would be the beginning of her new life.

She had contacted Amanda Russell about the apartment rental on Primrose Lane and arranged an appointment to see it at five-thirty after the woman got home from work. Perfect. It was Tuesday, and that gave Nora time to see Julie and Arlene at the park.

She glanced at the digital clock on her dashboard. Three-ten. She'd get there just in time to spend a half hour with them before Evan picked them up. She couldn't wait to see them both, but was nervous about Arlene's reaction.

As she drove into a space at the Main Street parking lot, she immediately caught sight of Julie running across the wood-slatted, wobbly bridge. The delight in her eyes caused Nora's eyes to well with tears. God, she loved that little girl. Her heart swelled with pride as Julie jumped off the platform at the end of the bridge and bolted across the playground to the net ladder. Looked like all those soccer practices had paid off. The kid certainly was quick on her feet.

Nora left her car, wrapping the collar of her jacket tightly to her neck. The mountain winds were reminiscent of those whipping through the deep canyons of the city. From her time spent in Cedar Ridge, she knew living at this higher elevation would be colder than she was used to, but she didn't care. She would be close to Julie and Evan, and that's all that mattered. Her heart danced just thinking about him. For someone who never wanted a permanent relationship, she was now determined to do everything she could to spend the rest of her life with him. With any luck, he would have a change of heart once he realized she was trying to help. Maybe if the stars were in alignment, things would go her way.

"Nora!" Julie yelled when she noticed Nora walking toward the jungle gym. And the same way she ran to her father that first time Nora found out she was Evan's daughter was the same way she ran toward Nora now.

Nora squatted with open arms, and as Julie made contact, the two of them tumbled to the ground in a giggling, joyful mess.

"I missed you!" Julie squealed as the tassels of her hot-pink, knit hat brushed Nora's face.

"I missed you, too." She tickled Julie's ribs although she was sure the Julie didn't feel it under the heavy layers of her jacket. The child shrieked the same delightful way she did when her father rough-housed with her on the living room floor.

"This is the bestest day." Julie tried to wrap her short arms around Nora and shimmied her way up to kiss her cheek.

"I think you're right. This is the bestest day." Nora helped Julie onto her feet. Holding hands and swinging their arms, they walked toward Arlene who was seated on the wooden park bench near the swings. Nora hoped with all her might that Arlene wasn't still upset with her.

"It's about time you came back." Arlene stood and greeted Nora with a fierce hug. "The place hasn't been the same without you."

No longer put off by Arlene's outward shows of affection, Nora looked forward to her hugs and whole-heartedly returned the gesture, grateful that Arlene was truly happy to see her. "I would have been back sooner, but I wasn't sure if it was a good idea. Thank you for letting this pumpkin princess call me. It was the bestest." She tapped Julie's nose with a fingertip and the little girl hugged Nora's arm.

"Come on, let's have a sit." Arlene motioned to the bench. "Sweetie, why don't you go on the swings while Nora and I have some grown-up time?"

"O-kay." Julie nodded, reached over to give Nora another

quick kiss on the cheek and then she hesitated. "You're not gonna leave, are you?"

Nora shook her head. "No way. I'm here for good."

"Yay!" Julie exclaimed and off she bounced to the playground.

"I miss her *so* much," Nora said as she watched Julie hop onto the U-shaped swing. She turned her gaze to Arlene, anticipating the worst. She could handle a lecture on what a terrible person she was for deceiving all of them. But, if the lecture was on how disappointed Arlene was with her, that would break Nora's heart. She couldn't blame Arlene. Nora knew she deserved whatever Arlene was about to say.

"She missed you, too, and so did her father."

Nora let out a heavy breath. "I'm sorry. I screwed up. It wasn't my intention. I *never* expected to fall in love with this place, or with all of you."

Arlene patted Nora's gloved hand. "I know. And I also know you're trying to make amends. Evan's going to deal with it tonight. Planning board called an emergency meeting because of your help." She squeezed Nora's hand. "Thank you for that."

"It was the least I could do." Relief in Arlene's understanding filled Nora's heart with hope that she could and would be able to salvage her relationship with the Cavanaughs, especially Evan. "I don't want MoonBurst here anymore than all of you. Does Evan think it will work?"

Arlene shook her head. "Not sure, but he's hopeful. We should know after tonight."

Nora noticed Julie creeping closer to them. "Can I please come near you now?" she asked her grandmother.

"How can I say no when you asked so nicely?" Arlene said and beckoned her. "Come on over."

Julie hopped a few feet, then sprang toward them and fell onto Nora's lap.

Nora held tightly, never wanting to let go. She gave the hug a little extra measure in silent thanks for Arlene's acceptance and forgiveness.

"Are you comin' over for dinner tonight?" Julie asked.

"Oh, honey, I can't. I have an appointment." She was disappointed to pass up a Cavanaugh family dinner, but it was also too soon. She had a lot to clear up with Evan. But the anticipation that the apartment would soon be her new home and that she'd be closer to Evan and Julie made her almost giddy.

"After the appointment, can you come to my game?" Julie pouted. "Daddy can't come."

"He can't?" Nora smoothed a wayward hair out of Julie's eye. "Isn't he your coach?"

"Gramma's gonna coach us."

Arlene snorted. "Only until your father gets there. Lord help those poor kids. The only thing I know about soccer is that the ball gets kicked into the net."

Nora chuckled at Arlene's comment. "You'll do fine. But isn't it too cold to play at night?"

"It's the indoor winter league played at the community center."

"That makes sense." Nora nodded. For such a small town, Cedar Ridge certainly had enough to keep kids busy. Just another reason to love this place.

"Hey, I could use some help." Arlene elbowed Nora's upper arm. "What do you say?"

"Pl-lease, Nora. Pretty please?" Julie's pout and puppy-dog eyes weren't necessary. But they were cute.

"Of course, I'll do it." She bent her head to lean closer to Julie's. "Did I ever tell you I played soccer when I was a kid?"

"You did?" Julie's eyes lit with surprise.

"Yes." Even though she wasn't a great player, she

remembered how much fun it had been. "Between me and your grandmother, your team is in for a real treat."

"Do you think we'll win?"

Nora tried to give Julie a positive smile. "I hope so."

"Yipee!" Julie bounced and jiggled on Nora's lap. "We're gonna win!"

Uh-oh. What had she gotten herself into?

God, if you're listening, could you send us your best ringer?

~ ~ ~

Evan fiddled and rolled the hard copy of the e-mail Nora sent him between his hands. A file folder lay on the table in front of him with enough copies to distribute to the planning board. However this emergency meeting turned out, he'd be forever grateful to Nora, even though this situation with MoonBurst had been her fault in the first place.

She'd come to town to put him out of business. Did a damn good job of it, too. The board and council all but signed their approval to the coffee giant's application to occupy the Baxley building, three blocks away from the Bean & Brew.

But if it wasn't for Nora, he wouldn't have the ammunition to possibly stop MoonBurst before they could begin. He had tried hard to put her out of his mind. Pretended—like he had with Miranda—that Nora didn't exist. But after his mother called him out for not letting Julie talk to her, he'd done some deep soul searching. He couldn't ignore Nora any more than he couldn't acknowledge Miranda. Nora had taught him that Miranda needed to be resurrected, if only to let Julie know that she did have a mother. Even though Miranda was no longer an immediate threat—thanks to Nora—he planned to tell Julie about her mother. And now he needed to apply that same lesson to his childish attempt to banish Nora from his mind and his life.

Evan kept his eyes on the rolled paper he held. Nerves churning, twisting his gut, the tension ran through him in fits of frustration, so he kept it at bay by continuing to roll the paper over and over.

"Hey, buddy, you okay?"

Evan glanced to his right as Adam patted his shoulder. "Yeah, man, I'm fine."

"Bull," Adam said in a low voice. "You're a mess."

"Wouldn't you be if someone was about to steal your customers?"

"Damn straight. That's why I'm here. You have my vote. And if I have to, I'll put my two cents in."

Grateful for the support, Evan was also grateful that if anyone could get the board to see his side, it was Adam. He'd championed a few issues since the village revitalization came into existence and was on the village council. He was an all-round great guy, but more importantly, Evan was proud he was a friend.

Tapping his gavel, Ronald Whitmore from the planning board, began, "As board chair, I officially open this meeting. The only issue on tonight's schedule is the matter of approving the MoonBurst Coffee Corporation's petition to operate a business on the premises of 34 Main Street. A citizen wishes to address the board and council regarding this anticipated approval." He looked directly at Evan. "Please state your name and address for the record."

This is ridiculous. But, he guessed it all had to be legal, so he stood. "Evan Cavanaugh. 8 Deer Path Trail."

"Your concerns regarding this issue are . . ."

"One of the reasons you all seem to think MoonBurst is a good idea is because you think they're going to employ only Cedar Ridge residents in their store. They are not."

"Evan, I know this is hard on you," Whitmore interrupted, "but they assured us they were only hiring residents. They're going to need thirty-five people to run the store for their hours of operation. They went as far as to say that if people from neighboring towns applied for jobs, they wouldn't hire them unless no Cedar Ridge residents were interested. With our unemployment rate as high as it is, this would help the community immeasurably."

"Really." Evan chuckled to himself. "I have proof that's not going to happen." Evan retrieved the file folder that lay in front of him and began distributing the copied e-mail to the board. "You're holding an interoffice e-mail that was sent to the members of the MoonBurst Coffee Corporation's Sussex County Expansion Project Team. Notice the second paragraph."

Evan read the text aloud, "'Only Cedar Ridge residents will be hired in the capacity of maintenance, which shall consist of two part-time positions in the evening. The thirty-five remaining positions will be filled by current MoonBurst Coffee Corporation employees. This is to ensure quality and consistency of product and services.'"

An audible gasp sounded through the room, then Adam said, "Damn. They were screwin' us!"

"That comment will be stricken from the minutes," Whitmore directed the board secretary.

If it weren't such a serious matter, Evan would have laughed at Adam's comment. "As you can see, they're not going to do what they promised," Evan simply said.

"Let's not jump to conclusions." Whitmore fumbled with the paper, turning it over, but noticing the back was blank. "Where did you get this?"

"From Eleanor Bainbridge. You all know her as Nora. She worked for the company." As he explained the situation, his stomach turned in disgust. He knew rumors flew around the village about how Nora had betrayed them all, so he wanted to give the board the real story. And as the words left his mouth, he realized he needed to really listen to those words.

"She's sorry for what she's done to Cedar Ridge, and because of it, she quit her job with MoonBurst and sent a copy of this e-mail so we could stop them before they hurt our village."

He answered questions, gave a few comments, and then sat, knowing he'd given his all, and so had Nora. He decided that as soon as he was finished here, he'd go to Julie's soccer game then he'd make arrangements with his mother to babysit so he could go to New York to see Nora.

His words to the board had hit home. Nora had organized the protest and had armed him with the e-mail. In short, she gave him what he needed even though he told her he didn't want anything to do with her. Probably hurt her as much as she hurt him. He needed to see her, needed to see if the relationship they had been building wasn't a lie. She had fought for him, proved her loyalty to his family by helping him keep Julie, helped his town, and now it was his turn to fight for her. If she'd have him. But first he needed to see if his business would stay intact. Evan clutched the rolled paper in his lap, hoping he'd done enough.

It was up to the board now.

Adam gave him the thumbs-up. And without further discussion, the board began roll call for the vote.

Chapter 18

It all came back to Nora as the game progressed. To score, two forwards needed to move the ball. But at age six, Julie's team, the Bulldogs didn't know a forward from the guy selling popcorn in the bleachers.

Loud cheers echoed through the community center gymnasium when the opposing team slammed the ball into the Bulldogs goal. Again. As the Astros celebrated, the freckle-faced Bulldog goalie burst into tears.

This was *not* how Nora remembered it. But she kept reminding herself she had been on the winning team all those years ago. This was how her opponents felt when her bantam team took the field and shut them out.

"Got any ideas?" she asked Arlene.

"Me?" The older woman aimed a thumb to her chest. "I only understand goals, nothing else. We need divine intervention on this one."

"I agree, but unless God can send us a coach right now, we've got to figure out something. Short of having our team huddle around the ball, there's no way we can stop that tall redhead from scoring again. How old is that kid?"

"Nora?" Julie tugged on the sleeve of Nora's sweatshirt.

"What, sweetie?

"We're gettin' killed." The frustration in Julie's voice caused Nora's heart to tighten. She needed to do something. But what? The Bulldogs had to gain control of the ball, but not all of them at once. But maybe.

"You know what? I have an idea." She took hold of

Julie's hand, signaled a time out to the ref, and gathered the team along the sidelines into a huddle.

"Please, let this work," she whispered to herself then told the team her plan.

~ ~ ~

Damn, Evan thought. He'd arrived just in time to see a goal scored on his team. He quickly scanned the scoreboard. They were being shut out, seven nothing.

The look of panic on his mother's face told it all. She was in over her head. Just as he was about to sprint over to relieve her, he stopped short.

"Nora?" he said to himself and held back, watching his mother converse with the woman who had turned his life upside down.

When Julie approached her, his heart twisted at the frustration on his daughter's face. Nora took her by the hand and corralled the rest of his team like a mother hen gathering her baby chicks. When she knelt in the middle of the huddle to talk to the team, she disappeared from his sight. Curious to see how she handled the team who was getting the crap kicked out of them, he realized he'd love to hear what she was telling his players.

Sure, he could jump right in and take over, but he wanted to see if she could fix this mess. It seemed the woman who described herself as an idea-driven creative gopher had a way of cleaning up bad situations. He wanted to see if that talent transferred itself to this jam.

The ref blew his whistle to restart the play, but the Bulldogs still surrounded their substitute coach.

"Let's go, Bulldogs," the ref warned.

The whistle sounded again. Evan was glad the ref was Parker Green, Adam's business partner. Parker was younger than the rest of the refs and, luckily, more patient.

Parker scrubbed the back of his neck, then glanced Evan's way. When he raised his chin with a nod, Evan held up a hand to hold on, then smiled and shrugged. At this point, there wasn't much Evan could do. Besides, he wanted to see what Nora had up her sleeve.

With a roaring shout, "Bulldogs!" the players broke the huddle and scattered across the shiny gym floor as if they knew their positions. They sure did seem amped up to get the game going. Whatever Nora said had them raring to go.

When the ref blew the whistle, the entire Bulldog team ran toward the ball, positions forgotten. Damn! They were doing it again. No matter how hard he had tried in the past, they still chased the ball together like a group of lemmings aimlessly following the pretty white-and-black ball. But . . . *Hey! What are they doing?*

Justin, the tallest of his players, kicked the ball toward Elise. Elise held it between her feet until the entire team pushed and shoved their way around her. As one cohesive group, they moved toward the Astros' goal protecting the ball against any Astros player who dared to get near it. When tiny Bailey Bradford attempted to push an Astros player away, Evan knew Nora had thrown caution to the wind and told his team to guard the ball at all cost.

When the first attempt missed the goal by flying out of bounds, his team regrouped and swarmed the ball again like bees guarding the hive. He had trouble seeing who had the ball, so he quickly ran to the sideline where his mother and Nora called out directions to the players.

He purposely stayed a few feet away, not wanting either woman to notice him. They were doing a decent job and his pride for both of them had him hoping this crazy idea would work.

"Bailey, NOW!" Nora yelled. Within seconds, Bailey's foot connected with the ball and the ref's whistle blew long and hard.

"Goal!" he announced with his arm pointing to center court.

Evan pumped his fist back hard. "Yes!" His team had actually scored a goal. He watched the melee of players rush to the sidelines. When they reached his mother and Nora, they practically knocked the women off their feet. Julie, on the outside of the crowd, yelled for Nora.

He searched and then spotted Nora's head of black hair surfacing from the middle of the players toward his daughter. When he was able to see her face, she was calling back to Julie. When she finally broke from the crowd, the two embraced, jumping up and down holding hands. Nora picked Julie up and hugged and kissed her.

The sight solidified everything he'd been thinking since he left the planning board meeting. Nora had saved the day by providing the tools to block MoonBurst, saved him from losing his daughter, and now she taught Julie the lesson to never give up. She was a great role model for Julie. And she obviously loved her. And Julie loved her right back.

As hard as he had tried to fight it, opening *his* heart to her was the best thing he could have done. She was real and warm and loving. With Nora, his life—and Julie's—was whole and complete. Neither of them could live without her. And dating was out of the question. He wanted her in his life forever. Now, *he* needed to make things right between them.

~ ~ ~

"We did it!" Julie squealed. "You're the bestest."

"And you're the bestest." Nora snuggled Julie close, then spun her around until Julie giggled. She loved the unabashed joy this child possessed. After being apprehensive about helping Arlene with the team, Nora knew she'd made the right choice. In fact, once she settled in as an official village resident, she intended to volunteer for whatever Julie wanted.

Being with Julie brought more contentment to Nora's life than she ever thought possible.

Just as the excitement waned, Nora noticed the broad, familiar stance of Evan near the sidelines and her heart kicked back into excitement mode. Unable to read his expression, she gently placed Julie on the floor and pointed the child's attention in his direction.

"Daddy!" Julie bolted across the gym's shiny hardwood, almost tripping as she reached her father. "Did you see? Did you see Bailey's goal?"

He scooped her into his arms and Nora nearly melted at the sight of the two people she loved most in the world. She, too, wanted to run into his arms. But there'd be no welcoming hug waiting for her. If she was going to live in Cedar Ridge and be a part of Julie's life, even though she messed things up, she needed to make amends with Evan. And if she was going to start over and remake her life, she might as well begin now.

She squared her shoulders and walked toward him, trying to channel all the Cavanaugh bravery she'd witnessed over the last few months, reminding herself that she had shed her life as Eleanor and became a new woman. When she came within speaking distance, she extended her hand.

"Hi. I'm Eleanor Langston Bainbridge. Most people call me Nora."

Evan glanced at her, then at Julie, who smiled broadly and nodded her approval. He hesitantly extended his hand.

Nora reached for it and gave her best firm handshake. "I filled in as coach for this game. Your team did pretty well."

His hazel eyes locked onto hers but she was unable to read their meaning. "I'd say they did great. First goal of the season." Then his gaze traveled back to his daughter. "What do you say to Ms. Bainbridge for helping your team?"

"Thank you." Julie chuckled behind her two pudgy hands.

Nora couldn't hide a giant smile that radiated toward the child. "You're very welcome, Miss Cavanaugh."

Julie squirmed, and Evan lowered her to the floor. "Can I go see Gramma?"

"You can. But wait until she's finished talking to the ref, okay?"

"O-kay." She nodded and ran in Arlene's direction.

Nora raised her eyebrows and turned her gaze toward Julie. The awkward silence between her and Evan filled the air with a tension as thick as the gym's painted, cement-block walls.

"Thank you for helping Mom. She's not too comfortable with the game."

Nora chuckled. "Neither was I, but we muddled through it."

"It was a big help. I didn't have to worry about the team while I was at the meeting," he said, his eyes trained on his players running around the gym in an impromptu game of tag.

"I'm glad." Nora wondered how the meeting went, but he seemed to be holding back. Had the e-mail worked? She desperately wanted to ask, but she'd done enough to screw with his business. She was lucky he was even talking to her. The last time she had seen him, he told her to never come back. *Baby steps*, she reminded herself.

Nora inhaled a deep breath when she noticed a slight frown at his mouth. He clearly wanted nothing more to do with her. "Well . . ." she exhaled loudly. "I guess I better retrieve the balls and gather the roster clipboard for you." She started to move away.

"It worked."

She stopped and turned to him. "What?"

His eyes aimed off into the distance, not even looking at her. "The e-mail," he said casually. "The board rejected MoonBurst's application."

Then what was wrong with him? Wasn't he happy? She wanted to jump for joy, and it took all her energy not to shout with glee that Evan no longer had to worry about losing the Bean & Brew.

Her insides bounced and flipped, and it took great effort to fight the urge to hug him right then and finally tell him how much she loved him. She bit her bottom lip to keep from shouting out loud at how happy she was for him, so she turned away so he wouldn't see the excitement she knew clearly showed on her face.

And then she felt his hand on her shoulder as he gently turned her around to face him. His stern expression slowly morphed into a smile that lit up the entire gym.

"You set out to ruin my business. But then you helped save it," he said while drawing her into a hug. "I'm eternally grateful."

Not sure if it was a joke, Nora waited a few seconds to see what he'd do, so she let her arms hang limply near the sides of her hips.

When he tightened his hold, he whispered, "I missed you."

"Oh . . ." Tears filled her eyes and her hands knew exactly what to do now as they wrapped around his waist. "I'm sorry. So sorry. I didn't mean—"

His lips came down on hers in a tentative touch, and her whole world opened. What she'd been too scared to hope for suddenly became reality. The only time she was truly happy was with him.

Evan and the Cedar Ridge spell wound around her heart, forcing her to abandon her emotional walls to let others in. Evan, Julie, Arlene, and the rest were the family she always dreamed of. No promotion on the 23rd floor or anywhere else would ever compare. This was what life should be about. And the man feathering light kisses on her lips was who she always needed, but never knew she wanted. Now, she never wanted to let him go.

"I love you, Evan."

"I love you, too." And his lips met hers in a promise that her life would never be the same. "Will you stay in Cedar Ridge?" he asked.

Nora nodded. "I signed a lease for Amanda's apartment this afternoon."

"Really?"

She nodded again. "Yes. I've sent out a few resumes last week."

"You're looking for a job?"

"I have to support myself. If it's one thing I don't need, it's a man supporting me."

"Well, then, since you're a great idea person with coffee company experience, I could use your *talents* at the Bean & Brew." He wagged his eyebrows at her as he slightly loosened his hold. "How do you feel about a man signing your paychecks?"

"Um, that, I could do," she automatically teased.

"Good. How do you feel about dating your boss? Do you have an issue with that?"

"Oh, that could be a problem. I'm not good at getting emotionally involved. Dating's not an option."

"Good. Because I'm not interested in dating." He tightened his arms around her and his lips came down on hers in another long, satisfying kiss.

When he finally eased his lips from hers, he asked, "How do you feel about marriage?"

Nora's heart soared with emotion. She'd found the one man who truly loved her, the one she wanted to spend the rest of her life with. She'd finally found a home, a place where she belonged: In his arms.

"I thought you'd never ask."

Short Bio

Leigh Raffaele's life mirrors Goldilocks's. Growing up in the suburbs had been a little too soft. A short stint in the city had been a little too hard. But a recent move to the country proved just right.

Married to her college sweetheart, she now lives on a farm in the mountains of Northwestern New Jersey with acres of pastures and woodlands, 20+ goats, a dozen chickens and two dogs. She's biased—as all grandmothers are—in that she has two beautiful granddaughters who call her Farm Mama.

The mother of three grown sons, she says raising them was such an adventure, she'd do it all again in a heartbeat. Cub Scouts, Boy Scouts, softball, guitar lessons, trumpet practices, drum rolls, marching band, WWE Wrestling, camping . . . boys are so cool!!! And then they grow up to be the heroes in her books!

She loves jigsaw puzzles, coloring, and is addicted to an odd combination of Hallmark movies, HGTV's *Fixer Upper*, and Discovery's *Alaskan Bush People*.

To "talk" to Leigh about her books, The Goats, her crazy obsession with her TV shows, or whatever floats your boat, contact her at LeighRaff@aol.com.

CPSIA information can be obtained
at www.ICGtesting.com
Printed in the USA
BVOW09s1043150418
513434BV00016B/170/P